Alas! The Poor Yoricks

A mostly sympathetic stumble through an imagined Roman Catholic moment in the 1980s

A Comedy by

James Louis Fortuna, Jr.

Lightnin' Bug Publishing, 2022

Lightnin' Bug Publishing
Statesville, North Carolina

Address all correspondence c/o Lightin' Bug Publishing, lightninbug@att.net.

First Lightnin' Bug Edition: 2022

ISBN: 9798848060553

Many of the jokes presented herein were gleaned from public domain documents collected by Project Gutenberg, whom the author gratefully acknowledges.

"There's a divinity that shapes our ends,
Rough-hew them how we will–"

--Hamlet, Act V, scene II

This novel is dedicated to:
Catherine Compton Fortuna

PROLOGUE

Midway through an amusement park at the cross-roads of Heaven and Hell is a plain brown tent with mud-stained canvas flaps and the faded faces of clowns painted along its sides. Not many tourists bother to stop there; mostly hurrying back and forth to see the more spectacular shows and rides, they barely glance at the little Monk who sometimes juggles fruit or boxes and sometimes dances on a narrow stage set hard beside the ticket booth. The Monk has tiny bells upon his robe and juggles very well indeed and dances with a step so light he seems to float upon the air. He sometimes plays a fiddle and he sometimes sings a song and if you come in close enough to hear, he'll sometimes tell a story too, sometimes sitting in a chair for hours at a time. But few stop long enough to watch and fewer yet to hear and fewest out of all the rest will follow him between the dirty flaps when it comes time to go.

And every day and every night he's there; with few or many it seems all the same to him, a fiddle tune bowed lively up and quick or tuned down sad and sweet, a tap-tap-dancing on the hollow stage and juggle up whatever comes to hand, it's all the same and never changes with the weather or the time of day. But some-times when the other shows and all the rides are full, especially then or when the lines are long and cook-tents have run short of food, a larger crowd will gather there with nothing else to do.

"And welcome every one of you," he always cries,

"and welcome welcome every one," he'll cry again and tell them all to "hurry hurry hurry" in, in close to "hurry hurry one and all" and "listen to me, listen now" and "tell me what you think you hear."

His voice is always funny-sounding at the start but no one laughs the more he talks and talks, a story strongly building with each word, of doors the most and all the things one meets just on the other side, the things one chooses to let in or goes to see or follows after in a heat, the journeys ended and begun in simple stepping over place to place. Of doors the most—the stories all have doors within their telling somewhere, right away or later on or like the wind from first to last unseen but touching everything at once. He talks of doors the most.

And then he dances in a jingle-jangle for a while up on the stage, and bows a fiddle tune up high and fast and goes inside the tent to wait and see who might come follow to the Throne of God.

CHAPTER ONE

Heinrich Cardinal Spitzmulcher was furious. He had waved Darby Ross into an overstuffed easy chair near the door and continued to pace and sputter out bits of words and phrases at the blaring television set mounted chest-high in the dark wooden paneling of the far wall. Darby already had waited for over an hour in the foyer and his wife was expecting him to be on time for their daughter's birthday party. He had missed the previous fifteen. The Cardinal's words began to come together as the screen turned full of a familiar round face.

"*That's* what I mean—there—hear it? And look at his face—look at that—that smirk! See it? And the sarcasm in his voice—can you hear it, Ross? And now a documentary—in my own Archdiocese—*here*, Ross! It's spreading *here*!"

"The Poor Yoricks, Your Eminence?"

The Cardinal's lean face had lost all color but a deep, near purple smear along his close-shaven cheeks.

"Who—who else, Ross? Who else? Who—who—"

His voice pitched upward, higher and cracking like an owl that had missed its prey. The room was too hot and the television on so loud it hurt Darby's ears. The round face on the screen was telling a joke.

"It's grown then—since my report?" Six months ago, a fourteen-page transcribed result of three days spent in Slackbridge, Georgia—four major headings culled from tape after tape of rambling dialogue and jokes so old the punchlines wheezed. He wished now he somehow could have dodged the Cardinal's call and never gone to see the Yoricks' Laughing Place. The round face had disappeared, lost among a staggered chorus line of dancing men in identically colored blazers, a green and red plaid that seemed to flash and crackle in collision with the deep pink of their slacks.

"Look—just look at them!"

"Have you read my report, Eminence?"

"Report? Report!" He suddenly stopped mid-stride, tall body tensed beneath his red cassock and one long finger jabbing at the air toward his desk. "That's all there are, Ross! Reports—letters—paper. And nobody tells me what I want to know." He came in close, partially blocking the dancing men and their bob and jump among what looked like some factory's loading-dock crew. "And *yours*—yours was the worst, Ross. The worst—visions and Papal blessings—joy and peace like candy canes along a chocolate road—it told me nothing. Nothing!" The round face was back, briefly visible as the Cardinal shifted his weight from foot to foot and frowned his own face into a mass of wrinkles deep and shallow. "No hint of the blasphemy there—there—" he waved a hand out behind him like he was pushing away some unwanted visitor, "the scandal for the world to see—"

"But—but your Eminence—the Congregation for Religious and Secular Institutes granted Father Bede full—"

"Riga—Riga did that."

"Yes—Cardinal Riga—but Pope Hilary—"

"Doesn't see it every day. Doesn't see what's happening. I need proof, Ross. Proof." His face was twitching now, cheeks the deeper purple color they got just before he lost control, before he cut short an interview and called in his secretary to clear the room.

"Proof, Your Eminence?" Darby scanned the face for

4

signs of something beyond the immediate anger, something to tell him how far he could safely go. He already was late for the birthday party.

"Yes proof—yes—something to stop it. To stop it clean. It's spreading quicker—quicker than I thought possible. It's crossed into Florida in strength—they've acquired a house right here in San Cristobel," he half-smiled and then brought back the frown. "Oh, I have them under close surveillance to be sure. Yes. And—yes they are following the canons regarding consultation and pastoral visitation. Riga has seen to that. But they answer directly to Rome, Ross. And the main house—the Slackbridge one—is not within our jurisdiction at all. Again—Riga. It's been cleverly done, Ross. Cleverly arranged—effectively arranged—to keep us from exerting any real control. Even *here*. *Here*! In my own Archdiocese. The oldest in America." He sighed and put a hand on Darby's shoulder, ring slipping sideways and its massive stone pressing into the cloth of his sweater. "And two new reports from Alabama and one each from Mississippi and Louisiana. It's growing like a cancer—just like a cancer." His voice trailed off and got lost in an explosion of rinky-tink piano and banjo rolls that came in with the rising list of credits filling up the screen. "I need proof. On Bede."

"Father Bede?" The face was there again, past the Cardinal's side, behind the credits as a smell of incense seemed to rise each time the ring came down on Darby's shoulder. The piano was sounding single notes with pauses in between to let the face on the screen be heard. The Cardinal was always the same. And Darby owed him everything he had.

"You'll go back to Slackbridge, Ross. To do a feature story for *Catholic Cross* or some such reason. Yes. That's exactly what you'll do."

"But, Your Eminence—what about the other visit? We spent nearly a day together. What if Father Bede asks why he wasn't even mentioned in my column?"

"Background. If anyone asks, you'll say that the other time was all background. And it was. It was background. For a future column perhaps. But this time," he folded his arms across his chest and tried to smile, "this time it's a series. A three-parter. Three full articles. Or," Darby thought he saw the Cardinal wink, "something more than that. Yes. Something weighty and important. You come up with the particulars. That should be easy enough to do. Yes? You'll leave tomorrow."

"Tomorrow?"

"Yes. It's all arranged. The Editorial Council has been duly informed. And you'll find proof, Ross. No matter how long it takes. I need this from you. I *need* it. Proof."

"Yes, Your Eminence." The face on the screen was free of the piano notes and credits, in close-up now with tiny jester's hat slipped down and bells atop one ear. The Cardinal had never spoken of his own need before. The voice from the television made Darby smile.

But seriously folks—

#

Darby Ross nosed the Cardinal's third car—a beeping, blinking, buzzing German compact—onto the Ponce De Leon Expressway and tried to relax. He had made it home in time to watch his daughter open her gifts. His wife had packed his suitcases quickly, the late spring sunset making everything look slightly blue outside the big upstairs windows and the sounds of teenaged girls mixing in with birdsong in the semi-darkness of the bedroom. His wife was devoted to Cardinal Spitzmulcher.

"Be sure you call and let me know how to reach

you."

"I'm not sure how long I'll—"

"And don't just eat hamburgers."

"It's Slackbridge—Georgia—again."

"So eat right—His Eminence and I both want you to stay fit."

Slackbridge, Georgia, was exactly one hundred and twenty-two miles due north of Darby's new country home on the Little Okra River. The house had been built by a recently failed rock star who only spent two days there during the ten years he owned it. Or so the real estate agent said. The bullet holes in the dining room ceiling and the lingerie cache his wife had discovered behind a sliding panel in the master bedroom spoke of a longer occupancy. But the price was fair and the view of the Little Okra from the kitchen/solarium was peaceful, and the peach-shaped swimming pool had made his daughter jump up and down and squeak like a beach toy going flat. They had lived there the past five months, fifteen miles from San Cristobel and the editorial offices of *Catholic Cross Monthly* and the almost daily shadow of Cardinal Spitzmulcher.

Darby had been Chief Editor of CCM for almost a year now, the magazine seeming to follow his own long and personal climb through bad housing, politics, debt and near-despair to become just last month the biggest Roman Catholic publication of them all—number one in circulation, number one in advertising, number one in orthodoxy and the hearts of everyone who prayed in Latin and spoke curses on the 60s for the damage done to Peter's Rock. And Darby Ross had just become their latest secular champion, groomed by Cardinal Spitzmulcher himself, jumped over the heads of his betters (men and women alike), and one more time picked up like a player in some Divine and well-timed comic sketch and put down fast and hard to act a part he hadn't trained to even think about. He owed the Cardinal more than he could ever pay.

#

The car was too small, and he felt his legs cramping. A multi-colored van went weaving by him in the left lane, a slender-faced girl down low in the passenger's seat, her long blond hair whipping out around the window frame and for some reason making Darby think about the first time. Over twenty years ago at least, the Cardinal back then a Bishop's secretary fresh from Rome and come to visit on a Sunday afternoon the vagrant refuse packed in tight, in holding tanks in cell blocks A and B and part of C in Duval County's cement jail set down among the thick dark oaks of Liberty Street. The van weaved into the right lane and blinked to take the San Cristobel exit, speeding off and leaving nothing but a stretch of empty road ahead, due north to Slackbridge and The Laughing Place of Father Solomon Bede.

The highway was boring. Darby tried the radio, but the buttons seemed stuck. There was no tape deck and the St. Joseph bubble-compass barely moved at all. He flexed his fingers and hummed a tune he used to know. But the first time memory kept coming back. The pines and water-oaks, the patches of palmetto and condos and tourist attractions and the big trucks sometimes rumbling up behind began to force that one day on him more and more until he couldn't focus on his journey's end. There had been ninety-two vagrants in the jail that day. Darby had been running away from school again, from the Catholic college his parents sent him to, from Dr. Aratowski's church history midterm, from everything. But he had lost his wallet in the Jacksonville bus terminal and wandered outside into what at first had seemed a party, lights and jumping men and more police than he had ever seen before. And later, Father-Secretary Spitzmulcher came to visit and had somehow never left his life again for very long.

The man, Spitzmulcher, had sounded old, even back then, and his eyes had almost never blinked. Darby gave himself away at lunch, reflexive Grace among his sweating, cursing, new-found friends at table 16-A.

"You're Catholic, aren't you, son?"

"I—uh—yes Father."

"Then what are you doing here?"

And the man had posted bond and sent Darby home; no, he had taken him home in the Bishop's car and stayed for cocktails, supper, and the tour of Darby's father's supermarket and the Pee-Wee Golf-A-Rama and the not-yet-finished Olde-Tyme Arcade-By-The-Sea with life-sized mermaid statues and a giant seahorse ride to scare the tourists who might stray the fifty miles it took to get there from the nearest beach. The second time had been in Jackson Square at dawn, a taste of bourbon curdling in his mouth and someone's half-smoked joint beside him on the curb. Darby had run away from his master's thesis, run away that time to help the Negroes go to school. But somehow, straining all coincidence, a nearly brand-new Monsignor Spitzmulcher, straight-lined and freshly shaven and smelling of cloves and cinnamon, had seemed to swoop down from the towers of St. Louis's Cathedral, his features sharp and beak-nose huge and every word he spoke a stabbing, jab and jab and jabbing into Darby's aching head until they came together in a cadence like a drumbeat on a hollow log.

And what of your mother and father
your promise
your soul immortal soul
your body holy temple that it is?
"I—I came to—I came here to—"
You come to Mass you come with me
with me and make your Easter Duty
and you
pray that your poor mother's heart
has not been broken full in two!
How long
How long since you last confessed?
"I'm—I—I'm only here to march—"
You come with me!

The offices had been cool and dark, and Darby had slept almost a day in some small room where muffled chanting and a boat horn far away had come and gone among his dreams like noisy neighbors in the stillness of a winter's night. His parents had paid for the bus ride home.

#

The St. Mary's River bridge sign surprised him, somehow seeming in his mind to be at least ten more miles down the four-lane sameness passing by outside. It was stuffy in the car, and he tried to open the windows, pressing the buttons beside the door handle several times but getting back only a hum and clanking buzz. The air-conditioner worked on the first flip of a rainbow-colored switch, and the cool stream from the tiny vent ruffled his hair. He would soon be in Georgia, moving through the piney woods on the shortest route to Slackbridge, two towns north of the Cardinal's immediate jurisdiction. He suddenly said the words aloud, for some reason in a sing-song cadence–"im-me-di-ate ju-ris-dic-tion"–the Cardinal's face there in his mind, beside him in the car, outside in the passing air–out over South Georgia up ahead and every place that Darby went, had gone, or hoped to go. He owed the Cardinal more than he could ever pay. His wife had said that very thing many times. And he agreed. Had come to agree. Had had to agree. Finally. After all the findings, all the sudden presences, appearances, coincidence long since gone and yet sometimes sadly missed like a lost friend or the solid ground of a math problem at school. "Im-me-di-ate Ju-ris-dic-tion: *Everywhere.*" Like the times past Jackson Square that one by one had made him what he was today. The times that he remembered more than all the rest, labeled now like video cassettes all ready for the screen. The third and fourth and fifth times–whirring in the cool air from the tiny vent–gone by like pavement underneath the car but leaving flashes of themselves to reinforce his debt–for missing Vietnam and for a wife-and-daughter and a home and freedom from the need to go to jail.

The St. Mary's River was down, high water line clear to see even before he started over the bridge, tangled roots and mulch clumps full of rock-like bulges up above the darkish water rippled here and there by swirls and floating tufts of grass. And then it was gone and Georgia had welcomed him briefly with a buckshot-pitted sign and the road he wanted had come clear of billboards and a parked and idling National Guard convoy–*Slackbridge* sign on the other side of Tyburn, Patches, Congo Crossing, with the mileage too far gone to read. "Im-me-di-ate Ju-ris-dic-tion: *Everywhere.*" The Cardinal–a man to reach down quickly, three and four and five times straight, stronger than coincidence, able to leap the barricades of whining doubt and fear and land sure-footed, never winded, not a drop of sweat upon whatever new-made habit he had worn—"Im-me-di-ate Ju-ris-dic-tion: EVERYWHERE." Father Bede should be pitied for having such an enemy.

Darby wiped his face and cleared his throat and turned onto the Slackbridge Road. He owed the Cardinal more than he could ever pay.

#

As he joined the Slackbridge traffic, the stop and start of the shift changes at the factories on the south side, Darby was glad the Cardinal had insisted he take the General Fund's credit cards. He didn't want to stay inside The Laughing Place itself, not this time, not with what he had to do in the way of finding proof. Whatever that might finally be. No, he needed a telephone he could depend on, not one that sometimes squirted perfumed water or puffed out mini-clouds of bright red smoke; he needed a place of privacy, to dial the Cardinal's special number, a place to type his daily log and organize the tapes he knew would soon be filled with interviews, brimful of voices, Poor Yoricks and Father Bede again but also with the ones who lived in town and in the housing projects out past the well-kept lawns and the pecan orchard, the pines and oaks and shaded pathways of the grounds on which the Order's main house and its pre-fab dormitory sat close together in the figure of a bloated cross. The Order had grown, was growing yet, already nearing fifty brothers full-time and a crowd of hundreds more there in a kind of loose novitiate, the whole a mix (or "stew" the Cardinal said) of secular institute and some strange form or near thing to a society of apostolic life. Darby couldn't tell just what it was, his three days there a whirl from dawn to sundown in which aging stand-up comics punched out their jokes and gags and sketches, playing to each other and the younger crowd, standing on tables and stairwells and porches and at night upon a good-sized stage inside a barn-shaped building bulging like a monstrous toadstool in a clearing near a frog-choked lake. He had never laughed so much in his life.

But his time with Father Bede himself had been too brief, cluttered with the endless-seeming stories that he told, the tapes of little use in writing a report, the one half-serious time too late in coming and delivered up so softly that the microphone had gathered only clanging cow-bells and the jangle of the little jester caps the brothers wore. The words themselves were lost but memory gave a sense of phrases feeling like a whispered prayer, the balding priest gone quiet in the midst of all the noise, his eyes still bright and at their corners dark skin creased by wrinkles big and small, his mouth a moving smear of pink and red:

He had seen a vision or had heard a voice–

He had dreamed a dream or felt a tug and urging on his heart–

He had been reached perhaps among his duties as a high school teacher, had been pulled up from his English classes at Our Lady of the Flight to Egypt–

Had known at once clearly what he had to do or had waited on a confirmation–

Had acted, waited, saw or heard–

Until it happened, Cardinal Riga there somehow to hear and judge it worthy of the ear of old friend, school-mate, brother priest and Pontiff, Hilary (the second of that name but first come forth from wild America)–to cut the corners of so many canons that it seemed a lightning bolt had flashed from Rome down to the piney woods of Georgia, to Father Bede there waiting to begin.

And its founding, the approval of the Poor Yoricks by the Holy See and gifts of land and buildings from a source Cardinal Spitzmulcher had not yet pinned down, had gotten two whole columns in *L'Osservatore Romano* and a special write-up in *The Slackbridge Times and Daily Ledger* longer than the one that Billy Graham's Crusade got five years before.

Darby slowed and then stopped as two red-suited security guards stepped off the shoulder of the road near the open gates of a furniture factory parking lot. The shift change began slowly but soon picked up speed, most of the cars and trucks looking new or freshly washed, drivers shaking their heads and laughing and a faint sound of jingling bells there also toward the end, a group of Poor Yoricks suddenly visible near the guard booth, their green and red plaid blazers flashing in the sunlight as they danced and waved the workers home. Darby smiled and accelerated slowly, the Yoricks blurring as he passed. The last car to leave the lot was now in front, a torn bumper sticker there flapping in upon itself like awkward hands applauding everything behind. A motel sign seemed caught by kudzu just ahead: THE BIDE-A-WHILE OVERNIGHT, *MAJOR CREDIT CARDS ACCEPTED.*

#

The motel room was decorated in what Darby finally decided to call "nautical circus"—seascapes and carrousel prints on the walls, seahorse lamps beside the bed and the cover of the Gideon Bible polka-dotted, elephant heads for tap handles in the lavatory and a smell like disinfected sawdust puffing through it all each time the air cut on. The coverlet on the bed was striped red and white and the carpet felt spongy, bits of different colors scattered in the places he could see, confetti-like dots and blobs that sparkled faintly in the lamp glow from the nearest seahorse. The television set and re-mote control were hidden in a painted cabinet with one door nearly cracked through in the middle, the whole front making up a stylized whaling scene, distorted long-boats riding in a boiling sea and giant flukes spread side to side above the standing men like a fat canopy. The sound was tinny and the screen too bright, a western shoot-out flickering for a few seconds before dissolving into a car lot, a tall man there dancing on a pickup hood while dwarfs in motley bounced on Pogo sticks and waved out at the camera down below. The tall man was in a plaid strait jacket.

Best deals in the whole southeast—we're crazy I tell you! Crazy!

The telephone felt greasy, seahorse light making its pinkish surface look wet. The Cardinal's secretary took the call and thanked him and said to please hold, his voice turning high-pitched, tinny like the tall man on the screen or the fat desk clerk in the motel office when he finally found the key. The clerk's cheeks were a deep red and he spoke slowly.

"You plan on staying long, Mr.–Mr. Ross?"

"Depends. It depends."

"Bidness, huh? You here on bidness I bet. I can al-ways tell. I like to study people. Guess at what they do? You in fabric I bet ya. Fabric or maybe furniture. Right?"

"No. I'm a reporter. I'm with–"

"Oh. Reporter huh? Well–it's Room 117, Mr. Rust. That's down yonder by the satellite dish."

The Cardinal's voice was nearly on a pitch with the television and Darby lowered the volume and sat down on the edge of the bed. On screen, the dwarfs seemed to be trying to free the tall man from his strait jacket.

Try to keep it low profile, Ross. But if anyone presses you—really presses now—be forthright—they already know your connections. Just say you're writing a book.

"A book, Your Eminence?"

Yes. Book. We've decided that's best. A book. And it's true enough. You are writing a book.

"I am?"

Yes. And you need background. Like your first visit. Only deeper this time. You need more and that's where you'll find something solid. He's from there. From Slackbridge. Near there. From—from a place called—let me see—yes—Ailey. That's the ticket. You go to Ailey, Ross. Start there. But don't bother about his time in Philadelphia. His training. His teaching. That's covered. That's not important now. I want the home part. We'll find something there. In what they think. Start with what the people there think. Do you understand?

"Yes, Your Eminence."

And Ross?

"Eminence?"

Stay alert. Stay on top of what he's doing now as well. Do whatever it takes. He's sly. He has powerful friends. And spies are everywhere. You do know that? About the spies?"

"If Your Eminence thinks that there are—"

Yes. But we have word that he likes you, Ross. That's the latest word we have. In spite of me, he likes you. He even reads your column regularly.

"He does?"

Yes. And all that is to the good. But stay alert. Don't let him pull you in. He's crafty, Ross. A master at playing the innocent. At playing the simple fool. He'll try to get your help. But don't get involved. No matter what he tries. I trust you, son. Don't fail me.

And the phone clicked dead.

"No, Your Eminence."

The screen seemed to be pulsating, images expanding and shrinking to a beat of drums and blare of trumpets, flashing colors finally settling down on one last shot of the dwarfs and their tall friend, everybody bouncing now on Pogo sticks and the car hoods rising and falling like the beaks of fat crows feeding in a cornfield. And then Father Bede was there, jester's cap straight and his round face looking deeply tanned and his eyes wide above a nose whose tip bulged red. The background seemed to be of stained glass, windows or a curtain shaded cross-like in its middle. Darby turned up the volume and loosened his tie. A rinky-tink piano was tapping into silence.

"Joke Break Joke Break! With thanks and with a grateful tip of the cap to Father John Lima, a true lover of good humor. Joke Break Joke Break—and wherever you are and whatever you're doing—make it Good!

"Ok—see—Little Bobby was asked by Sister Bridgett where God lived. The youngster thought and thought and finally, his face lighting up, replied: "In the bathroom." Sister Bridgett's face got very red and then she asked him why he thought such a thing. Bobby quickly said: "Because every morning my Dad pounds on the bathroom door and yells: 'My God are you still in there?'"

"Ok—ok—what do you want from a volunteer? At least I'm trying. Are you? Ok.

"Ok—look—here's the second one. And remember now—be kind and pass it on. You never know. Like Hebrews 13:2. Hebrews? It's in the Bible. New Testament. Toward the back of that big book your mother gave you?

Y'know—the one you use as a doorstop? The book, not your mother. Look it up. Hebrews 13:2. Ok?

"Ok—here comes Number Two—gasp! Are you ready for this? Ok. See there were these two men seated in the lobby of a hotel in Mowbridge, South Dakota. One of them was a cowboy and the other one was in a business suit. The cowboy turned to the businessman and said: "Look here, pard'ner—"

But the television screen went blank and then came back on and went blank again before finally settling down into Father Bede tap-dancing with the bells jingling loudly from his cap. And laughter came from somewhere, staggered and muffled from where the wide eyes blinked and stared. The screen went dark and a deep voice rumbled its way through the piano notes and a rhythmic thumping like a dancer on a hollow stage.

This has been a Joke Break courtesy of The Poor Yoricks and this station. Stay tuned for Red Clay Division Wrestling on WGAR—your Sports' Connection.

Darby clicked off the set and fell back on the bed. There were tiny silver stars painted on the ceiling, in clusters and strips from door to far wall, and water stains among them shaped like flying ducks and geese. He would call his wife after he rested. And he would need a map to find Ailey.

CHAPTER TWO

There had been too much activity in the Old Ailey Cemetery and Darby parked the car beside a blighted camphor tree and went to find the reason. The reason was given by a tall, sunburnt man in faded overalls whose face seemed too small for his lips and teeth. He was standing on a mound of red clay, two men below him struggling with a length of thick chain. About fifty yards away, a crane and bulldozer sat chugging on idle near a line of yellow trucks.

"Movin' 'em. Ever one. Takin' 'em to Mt. Gerezim. They're flooding this here. Mind your shoes—mud's slick."

"Moving the graves?"

"Coffins—yes sir. Can't use th'dirt." His teeth showed big and white, lips flapping up in the corners and bunching together. "Big lake comin' in here. Slackbridge got a grant. Doin' it to us again. Fed'ral money. This right here is th'last. Scattergood family."

"Pardon?" The man seemed to talk through his teeth, keeping them almost together and forcing the words to come out the best way they could find. The two men in the hole were cursing softly as they scraped the chain along what looked to be the burnished casing of an artillery shell.

"Scattergoods. Judge Tyler P. and Miss Della. They been here for years. Yes sir. Th'kids're all somewhere else. You know how kids are these days." He shook his head and peered over into the pit. "Easy there now—

don't scratch it all to hell. That's high-grade bronze y'got hold of."

"Shit!"

"Just go easy. Won't do to drop another one." He shook his head again and flicked at a lock of nearly silver hair that had jiggled down to almost touch the bridge of his nose. "Happened yesterday. Crane driver hit the wrong gear an' th'chain broke." He winked and nodded toward the hole. "Happened over there." He pointed at a trench-like gash in the light green grass, clay wet-looking beneath and to the side of a row of stacked headstones that sometimes sparkled when the clouds let in the sunlight. It was still early, not even 9:00, the air cool and damp. The cemetery wasn't on the map the motel manager had given him. The manager had seemed a bit uneasy at first.

"Nothing much to see there, Mr. Rust. Used t'be the County Seat but Slackbridge took that away. Years ago. Nothing much doing out there anymore. Waste of time."

"Thank you."

"Sure. Keep it. One thing I got is maps. You want one of Confederate shrines?"

"No thank you—this will—"

"It's real pretty. UDC put it out. Daughters of the Confederacy? Wife's into that stuff real big. It's free. The map? I got fifty, sixty of 'em. You sure?"

"Yes. But thank you."

"Ailey, huh?"

"Yes. Is it far?"

"No sir, it ain't. Ten, fifteen miles on that same road you came in on. North. But like I said, nothin' much there to see. Confederate statue ain't even over there no more. It came here when we got th'County Seat. You doin' a War Between the States story?"

"No–no, I'm not."

"Didn't much think so. Wife wanted me to ask. So, I asked. Look–there ain't even a good place to eat in Ailey. We got the MacDonalds an' Burger Boys. An' th' Dan D. Pig. Nothing like that up there in Ailey."

Graveside, the man in the overalls squatted down, boot toes nearly covered by clay and grass as he steadied himself with one hand and smiled.

"Yessir–dumped ol' man Bede onto th'water barrel." The laugh sounded like a bird cry caught in phlegm. "What there was left of him, that is. Them two ol' boys down there in the hole forgot to twist 'er down."

"Go to hell, Tucker!"

"Now now, boys."

"Did you say, Bede?"

"Yep. I did." The man slowly turned away his face and spat a brownish gob of something in the direction of the stacked headstones. "Bede. Marcus A. Bede. Sounds worse'n it was, a course. Boys there're young. Y'know. They didn't mean nothin' by it. Accident pure as can be. I like t'tease 'em. Only accident we had too. So far. Four hundert moved so far." He raised up slowly and wiped his mouth. "An' only ol' Marcus tried to get away. Th'only one. An' you should a seen it! Come down in a clump, bones mostly. But I'd a known that skull anywhere. Steel plate in the side. World War One. Everbody heard a that steel plate. I'm foreman here. Conroy Tucker. Foreman, Ailey Reburial Project." He let his teeth show, words still seeming to stick together and scraping out in a hiss and pop.

"Foreman a Hell, Tucker!"

"Now now, boys." He ran his hand over his mouth and winked. "You just make real sure that chain goes all th'way around that thing this time. Wouldn't do t'lose th'Scattergoods." He stepped close to Darby, the clay sucking at his boots and his laugh a rasp, dry now and wheezing. "'Specially since Miss Della's Foundation give th'land for th'lake. You a loved-one, Mister—Mister?"

"Ross. Darby Ross. No—I'm—I'm writing a book." He could feel the Cardinal behind him, somewhere nodding in approval. "I'm a writer."

"You don't say." The teeth looked even larger up close, canines prominent and the lower lip downturned like Poddy O'Malley's, the Assistant Editor, the ambitious young flatterer back at *Catholic Cross*. He made a mental note to keep a closer watch on Poddy. But San Cristobel seemed a long, long way from Mr. Tucker's smile. "Writer, huh? Hey boys—man here's a writer."

"Go to Hell, Tucker!"

"No use in that—they'd just send 'im back!"

"Now boys," he waved a hand out to the side like he was shooing away a fly. "Thought you might be a loved-one, Mister—what was the name again?"

"Ross. Darby Ross."

"Yessir. Y'see, Mr. Ross—we've had a few loved-ones come by since this here started. We've had our share." He frowned and pulled at his overall straps. "Mostly against. Had a few threats too. But that's all over now. This here's th'old cemetery anyways. Not too many loved-ones left behind to say much of nothing about anything. You heard a ol' Marcus?"

"What?" Darby stared full into the man's eyes, their color a blue so pale it seemed the irises had disappeared.

"Bede—you seemed to know him. Looked like you

did anyways there for a second."

"No–I mean I know a Bede. Not Marcus but–"

"Then it's got to be Sol, right. Got to be him. He's th'last Bede left. You know Sol?"

"Yes–I–yes I do."

"Who don't? Right? 'Specially now with him on the tee vee. Is it Sol you writin' about?"

"In part–yes."

"How about that." He shook his head. "Sol Bede in a book. Shoot fire–me an' him go way back, y'know? Grew up together."

"You did?" Darby's stomach tightened. He hadn't thought to bring along the tape recorder, resting down among the papers in his attaché case on the back seat of the car. He felt the Cardinal's eyes behind him, glaring at this early foul-up in the land of proof. And he knew that Poddy would be nearby and laughing, fat lips and all the rest, his own eyes glittering with the thought of Darby's failure.

"First grade through high school. All th'way. And y'know what?" He moved a step close, voice dropping as if to hide his words from the men down in the pit.

"No." Darby decided to write up everything as soon as he made it to the car, to salvage as much as he could. Shorthand would do it. He felt the Cardinal smile. Poddy didn't know shorthand.

"He ain't the same now, a course. You hear that bathroom joke last night?"

"Yes."

"That's what I mean–he's different now. Not like he used to be at all. He wadn't never funny like that back then. Never. He was serious. All th'time. Never funny. Not like now. Miss Peese–Miss Hattie Peese, our sixth an' seventh grade teacher called him 'the Pickle.'

Y'know? Sour? Like one of them Jew pickles?" He cleared his throat and chuckled. "Now–she–hah–*she* was somethin' in this world, I tell you." The men in the pit were singing, chain clanks and scraping sounds keeping a rough time with the rise and fall of the words.

Do it do it doit–do it do it–do–da da da
Doooo it–doooo it–nownownow–now–now–

"Music." He sniffed and slapped at a sweat bee hovering above his arm. "Yessir–Miss Hattie was a mess. Like ol' Marcus. Now *there* was a card–that man loved a joke better'n supper. An' his wife, Juney, was just as bad. Lord," he raised and lowered his head, a quick sharp movement like something had jarred loose and needed to be put back in place. "Marcus even pulled one on the Klan. Back in '37. The year Sol an' me was born. They still talk about that–th'old timers. An' them other things. Th'goat he dressed up an' put in th'Sheriff's car. An' them hogs he painted purple an' called 'runaway grapes.' Lord," he wiped his eyes and let the laugh rise up to a near shriek. "My–my daddy loved that one th'best. Purple pigs all over th'woods an' Marcus takin' out a ad in th'town paper offering two hundert dollars cash to anybody who'd catch 'em and turn 'em into wine. An' that one was back in Prohibition too. Oh my God!"

Doooo it–doo it now–sweet bay-bee do
T'me t'me t'me–do do dooo–

"Did you say something about the Klan?" Darby wasn't sure which way to go, the Cardinal seeming to have gotten lost among dry coughs and the singing from the pit.

"Yes–oh my God–yes! Y'see Marcus was Cath'lic. Bedes was big Cath'lics all along. Had their own chapel– and a priest come in about every two weeks to do whatever it is they do. Cath'lic. Way back to th'beginning, my daddy used to say. Lived here since there was a here an' a big fambly too. Until Marcus' time. An' he just had th'one boy. An'—well, Sol went off and got turned into a priest hisself an' they ain't supposed to have kids. Right?"

"Yes." The Cardinal's face was frowning now, impatient, Darby knew it was, frowning somewhere near at hand, hidden but listening close to nothing even like the sound of proof.

"It was '37—summertime. Nigras done something. Who knows what. Got somebody all upset. An' th'Klan took to night-ridin' an' marchin'—hunderts of 'em. Come in here from everywhere.

"Now Marcus, bein' Cath'lic y'know, didn't like th'Klan. No sir. Most folks just kept quiet, y'know what I mean? Safest way. But not ol' Marcus. He was allus popping off about 'em. Pokin' fun. Laughin' at them when they marched through town. Klan was real powerful around here back then.

"Anyways, they took to gatherin' in this pasture right next to Marcus's land near about every night that whole summer. Y'know. Usual stuff. Cross burnin'. Speeches. Sometimes a little drinkin' an' socializing. Until August come. August sixth, it was. A real hot night. An' they was really getting' worked up. Whole bunch of 'em. Big crowd from town too—both towns—Ailey and Slackbridge both. Gawking mostly. Y'know—somethin' to do? Car lights on, torches, cross burnin', full moon. An'— oh," he put his hand on Darby's shoulder, "did I tell you that Marcus raised hounds?"

"No."

"Well he did." Mr. Tucker squeezed Darby's shoulder and drew back to hug himself and chuckle. "An' big-time too. I mean, he must have had a hundert of 'em. Best Blue-Ticks an' Walkers in th'county. Well that summer he had him about—oh—fifteen or twenty bitches in heat, put-up–y'know–iso-lated. An' they was ready. Man they was prime. The time done come. Now or never, y'know what I mean?" He stamped his boots on the clay and blinked his eyes, face getting redder and redder.

"Yes."

"An' you can probably guess what he done–Lord– right when the whoopin' an' hollerin' was goin' full blast–he–Lord–he set them bitches free under his fence–and–and–they–they all run for th'light a course an'–an' then he let their boyfriends go find 'em. Oh my God!" His face was purple in places, the red so deep around his collar that the skin looked freshly scalded, and the laughter turned so loud it stopped the singing in the pit.

"Tucker? Hey Tucker!"

"He–he–oh my–" Tucker suddenly knelt down on the clay and slapped at his thighs, "they started in on one another all over the place–everywhere–dogs an' them Klan sheets–yellin'–runnin' around–th'cross got knocked over an' th'grass caught fire an'–oh my God did everybody laugh–an'–wait–an' then right in the middle of it all ol' Marcus come walkin' up and says in that big voice of his–says it real loud so th'people from town could hear–says: 'Anybody seen any dogs over here? Couple of my pups got loose.' Oh my sweet God–Daddy said he could a heard th'howlin' clear to Slackbridge– he–he loved to tell that story–oh my–" He reached in his back pocket and pulled out a torn red bandana and held it to his face until the laugh began to turn to coughing and the singing came back softer from the pit.

Be be my–my sweet ba-bee–be my bay-bee

Come a come a come-a be my bay-bee now–

"Did they do anything?" For Darby, proof seemed far away, the Cardinal no longer there to hear.

"What say? God!" Tucker slowly got up and brushed at his knees. He wiped at his nose with the bandana.

"The Klan–did they do anything?"

"With all that courtin' going on? No sir. That come later."

"Later?"

"Yes sir. They shot him dead 'bout a month later. No proof a course. But everybody knew. Lord. He was somethin'. An' Juney–the wife–was just as bad. Lord." He folded the bandana and slipped it into his back pocket. "She used to paint watermelons red an' sneak 'em into the strawberries. Lord. Stuff like that. She died just last year. They're both over to Mt. Gerezim now. I put ol' Marcus back in his box personal. He'd of loved seein' all that water barrel stuff though. He'd a pure loved that."

"And Solomon?"

"Sol? What about him?"

"Did–did," Darby felt the Cardinal come close again, tentatively, hanging back in case things turned out wrong, "did he ever get into any trouble?"

"Sol? Trouble? No sir. Nothin'. Like I said–he wadn't funny at all. Not at all. Not growin' up. Serious. Real serious. The Pickle. 'Pickle Bedes' was what Miss Hattie called him." Tucker turned to peer over into the pit. The singing had stopped and the men were grunting amid the clank of chain on metal. "And that's pretty much what he was. You goin' put all this in your book?"

"I don't know. Maybe." The Cardinal was gone,

swept back to the car on a rising breeze come up from where the gravestones lay, Poddy O'Malley clinging no doubt to the hem of his best red cassock and the sunlight causing moving shadow spots out across the grass and clay.

"Well if you do—do it right. It's Conroy with a 'C'. An'when you see Sol again, tell him that Conroy Tucker says come visit. Conroy, the gravedigger's son—he'll know me that way. You do that now, ok? Conroy Tucker. C-o-n-r-o-y T-u-c-k-e-r. Ok? Oh and look," he lowered his head, "I'd 'preciate you not tellin' him about his daddy—falling out like he done—y'know? It was a pure-tee ol' accident an' no sense worryin' him none. He signed th're-burial papers while he was still up north an' I believe in lettin' sleepin' dogs lay. Ok?"

"Yes."

"Y'see—I've known him all my life but—but—well, he's different now, y'know? Different. Not as good as his daddy. Or his mama. Nothing near that good. But still good."

"Yes."

"Good in his own way. He's a Bede ok."

"Yes." Darby stepped toward the car.

"An' you can't never tell what a Bede's gonna do. My daddy always said that. You just can't never tell about a Bede."

CHAPTER THREE

The Old Bede Chapel had been nearly covered by kudzu and a strange variety of honeysuckle that smelled right but looked all wrong. A recently erected historical marker had pointed the way to the building itself down a hand-cut trail among the thick clumps of leaves and oversized flower petals that seemed to be just before covering the rest of the wood and stone and leaving nothing but a larger bulge to show where they had been. But the Ailey K-6/ Junior-Senior High School complex was free of vines and its grounds filled with rushing people leaving for the day. The Chapel had been nearly lost in its dark and tangled clearing, but the school sprawled and sparkled in brick and shining steel over several acres of rolling farmland on the far side of the Ailey business district. Darby had not stopped for long at the Chapel, but he parked the car in the school's visitor lot and went to find the principal.

He had spent the past few hours back in Ailey, mostly as a careful listener, a silent guest at Lola's Café, a browsing customer in Farmer's Hardware and in the Teletronics Video and the Pretty Pig Supermarket, an attentive tourist in the Court House square and on the cool inside, with court no longer held there but old men in the hallways just the same and enough deputies and office workers to make it seem that nothing much had changed. But even he could tell that everything had changed, a feeling in the air or in the way the people spoke much like it was on Sundays when the Latin was

all gone and priests turned around to face their flocks
and altar rails came down and nuns began to look like
Joan Baez and bishops didn't notice how few people
chose to listen when the Holy Father spoke. Everything
had changed but like back in Ailey, structures stood the
same, a few things gone–the statue of a Confederate ri-
fleman and Bibles for the trials, the World War One artillery piece and pictures on the walls–but most things
went along without a need to look too closely anymore
at all the shifts and twists and turnings that had tried to
make the battered past stand strong enough to hold and
teach the new ones, runaways and lost.

He had spent hours listening, watching, in search of
proof—the people much like those back home, with Solomon Bede somehow a link among them all, among
their daily lives, their work and rest and hunger, their
confusion and their fear, perhaps become like Cardinal
Spitzmulcher had become for him, a constant that always sprang up with a timely word or way of going that
had not seemed possible before. The people loved his
jokes, each place a different one, the subject matter
changing but the laughter always there. Darby turned
down a long walkway that curved between two flag
poles and a statue of a purple pig.

The principal's office was almost cluttered with
aquariums of various shapes and sizes, some making
bubbling noises and others humming, a few with pinkish
water and in each a lighted castle seemed to reach up
toward the surface like a bloated version of the multi-
colored pebbles out around it on the bottom. The principal himself was a short, muscular black man with a
long scar on his left cheek, a zig-zagged purple bulge
from just beneath his eye down to his outsized chin. His
voice was loud and his handshake nearly painful and the

chair he offered Darby felt like marble, cold and hard. The fish in the aquariums seemed to be all the same species, a kind of miniature catfish.

"Is it a job, Mr. Ross?" His name was Thad Stevens and the way he sat on the edge of his chair behind the ornate desk made Darby feel he was expecting to be called away any second.

"Pardon?"

"A job. If you're here for that, I'm sorry to say you have most definitely come to the wrong place. Is it a job?"

"No—no—I'm a—"

"Good." He relaxed and settled back in the chair, metal creaking and his hands thumping on the armrests. "That's good. I'm glad it isn't about a job." He glanced over his shoulder and reached for the venetian blind cord. Dust puffed out the sides as he pulled the slats tight. "Can't be too careful."

"Sir?" The overhead light hummed and then sputtered, one of the long fluorescent bulbs about to go out.

"Then you're new here?"

"Yes."

"Oh. Well. Are you a parent?"

"No."

"Yes. Well. Then you can't know how it is." The man seemed to become more nervous the longer he sat behind his desk, face not yet twitching but his fingers drumming faster and faster on the armrests. "No. You can't possibly know. Why are you here?'

"I'm writing a book and—"

"Book?" He leaned forward and rested his forearms on top of a stack of yellow papers, legal-sized sheets that looked to be frayed and torn along their edges. "About what?"

"I–it's," Darby hoped the Cardinal would approve, "changes in humor. Differences in well–differences in–"

"Humor?" He seemed to tremble for a second before beginning to shuffle the papers, eyes still fixed on Darby and his face seeming to grow somehow darker. "Did you say, humor?"

"Yes. What makes people laugh. Regional differences. Changes in what people find funny. I think it'll be a long book." He sighed and seemed to almost feel Poddy O'Malley's breath on the back of his neck. He wondered if the Cardinal liked Poddy.

"Then," he quit shuffling and exhaled loudly; the fluorescent bulb crackled and hummed and then went dark, its neighbor taking up the slack with a buzzing pop. "Then you *have* heard about us." He stared for a moment at the nearest aquarium, a long bubbling rectangle with tiny silver catfish hovering there at various depths and staring back. "About Ailey?"

"I'm not sure I–"

"Was it my article in *The Georgia Educator*?" He smiled and began to tap his fingers on the papers. "Or the Stimulus Factor Symposium? Are you from the NEA?"

"No–I'm not sure you understand what–"

"Of course, it's gotten worse since the Symposium. Much worse. Since that cult started up over in Slackbridge–more children involved–more grade levels. It's coming earlier each year. It's–"

"Cult?"

"Yes. The Poor Yoricks. The Bede cult."

"You think it's a cult?" He felt the Cardinal's entrance, overpowering Poddy's breath and filling up the room with cloves and cinnamon mixed with incense and a scent of candle wax. But Darby hadn't thought he'd need the tape recorder here, not on his first visit. He had come to see if Hattie Peese were still alive, or any other teacher who might give him something he could use. "The Poor Yoricks?"

"I do. Yes indeed I do. Not that I think it's directly related to our problem here. Not immediately related anyway. Our problem is older than the Yoricks. But some of our recent graduates are over there with them. That Father Bede is preying on our problem. Using it." He coughed and blinked his eyes rapidly a few times. "Did you see our purple pig?"

"I–yes–but–" The Cardinal was not pleased, a second failure growing with each breath that Darby took, the witness clearly flawed and any solid proof elusive as the silver catfish when they chose to use the castles as their hiding place.

"I personally think it all started with that. Somehow that damned mascot–" He stopped tapping and clasped his hands together, thumbs scraping against each other almost rhythmically, moving back and forth and touching tip to tip. "I'm from Atlanta, you know? Court Order."

"Atlanta."

"Yes. I'm not from around here. Like you." He frowned and the thumbs momentarily stopped mid-scrape. "You're not a reporter, are you?"

"I'm writing a book."

"I'll just deny all this if you print it. Or sue you. It's a waste of your time to use anything *I* tell you." His eyes bulged and his head shook as if he had been hit by a low voltage electrical shock. And then the thumbs began again. "You're not a reporter?"

"Book." Darby swallowed hard and tried to avoid

the man's eyes. The Cardinal felt tense behind him, cloves and cinnamon and Poddy and candle wax now gone away for good and only the smell of incense left in the air. "I'm researching a book. Background."

"On what?" The purple bulge on his cheek seemed to grow larger, cheeks puffing out a few times and the thumbs moving faster. "Oh yes—humor. You said, humor. You've heard of us then?"

"I'm not sure you understand—I'm here to get some information on Solomon Bede. On his past. This is my first time in Ailey."

"What?" He seemed puzzled, lips moving but no words coming out for a few seconds, hands nearly at rest until a long whistling shriek from somewhere beyond the closed window ended in a rumbling boom and made him jump. "My God—that's behind the gym! Three weeks early this year!"

"Early?" Darby watched him slump forward and begin to bury his face in his hands; but a siren wail brought him back upright in his chair.

"They usually wait on the fireworks until the last week. It goes like that toward the end—stink-bombs, water balloons, fireworks—the last month of the school year. Every year."

"Every year?" Darby cleared his throat and glanced at the nearest aquarium. Something was different, the fish there seeming to have grown larger, fatter and longer in the bubbles and swirls. He wondered how that was possible, turning a little to stare into the pinkish water at what appeared to be a catfish head a full inch wide, whiskers thick and curled in circles at the tips. And then he noticed the light, a lavender-colored bulb that stretched across the back of the tank. He had been seeing shadows in the water, distortions, nothing real at all.

But Mr. Stevens was breathing heavily. And the Cardinal felt impatient.

"Yes. Every year. Yes. And no one knows why. Or they won't talk. I've been here ten years. First Black principal after desegregation. First Black principal in the whole county there for a while. Court Order. Jim Crow died hard here. But he finally did it. They shut down all the schools and reopened here. One by one. 1967. One school for this whole end of the county. With that damned purple pig as part of the deal. Somehow. Part of the land donation–part of the agreement. Did I mention that I've been here for ten years?"

"Yes."

"Ten years." He shook his head and whistled. "Court Order. Administrative Affirmative Action. Ten years ago. My immediate predecessor lasted only five. And his– three. And I'm told the first several years there were five or six others. All gone. But the pig's still here. Oh yes. Yes sir. The damned pig can't be moved. No sir. And," his face seemed about to smile, lips poised to draw back and expose his teeth, eyes wrinkling in the corners, "*I'm* still here. Ten years at the Purple Pig is a state record." The smile aborted as another whistle and boom made him wince and let out with a sound like a puppy squeezed too hard. "My God!" He stared straight ahead, seeming to have noticed something behind Darby's chair. "It could be supernatural, you know. It *could* be that. Right?"

"I'm not sure I understand what–"

"All of it–the pig might be the cause. It's possible, isn't it?"

"Well–I–"

"I know–I know. But I've gone at it every other way– I'm trained in sociology, y'know–with an abnormal psych minor. I've tried every other theory. And that's all I'm left with. The statue itself. Do you believe in the supernatural?"

"Well." The Cardinal had almost become audible, a slight rustling sound that came and went and mixed in with the bubbling from the tanks. "Yes. Yes, I believe there's something beyond what we can—"

"Right. And it influences the natural. I know it does. I do *now*. I even dream about that damned pig. I dream it talks to me. Really talks. Tells me things. Stories. Jokes. It's more than a statue. Oh yes. Much more than that. Oh my, yes. My immediate predecessor suffered a nervous collapse. In this very office. Over Christmas break. The fish were his." He sighed and shook his head. "He knew. I know he knew. They finally found him sitting on the pig. Trying to bust off its snout with a gavel. They sent him away."

"They did?"

"Yes. I visited him once. That's how I know. The pig. It's all the pig. It mocks us, Mister—Mister?"

"Ross."

"Mocks us. Teachers, guidance counselors, bus drivers, custodians, secretaries. Mocks and mocks. Mocks everything we try to do. Every good thing. We've never won a football game."

"Never?"

"Not a single one. And you know why as well as I do— if you just think about it. Pigskin. Pigskin! It gets even. It mocks. And the students all listen and do whatever it says. That's why the practical jokes! Every day—all year long. And nobody will talk about it. No one. They ignore the problem. Ignore it. Like they ignore me." He rubbed a finger quickly down his left cheek. "Like they ignore my scar. Oh," he waved feebly at Darby, "I saw you staring.

36

Everyone does that at first. Cherry bombs. In the faculty lounge water fountain. An intricate prank. Timed. Special fuses. Back during the tension over a state holiday for Dr. King. No real suspects. No repetition and—and eventually ignored." He sighed and bit at his lower lip. "Like everything else. Ignored. Like—like—like it never happened, isn't happening now. That everything is fine. Like back before there *was* a purple pig. Even the deputies have quit coming out here—unless it's serious property damage." Another whistle and another and another and three booms almost all together brought Mr. Stevens up out of his chair and into a short-stepped pacing in between Darby and the desk.

"Why don't you just get rid of the pig?"

"Get *rid* of the *pig*? You can't do that." A muffled clanging of cowbells and two long horn blasts seemed to relax him, catching him mid-pace. He leaned against his desk, buttocks pressing into the wood and the shiny cloth of his pants bunching up along the beltline. "You can't. They'll stop you."

"They?" He could feel the Cardinal rising up to his full height, robes crinkling and his face a study in annoyance.

"That pig's got friends. Oh, don't laugh."

"I wasn't going—"

"I'm not stupid, Mr. Ross. You don't get to where I am being stupid. Not even in South Georgia." He shook his head and chuckled, the sound dry and raspy and the water in the nearest aquarium suddenly bubbling louder, the light clicking off to let the big fish break up and return to normal size. "I even live on the other side of the next county. Gated community. I commute. Sixty miles at a crack. Every day. I know what I'm doing."

"I didn't mean to–"

"Yes, and I know about humor, Mr. Ross. I know all about what's funny."

"I'm sure you–"

"Mark Twain. Samuel Clemens. He was funny."

"Yes."

"And Will Rogers."

"Ok."

"And Satchel Paige."

"Yes, I've always–"

"And Ogden Nash. James Thurber. Charles Addams."

"Yes, well–"

"And Lucille Ball and sometimes Desi Arnaz."

"Mr. Stevens, what I really need is–"

"But that pig isn't funny. And that cult over in Slackbridge isn't funny. And I'm Catholic myself, Mr. Ross. Did you know that?"

"No."

"Well, I am. Convert. 1963. It was the least I could do." He turned slowly around and began to gather up the yellow papers, pulling a battered briefcase up from the floor near his trash can and stuffing them into it. "Where were *you* when John Kennedy died?"

"What?"

"Don't you remember?"

"Yes–yes of course I do–I–I–" Another day the Cardinal found the time and way to pop up in his life, a minor episode not far from Number One, out on the road between the holding tank and Jackson Square, hitchhiking north for Thanksgiving, as far away as he could get from home and questions and the pressing in of duty. "I remember. But, Mr. Stevens, I–" The Cardinal was already leaving, incense nearly covered up in some strong scent like mildew.

"Well, I was in New York City, Mr. Ross. Eating a hotdog. At a Nathan's." He sniffed and seemed to be holding his breath, letting it out finally in a rush of words. "Just off Times Square. Mustard and pickle-relish." He wiped at his eyes and then snapped the briefcase shut. "I know humor. Oh yes. And it's not here. There's nothing funny here, Mr. Ross. Like at Nathan's in 1963. Nothing funny at all. I'm going home."

"I—can you just—" Darby hastily stood up and followed behind, the briefcase bumping gently into the side of his leg as he came even with it at the door.

"You probably mean well, Mr. Ross. Writing a book. That's a good thing to do." He opened the door and cautiously peered out into the empty lobby, right and left and up above before stepping quickly through. "But as far as I'm concerned, the only story here is that pig. That damned damned pig." He started for the front doors, body tensed and head moving side to side as if expecting something to spring out at him from behind the overstuffed couches and chairs or from the thick folds in the partially opened drapes. "That's all there is."

"And Solomon Bede?"

"Say what?" He stopped and turned around, carefully, eyes twitching and his lips gone fish-like as he took in air and let it out in slow, short bursts.

"Solomon Bede. He graduated from here, didn't he?" It felt good to finally get to why he came. "Ailey?"

"That crazy monk in Slackbridge?"

"Yes. Solomon Bede."

"He didn't graduate from *here*." He seemed just before losing his balance, legs seeming to wobble a bit as he shifted the briefcase into his other hand. "No sir. Not *here*. No chance of that. I think he went to school up north."

"But—" The Cardinal was returning, piece by piece this time, beak-nose first thing out and sniffing at the air.

"Anyway—we only go back to 1967 *here*."

"But the records?" The cheekbones had come through and just a glimmer of the Cardinal's eyes. "Students and teachers? Records?"

"Lost. In a fire. Everything before 1960. Lost. Whoever he really is—he never went *here*."

"Lost?"

The Cardinal seemed to slide away beneath the laughter, deep and strong as Mr. Stevens patted Darby toward the doors.

CHAPTER FOUR

Darby had found Hattie Peese's address in a phone book back in town, inside a rose-scented booth at Lola's Café. He had ordered the catfish special with an extra helping of fried okra (frozen), hushpuppies and an apparently inexhaustible supply of iced tea in a mug shaped like a mermaid. The waitress seemed bored and the few other customers quiet to an extreme, but the catfish sat well on his stomach as he drove the five miles or so to Hattie's white frame house. The cashier had given him directions.

"Ain't seen her in a long while. You a relative?"

"No."

"Well. You can't miss *her house.* It's the only one out there with a satellite dish. Front yard."

The dish was painted blue and Hattie was dressed in a high-necked gown with starched lace stars attached seemingly at random along the sleeves and down the front. She had been watching a large-screened television set that perched like an overgrown building-block on a rolling table at one end of her screened-in side porch. She looked him up and down and then asked him to come in. Darby noticed a police car slow and stop out where the road curved back to town. It had followed him at a respectful distance all the way here.

"'Bout time they sent you!"

Her white hair was neatly swept back into a bun that bobbled a bit as she talked, lips thin and face a sunken thing with purplish folds of skin that bulged down from the cheeks like finger nubs or bruises that had never healed. She had one blue eye and one brown one, a shade of brown that sometimes turned to red when the light came in just right. Her voice was steady, not quite shrill but pitched to be noticed.

"I'd about given up hope. Did they send you from the Atlanta office?"

"Pardon me, ma'am, but–"

"Well, just look at it for yourself. Look!" She pointed with her whole arm, fingers curled in toward the palm and the knuckles of her index finger leading all the rest. "And that's my favorite program too. *Louisiana Love Feast*. My absolute favorite. Jack Onan's hosting this week–but–just look at his face there–green! You ever see the like?"

"No ma'am, but I–" The screen was filled with a man's smiling face, green with flecks of red and blue across the forehead and down along his cheeks and neck, a woman there beside him with purple hair piled high and wide atop her chubby head. They seemed to be singing.

"And Miranda has black hair. Coal black. They're such a lovely young couple, don't you think?" She smacked her lips and then stamped her foot a few times, an end table jingling beside the couch and dust motes rising on a shaft of late afternoon sunlight. "But not like that! And it's been getting worse. Every day. I can't count on a one of my favorites coming in decently. Oh look–Jack's healing someone!" She clapped her hands together and croaked out a sound halfway between a squeal and a cough. The green-faced man's massive-looking hands were pressing down onto the blue hair of a skinny child in multi-colored overalls and a pink plaid shirt. The child's face was boiled-lobster red and he seemed to be fighting back, body tensed and twisting beneath the green pressure on his head. "Praise Jesus!" She wiped at her eyes and turned to face Darby. Her front teeth seemed to claw out at her lower lip as she talked. "So what do you plan to do about it? And—" she closed the brown eye and squinted up at Darby through the blue one just as the screen dissolved into a whirling mess of colored dots and solid bars. "And don't tell me about adjustments. I've read the manual three times through. I think you sold me a lemon. And I want you 'Dogstar' people to put it right. I got a valid warrantee too. You hear me?" She put her hands on her hips and opened both eyes wide. "Well?" The green-faced man was back, seeming to be shouting nonsense words at the obviously terrified child, a fat lady now behind and holding to his pink plaid shoulders with both hands.

"Ma'am, I'm Darby Ross. And I'm here to ask you a few questions. I'm writing a book." He had remembered to bring along the tape recorder, a hard bulge in his jacket pocket, new tape set to soak up proof as soon as any chose to come his way. But he couldn't feel the Cardinal here at all.

"What did you say?" She seemed to quiver, head to toe, a flutter in her cheeks that dropped down quickly through her arms and hands. The screen was filled with dancing people, hands raised high above their heads, a sectioned rainbow moving through the growing dots and re-emerging bars of solid color.

"I'm Darby Ross—"

"No—no, after that. I caught the name fine. What was that you said about a book—are you a salesman?" She stuffed a hand into a slit in the side of her gown and pulled out a remote-control wand. The screen went dark, one fat blue dot lingering for a few seconds past the dying of the other colors. "Encyclopedias?"

"No ma'am—no—I'm here about a former—"

"Bibles then. Are you a Bible salesman?"

"No—I—"

"Because if you are, I want you to know right now that I'm not the least bit interested. I have twenty Bibles in this house. Twenty, young man. And every one's a King James Version. Translated from the original tongues. No 'her' and 'she' about God—no monkey business—straight English—*translations*, not guesses!" She had become breathless, the quiver gone inside to make her words sound shaky, coated with a huskiness turned low and soft like a whisper. "You're selling Bibles, aren't you?"

"No, ma'am, I am not."

"A Mormon then! Good God another Mormon—where's your friend? You devils always pop up here in twos—where is he?" The voice was breaking free, its original pitch coming back in stages. Her eyes seemed bulged to a point near bursting, tiny blood vessels in the whites clearly visible in knotted swirls and patches almost purple. "You just leave, young man! I'm a Christian lady! Born-again, Spirit-baptized, tongue-talking, Bible-believing, faith-healed child of the Living God! You hear me, you devil?"

"I'm—I'm not Mormon, ma'am—"

"Then Jehovah's Witness—one of them? Right?" Her jaw was trembling with a force that made her lips smack together. "Then get away from *me*!" She stepped back and waved at him with her hands, fingers fluttering out like stiff flags. "Go on now—get! I will *not* have my home violated by your filth. And I will *not* listen to—"

"Please, Miss Peese, I—"

"No sir! My ears are not garbage cans and I'm

44

standing on the Rock of Ages and I *will not* listen—no no no!" She cupped her hands over her ears and began to do what looked like a little shuffle-dance, soft-soled shoes going swish-swish on the hard wood floor. "No no no!"

"Trouble here, Miss Hattie?" The deputy was tall and wide, shoulders and chest seemingly too much for what must have been the largest sized khaki shirt he could find. "Miss Hattie?" He shouted and stopped the dance.

"Huh? Oh. Oh my. Is that you, Lil' Ben?" Her voice took on a gentle quality, nearly purring as she smoothed at her gown and patted at her hair and stepped past Darby toward the screen door.

"Any trouble here, Miss Hattie?"

"What on earth are you doing way out here, Lil' Ben? You're not playing hooky again, are you—you young scamp? Because—because if you are I'll just step inside and call your—"

"No ma'am—Miss Hattie—Miss Hattie! Listen now— this is the deputy—remember? One of Sheriff Charblaine's deputies?"

"Deputy?"

"Yes ma'am." He rested a hand on the lintel and bent down to bring his face closer to the screen door. "From over in Slackbridge?"

"Slackbridge?" She looked from Darby to the deputy and then frowned, slowly, the skin wrinkling up in stages on her forehead. "Then what are you doing *here*?"

"I'm on loan this month. Look, Miss Hattie—are you having any trouble here?"

"Trouble?"

"Yes ma'am. With that gentleman there," he nodded toward Darby, the brim of his patrol cap scraping across the screen. "With *him*?"

"This man here?"

"Yes ma'am."

"My land no, Lil'Ben." She chuckled. "Why on earth would you think that?"

"Well you was getting pretty loud in here. An' I a'ready had a call to check on you. There's no trouble then?"

"No no no. This is the 'Dogstar' repairman, Lil' Ben. He's here about the dish. It won't bring in the color right. He's here to fix it."

"That so, Mister?"

"No." Darby sighed and wished he was back home, back on the bank of the Little Okra watching the hyacinths float and bob, his wife up at the house saying the second of her two Rosaries for the day and his daughter in the pool. Even the office—Poddy O'Malley and the not-so-secret visits by the Cardinal—seemed preferable to Miss Hattie and her deputy in a place where proof must never have been born. "No I am not a television repairman. No!"

"What?" Miss Hattie looked genuinely surprised. "You're not?"

"No, ma'am, I am not."

"Then who are you, Mister?" The deputy looked hot, hot and tired and long overdue for a beer. He pulled a cigarette out from behind his right ear and lit it behind cupped hands, smoke swirling onto the screen door and coming through in thick blue strands. "If you ain't her repairman?"

"Ask him if he's a Mormon, Lil' Ben."

"I'm a writer, Officer—I'm here about a former student of her's—Solomon—"

"Tell him I'm a Christian lady, Lil'Ben. For eighty

years. Tell him I even got a baby brother in the ministry of the Lord. Tell him about Baylor over in Jonesboro, Lil' Ben. Mt. Ararat Assembly. It's a great big church too. Go on now. Tell him."

"Tell her again, Mister." The deputy pulled on his cigarette and stepped back from the door. "She'll hear you directly."

"Miss Hattie—I'm here about Solomon Bede."

"What?" She fluttered at the top clasp of her gown with shaking fingers. "What did you say?"

"Solomon Bede. You taught him?"

"Bede." She gasped and sat down quickly on a nearby couch—plastic pillows making a popping sound and part of her hair-bun coming loose. A few strands of silver hair hung down the back of her neck like wind-frayed feathers. "Oh, my good God! Bede! Now I see it. I see it plain. Go away and leave me you devil!" She growled out the words, lips gone nearly colorless and her face splotching red. "Make him go, Lil' Ben. Like a good boy. Take him on home."

"Better leave her, Mister, for a fact. She'll go quiet in a minute. I'll call her grandson. He knows what to do." Shaking his head, the deputy tapped on the door frame and exhaled the last of his cigarette. "Best just come on out and leave her be."

"But—Miss Peese—" He patted at the bulge in his jacket, tape recorder somehow growing heavier the longer it stayed out of sight, "I need to ask you about Solomon Bede. I'm writing a book," he glanced over at the deputy and smiled weakly, "you see—a book—and I need background information on Solomon—on what kind of student he was and—"

"Make him go away, Lil' Ben. He's a devil. A demon. You can see that for yourself. Like the Bedes. I know him now. I can see him plain as daylight. Like the Bedes. He's Catholic, Lil' Ben. Like a dill pickle. Sour. Never smiling. Smug. Damning everybody to Hell. Idol-worshippers. Sour or crazy. Sour like him or crazy like his daddy. And his mama. Crazy. You're no good, Solomon Bede! You hear me? Pickle Bedes Pickle Bedes Pickle Bedes!" She had begun to rock back and forth on the couch, plastic popping and the gown hem swishing as she moved. "But—but the craziness won. Oh yes it did. The craziness got inside. Into our new school. Into our precious children. Pickle Bedes left. Oh yes—*he* went away. But the craziness got inside. It was his daddy. *And* his mama. And they got stopped. Oh yes they did. First one. Then the other. Stopped. But it—*it* stayed on. *It* stayed."

"I'm taking him away, Miss Hattie." The deputy put two fingers to his lips and winked. "He's going away now. With me. You just rest. Watch your programs and rest. I'll call Lester to come see you. Ok?" He field-stripped his cigarette and tucked the filter into his shirt pocket. The black and white metallic name tag read: **EARP, W.**

"A book?" She suddenly stopped rocking and stared hard at Darby. "Did you say you were writing a book? Did you?"

"Yes ma'am." Darby could feel the Cardinal fidgeting with his robes back in the car, tired of Ailey and the scent of failure.

"And the Bedes are in it?" She sounded like she had at first, when she had asked him in and let him watch the green man and his chubby wife.

"Yes ma'am."

"I see."

"We're going now, Miss Hattie." The deputy pulled open the screen door and nudged Darby outside. The door shut behind them with a slapping sound.

"Yes. Go do your homework, Lil' Ben. And maybe you can go to college. Maybe you can *be* something."

"Yes ma'am."

"And young man?"

"Yes."

"You go to Slackbridge. They say," she nodded toward the blank screen, "they say that Solomon's come back. You go talk to him about the Bedes. He's the boy you need to see. He was one of them. Oh yes. Sure as there's a fire in Hell he was. He never fooled me one bit. You go see him."

"Yes ma'am." It had gotten warmer outside, the sun still bright above the trees and no air stirring. Darby followed the deputy down the graveled pathway to the road, the man's broad back pushing at the sweat-stained khaki and his collar nearly lost to sight beneath a moving roll of fat. He opened the door to the Cardinal's car and stepped back to adjust his cap.

"She ought be in a home, y'know? Nice rest home somewhere. Oh—an' my name ain't Ben."

"I see."

"Yeah—she stays confused. Pitiful. But mostly harmless. You stayin' hereabouts?"

"Slackbridge."

"That's good. Real good. I live there myself." He smiled and ran his tongue quickly over his teeth. "Not a whole lot there but it's sure more than here. Here is nowhere, y'know. I'm from Richmond."

"I see."

"Virginia Highway Patrol." He kicked at an asphalt clump with a deeply polished boot toe and laughed. "Ten year's worth. But th'wife wanted to live closer to her mama. You know how it is."

"Yes."

"What is your book about anyways?"

"It's–it's about humor–a study of–"

"Humor, huh? You mean, comedy?"

"Yes–it's–"

"Jokes an' like that?"

"Yes, but not just–"

"Well, shit, man–you need to go to Macon."

"Pardon?"

"Macon–go on over there–two new clubs opened just last week."

"But–"

"Hey–you ain't a talent scout, are you?" He tugged at his tie, eyes seeming to bulge a little from the pressure.

"No–no, I'm not."

"Too bad. Y'see, I'm tryin' to break into show bidness. I already won the First Blood Contest at th' Many Ha-Ha Club. In Macon? Statewide competition too. I do combat stuff." He swallowed hard and made the tie knot bob. "I was in the Nam. Early. '64-'66. Marines."

"I see."

"But hell now I've always had a sense of humor. Always. I got a whole act worked up. Combat stuff. Like– oh let me see–like: 'How many Seals does it take to grease a Slope?'"

"I–uh–I really need to–"

"Ok. Ok. But look–no foolin'–you go to Macon on that comedy thing. Not here. Hell man, there's nothin' here but low grade stuff. Slapstick an' bubble gum. An' them flaky monks. Amateurs. No honest-to-God clubs in th'whole county. Nothin'. No–you go to Macon if you want some real fun."

"Yes. Thank you."

"Don't mention it. Glad to help. I could tell you wasn't from around here. Us city boys got to stick to-gether. Right?"

"Yes."

"An' look—while you're in Macon, catch my act. I work Friday nights—Many Ha-Ha Club. Highway 602 North. You want to write that down?"

"No—no, I'll remember."

"Real good. Many Ha-Ha Club—Friday nights. Name's Earp. No shit. Wyatt Earp. Real name swear to God. Catch me in Macon. You'll bust a gut."

CHAPTER FIVE

The motel manager had smiled when he said it—"Big Red called"—and then: "Big Red called while you were gone"—his face approaching laughter as he added, "Sounded real important, Mr. Rust—like a movie star. Just now hung up. Five minutes tops. San Cristobel, Florida. Big Red. Said he was in San Cristobel, Florida and that you would know the number." And then he had handed Darby a small sheet of blue paper with balloons bunched in the corners and a faint outline of a seahorse in the middle and **WHILE U WERE OUT** printed all across the top. The manager had wanted to talk, settling back on his swivel stool behind the front desk and pouring himself a cup of weak-looking coffee from the 'Complimentary Pot'. But Darby got away after the first sentence.

"Hey—you all making a movie down there in San Cristobel?"

#

His room had been cleaned, a smell of lemon in the air mixed with some strong odor like detergent, the bed changed, or at least the coverlet, now a patchwork quilt with clown faces in each square and the stitching multicolored, golds and blues and reds in thick stripes like candy canes. It made a crinkling noise when he sat down. The telephone still felt greasy. Cardinal

Spitzmulcher answered on the second ring.

Anything, yet, Ross?

"No, Your Eminence. Nothing solid. Not yet."

Did you say—nothing?

"Yes, Your Eminence."

Do you watch television, Ross?

"Eminence?"

Television. Do you watch it?

"Yes. Yes, of course, Eminence. There's one in the room here."

It was on this morning's national news.

"What was, Your Eminence?" Darby could hear the anger building, the Cardinal's face by now, he knew, tensed, jaw tight and teeth grinding in the pauses between words.

The tour. Didn't you see it? All three networks.

"No, Your Eminence—I—I didn't watch the news this—"

Well they're going on a tour, Ross. Did you hear me?

"Yes. Tour?"

Something called the Denapoli Circuit. One of Bede's clowns called it that. Denapoli. Monsignor Gramland knew about it. His father was a juggler. Denapoli meant the little places. The places no one else would go. The show-folk called them Denapoli. No one knows why. Perhaps as a joke. Vaudeville, Ross. It's a vaudeville tour! In the 1980s!

"Vaudeville?" Darby pushed away thoughts building of jugglers and big-shoed comics squirting water at the dancing girls.

Yes. Monday. They're leaving on Monday—Bede himself and what he calls the Second Bananas. The pause seemed longer than it really was. *And you'll go too, Ross.*

"On the tour, Eminence?"

Yes. But first you'll attend Mass. At Bede's—his barn

or whatever it is he uses for a chapel. Sunday morning. 9:00. You'll attend Mass there.

"Yes, Eminence."

Perhaps you won't need to tour with him if there's real blasphemy—if he blasphemes during the Holy Mass. If there's any profanation. You watch for that. For blasphemy. I'm not expecting any, but be ready just in case.

"Yes, Eminence. Blasphemy." He tried to picture Father Bede in baggy pants and pork-pie hat, shuffle-stepping round the altar while the brothers clapped and sang, acolytes all Groucho-bent or honking-Harpos bleating out a tune on rubber ball-tipped horns to help the choir sing "Lydia."

Public blasphemy will stop him where he stands, Ross. So look close for anything irregular. The pause was longer this time, letting in a sound of tolling bells, the seminary chapel warning of the coming of the night. *I think he's too clever for that. I do. So—you know how to proceed.*

"Yes, Eminence." An earlier assignment. Five years ago when *Catholic Cross* was nearly broke. He had come to its rescue with a series written from the inside of the Jesus-Quest Charismatics, articles that pointed to their photogenic leader's wayward plunge toward alcoholism, egomania and the dank, lush ground of schism. Circulation had tripled during the series and Darby and the *Cross* were on their way. The priest then, Father Raphael "Pogo" Craps, had later been recycled as a friar somewhere in the mountains of Virginia.

In other words, be prepared to join the tour. Be ready for that.

"Where does this tour—"

It's all settled here, Ross. You have our total blessing and support. My friends are on full alert. They can help you if you need it. Like it was before, only more so this time. We think you'll be mostly in the South. We think that's what he'll do. But be prepared for anything. Did you think to check your room for bugs?

"Eminence?"

No. I can tell you didn't. But don't worry—we did. Today.

"You did? But, Eminence how was I—you didn't say to—"

My friends are ready to help you. But you will be the closest to Bede himself. And he'll take you with him, Ross. Yes. He'll do that. This tour is more than it seems.

"But Eminence, how long will I have to—"

And Bede—he's not what he seems either, Ross. The pause was filled with a low humming sound, a nearly musical counterpoint among the last of the muffled bells. *Oh. And I have told your wife to expect you back home in about a month.*

"A month, Eminence?" Poddy's face seemed to flash out smiling from the television cabinet, eyes dead center of the whale's fat flukes and Darby's house on the Little Okra also there, shuddering somewhere past the biggest longboat, fragile-looking, delicate, like his memories of the past.

She understands perfectly. You have a jewel there, Ross. A soldier's wife. Did you hear me?

"Yes, Eminence."

And it gives me great joy to see you children doing so well. After your long struggle. The humming returned in a tune that seemed familiar but broken, a shudder and a jerking there at times too low to comfortably hear. *And your beautiful daughter—how old is she now?*

"Sixteen, Your Eminence."

Ah, Sweet Sixteen. It seems only yesterday that I

baptized her. In that leaky church—when you were out of a job. Only yesterday.

"Yes, Eminence."

He'll show us what he really is, Ross. On this tour. And we haven't given up on his past. We're still searching—for what I know is there. Something. We'll find it. But you go with him. Stay close to him. And use pay phones. Did you hear?"

"Yes, Eminence."

Oh yes—Poddy O'Malley sends his best. Did you know he's receiving his Silver Beaver from the Boy Scouts this month?

"No—I never knew he was in—"

And he's Scoutmaster of the Year as well. For the Archdiocese. We're very proud of Poddy. He's a fine young man. A fine example to the youth.

"Yes, Eminence."

You were wise to hire him as Assistant. He has our complete trust.

"Yes." But Poddy had not come through personnel, instead appearing full blown on the day the old Assistant Editor retired, his patron undiscovered until now.

Go with God, Ross. Keep alert. We think that Pee Dee Crossing will be first.

"What—beg pardon, Eminence?"

On their Denapoli. It's northwest of you. Not far. About sixty miles. Ball-bearings. Did you hear?

"Yes."

There's a small plant there. And a souvenir factory. On the Timaquan Indian Reservation.

"Indians, Your Eminence?"

Yes. Our loyal red brothers and sisters. Jesuit-trained. The old Jesuits. It's still a first-rate mission. The pause flickered and was gone. *Ah yes—your blessing. Are you kneeling?*

"Yes, Eminence." Darby quickly dropped to one knee, elbow resting on the bedside table near where the polka-dotted Bible had been, a shell-shaped ashtray now there in its place. The Cardinal's voice was getting hard to hear, a crackle on the line like distant pops of lightning out before a building storm.

Dominus vobiscum—

"Et cum spiritu tuo."

Benedicat vos omnipotens Deus, Pater, et Filius, et Spiritus Sanctus—

"Amen."

Pax Domini sit semper vobis cum—

"Et cum spiritu tuo."

Good. Very good. Now go—'Ite'—go and make me proud of you. Prove my long-time trust was rightly placed. And Ross?

"Eminence?"

Remember about the pay phones.

The receiver was nearly hot and Darby's ear felt numb, a tingling that even rubbing didn't help. He sat down on the bed and noticed that his socks were different colors, a brown and green that in the seahorse light looked nothing near the same.

CHAPTER SIX

The Mass had not been irregular in any way, no jester-caps in sight, the brothers joyous but their voices well-controlled, the chapel cramped but tasteful—everything in order, Holy Family carved in dark wood polished so they glistened in their niches, Stations of the Cross just where they should have been, the sanctuary light full-strength inside its rose-etched glass, the altar well-provided—tabernacle, cloth and candelabra and a giant crucifix above it all with Christ there nearly life-sized in His public time of suffering and pain. There had been nothing irregular, no blasphemy or disrespect, the homily straight teaching on St. Joseph and the need for more novenas and an ending near-Franciscan plea for labor's dignity and for peace. Holy Communion had proceeded without hitch or glimmer of the mockery the Cardinal seemed to hope would show itself, Fr. Bede's eyes filled with love and trust behind the Host and Darby's 'Amen' joining with the others, a feeling in the room much like the times on Christmas Eve he served as altar boy and daydreamed of the presents soon to come. Darby had been the only visitor and a green-robed brother had gotten to him when the Mass was ended, handing him a note from Fr. Bede. The handwriting was nearly childlike, an oversized scrawl of printed and cursive letters jumbled like a message made from newsprint headlines pasted hurriedly together.

CoME bY OfFIcE. wE Can TalK—

The brother was young, barely in his twenties Darby

guessed, tall and broad-shouldered in the way of football linemen, teeth large and white and even and his eyes laugh-wrinkled in the corners, shallow lines and indistinct at times but clearly formed and ready for the years ahead to make them firm and lasting. He walked with a bouncing step that rippled the cloth across his back and made his lowered hood rise up a bit like a wayward collar needing to be ironed. He left Darby in a cubicle that opened off the sacristy, clicking on a single bulb suspended from a roof-beam, its harsh light showing the windowless room to be bare except for two straight-backed chairs, a battered table stacked with dog-eared books and a frameless bulletin board just inside the door with a sheet of yellow paper thumbtacked to its middle. The writing on the paper was a bolder version of Darby's note:

JOKE OF THE DAY

<u>Breathless Patient:</u> Doctor can you help me? My name is Arkswalter!"

<u>Doctor:</u> "No. I'm sorry. I simply can't do anything for that."

Fr. Bede's voice outside in the sacristy sounded softer than it had back during Mass, his words not clear but laughter following on the pauses, several other voices joining in and then gone silent, louder laughter in the places they had been. Darby reached into the breast pocket of his sport-coat and clicked on the Cardinal's mini-recorder, the one that had arrived with a small sack of quarters just as he left for Mass that morning. The driver of the special-delivery van had reminded him of any one of the San Cristobel seminarians as he bowed and winked and left without a word, the Cardinal's presence somehow going with him, leaving Darby on his own. The tape was good for ninety minutes.

"Mr. Ross?"

And there he was again, like months before dressed now in Yorick-fashion, vestments gone, plaid-coated and with lavender pants this time, his tiny jester-cap placed down upon his head just where the hair no longer grew. Darby knew that he would need to take in everything to give the tape a frame. The Cardinal would expect all that and more. Descriptions, details that would help him see, the feel if possible and smell and even taste of what the tape would hold of sound.

"Yes. It's good to see you again, Father Bede."

The hand felt warm as Darby squeezed once and brought his own hand to his chest just in time to pat back down the top of the recorder, its buttons snagged in a rough place on the otherwise smooth lining of his coat.

"And I trust that all is well at *Catholic Cross*?" He motioned for Darby to be seated in one of the straight-backed chairs, the one nearest the table and its books. The book on top had a badly scuffed leather cover, its title illegible, only a gold-embossed *comedia* left intact and bits of other letters out behind like flecks of glittered dust. Fr. Bede sat down quickly, bells jingling on his cap and his blazer sleeves almost alive with light reflected from the large bulb overhead.

"Yes. I'm sorry we haven't–"

"No need for that." He smiled and Darby noticed that his face seemed blurred–no–proportion not quite right, something, nose and mouth perhaps too close together or the eyes placed with no true concern for forehead width or where the cheeks began and ended and the ears–the ears left free to crinkle out a bit before made stiff with starch or baked until their surfaces looked glazed. Darby wondered what the face would do when he asked about the tour, about permission to go with it on the road. The smile grew wider. "All in good time. It *is* good to see you again as well, Mr. Ross. And you've come at an important time."

"I–I'm here to–"

"Yes, yes. We leave tomorrow."

"Tomorrow?" It was going to be too easy and the face had shifted somehow, placement of the eyes now closer to the nose, tip wider than before and passing back and forth from red to pink in surges like a blinking neon sign. It was all going too fast.

"Yes. You will travel with me. In the prop-van. It's easier to talk there. Our first tour should be fun. I believe in fun. And straight talk. I need it. Little or big. Like the candidate for Congress in a mostly rural state, not shy about telling voters why they should send him to Washington:

'I can plow, reap, milk cows, shoe a horse–in fact, I should like you to tell me one thing about a farm I cannot do.

Into the impressive silence, a loud voice came from the back of the hall, asking: 'Can you lay an egg?'"

And the smile seemed like a rocket burst upon the surface of a cloudless sky, the face for just a second disassembled, free to swirl its pieces right to left and drift them up and down before they had to come back where they started from, to let the laughter change itself to words. "We're opening tomorrow night. Third shift at Pee Dee Crossing. The older brothers this time. The Second Bananas only. A little tour. Will you stay the night with us, Mr. Ross?"

CHAPTER SEVEN

There had barely been time for a quick collect call to 'Big Red' before the motel manager and the maid service arrived, forcing Darby outside with the last of his bags. The maid had seemed almost desperate to plug in her oversized vacuum cleaner and the manager had insisted that Darby take along a sack of pecans.

"It's last year's crop. But still real good."

The sack and bags had been loaded into the trunk by a slender boy, an undersized teenager dressed in leather pants and wearing a cut-away tee-shirt with a faded image of Elvis on its glittered back. The sack weighed five pounds according to the white band around its middle.

"They prime too. Paper shells—best there is. Wife's idea."

"Thank you—thank her."

"Don't mention it—we try to please. Just glad I caught you before you left us. I meant to give 'em to you when you paid your bill. Sure you won't stay longer?"

"Yes."

"Well."

And then the teenager had pushed back a lock of greasy-looking hair and winked and came in close to Darby's ear, the whispered words almost too low to hear—*pax tecum*—said quickly while he opened the car door and winked again and walked away, the Elvis face there crinkling up among the glitter, shirt all filled with tiny flashes out across it as he moved. The manager ignored him as he passed and waved a pudgy hand while Darby fumbled for the key.

"You have yourself a good trip now, y'hear?"

His smile had looked painful, much too wide and forced to hold too long, the car at first refusing to start, beeps and buzzes mixing in with engine groans until it seemed that every gadget there had fallen sick at once and gone to shouting out for help. The smile, however, held up through it all and only died away when Darby finally got the key to work.

"And come back soon. Come back real soon now. Bye-bye—"

And the car had chugged and jerked and bucked a time or two, a backfire coming in to push it quickly past the office, black smoke out behind, past an empty linen cart and past the teenaged boy who seemed to bless him as he went, his fingers long and swishing through the air a Father, Son, and Holy Spirit flourished with a swirl at top and bottom like the one the Cardinal made when he was rushed or bored.

#

The car had settled down out on the highway, running smoothly all the way to the front entrance of The Laughing Place and signaled to a stop there by a fat novice who took the keys and helped unload the luggage and then shared what he had called a 'holy zinger' in a voice that sounded just like Elmer Fudd.

"So here it comes. Ready? Ok, ok: A customer complained to his barber that his hair was coming out. Every day. Big clumps. 'Can you give me something to keep it in?' He begged. 'Take this,' the barber said kindly and handed the customer a shoe box."

And he had left in the car singing, humming really, a ta-ta-*ta-ta* ta *ta* ta-*ta-ta*—burst of sound mixed in with equal parts of tongue clicks and a drumming with his fingers on the steering wheel. Fr. Bede had shaken his head and sighed, bells jingling softly as he seemed to appear from nowhere, Darby nearly jumping when he felt the pressure of fingers on his arm and turned to look down into eyes that changed from blue to green each time the sunlight made it through the clouds. The tape was a new one and Darby had just enough time to click it on while seeming to smooth down the inside of his coat.

"He has much to learn himself."

The voice had sounded tired, clear enough and strong but touched with what perhaps had been there from the first, a hint of sadness which was close to being weary. And he had not left Darby until after Vespers, a whole tape's worth of introductions and another noisy walkabout, the second tape inserted on a bathroom break to be prepared for what might show itself at prayer. The chapel had been filled with Yoricks, cap-less yet all dressed in glaring blazers and ill-matching trousers and in shirts that clashed with everything, bow ties on each and every one that Darby knew would flash out something like HELLO or squirt a stream of water on whoever seemed to need a closer touch. But there had been nothing irregular in the prayers, no blasphemy, nothing that the Cardinal himself would find offensive in the least degree. Fr. Bede had left him in a spacious guest room with windows opening on the pecan grove and closer by and to the right the well-kept lawn that ended somewhere in the growing darkness at the barn-like theatre, rehearsal hall, whatever it was called that this night had remained unused, empty while the brothers prayed for joy and happiness, for punchline strength and timing and above all for God's good humor going out before them into each and every place they had been let come in. Fr. Bede had left him in the spacious room, the tiredness, the sad and weary signs no longer there among the wrinkles and the creases making up a face as round as if it had been drawn that way by some cartoonist purposely intent on close economy of pen-stroke and of ink. But the face had stayed in place this time, not letting any part go wandering up and down, not losing its own settled placement even when it smiled just outside in the hall. The second tape was nearly over.

"Sleep well. We leave after Mass." And then a quick nightcap, offered almost shyly, the face's lips pursed both before and after. "Sleep. Ah yes. Afraid you are going to have insomnia? What are the symptoms?" And—the pause was just right, an eye-blink or a jingle of the jester-bells: "Triplets!"

And the laughter came from Darby, one hand reaching slowly for his inside pocket, fingers pressing at a bulge he hoped would stop whatever tape was left.

CHAPTER EIGHT

Darby eased down on the bed, his shoulders pressing into a firm pillow, into two pillows one on another against the ornate carved-wood headboard, big pillows, long and wide and angled in a way to give the best support for writing–the pen and paper ready (enough of both), the room quiet (the outside-the-room quiet as well), the mattress mostly hard and pajamas still smelling of the softener his wife had used for years–his luggage repacked, locked and the mini-recorder in his coat and primed to take in everything worth hearing, the travel-alarm wound and set for a time too dark and early to think about until it happened–the sack of pecans given to the cook–and details there enough for many pens and sheets of paper, details, all through the afternoon, coming one after another, questions too, details and descriptions, little things to bigger ones and back again to small.

The pen pushed out a heading and he saw his shorthand had gone rusty, the line impossible to read. He tried a few more times and gave it up, Poddy O'Malley smiling somewhere in a shadow of the Cardinal he was sure, but both of them kept away, outside, safely back too distant to make sense of what now tumbled out uncoded. He would flesh things out later, after the tour, after he was permitted to go home again, after he had checked to see that Poddy's office was the same one he had left him in. The writing was necessary at this stage.

And enough:
WHAT I KNOW:
Very little–much is the same, much different. There are bunk-beds in the dormitory, real linen napkins in the dining hall, a picture of Cardinal Riga and a formal portrait of Pope Hilary mounted on the staircase wall, a life-sized Sacred Heart statue in the kitchen and crucifixes nearly everywhere, a movie theatre where the stables used to be, a film-library (farces mostly–Three Stooges, Marx Brothers, and Jerry Lewis solos)–personal computers in the older brothers' cells, much electronic equipment–some of it still boxed, comfortable rooms for guests and less noise and confusion than six months ago. NB: There is a new chapel under construction, near the main one–a smaller version dedicated (it would seem) to Our Lady of the Flight into Egypt. Query: Who authorized the chapel statuary–running figures–St. Joseph in a long-legged lead, the Blessed Virgin (Holy Infant a bulged blanket on her lap) seeming to be clinging in terror to the mane of a galloping donkey?

---As noted earlier–the noise level seems to be down (especially in the main hall).

---The novitiate has grown in number–most appearing to be in their late teens/early twenties. NB: While every racial/ethnic background seems to be represented, most are short in stature.

---Various rumors seem to be false when placed against the discernible facts.

Rumor: That the Banana Rule fosters the sin of pride (i.e. assuming Godhead). Fact: Only God is Top Banana (the rehearsal/audition hall's emblem is three smallish bananas (attached), superimposed upon a giant banana topped with what appears to be a crown of intertwined thorns and bells). Moreover, the advancement in degree from tenth banana to second is rigorously monitored.

Rumor: That the present Second Bananas (excluding Fr. Bede) are not Roman Catholic. Fact: Only Roman Catholics in good standing are even considered as candidates for any degree above Fiftieth Banana (a kind of glorified prop manager). The seven Second Bananas at The Laughing Place are unmarried permanent deacons with backgrounds that range from rodeo clown to writer of government manuals.

Rumor: That there will be Laughing Places in every American diocese by the year 2000. Fact: While anything is possible, there is no plan for such expansion on the part of the present Ruling Bunch (Fr. Bede and the seven other Second Bananas). Any additional Poor Yorick houses are to be used strictly as hostels, temporary residences and not as training institutes–as places to shelter and feed traveling Yoricks and not as recruitment centers. NB: the Yorick house in San Cristobel is the only such hostel presently operational; negotiations, however, are proceeding in Alabama, Mississippi, and Louisiana.

---Fr. Bede–The Physical–The Known: He is short and slightly built (5'7", 115 pounds–to my own 6'3", 195 pounds) and his face is round, wide and round; his eyes are (I think) blue (but they might also be green); his hair is nearly gone on top–the Yorick-cap covers most of the bald, but not all, and the skin there is reddish with large freckles clearly visible even at a distance. His voice is a problem–in person sounding nothing like the near cackle of the television version (or the nasal twitter on the Cardinal's tapes) but softer, lower, calming. His hands are large, fingers long and slender; he uses his hands almost excessively while performing but in private talks, one on one, they stay mostly folded, never steepled or balled into a fist to make a point emphatic. He will occasionally touch someone, but such times are rare. His skin is smooth, a pinkish cast to fingers, neck and face. I have never seen him in short sleeves and cannot attest to the texture there. Physically he reminds me of a store clerk, a department store floor supervisor, or a head bookkeeper for a moderately successful retail chain.

WHAT I DON'T KNOW (didn't see):

Fr. Bede—the psychological/spiritual, The Unknown—And this is what the Cardinal will want most to know. But I couldn't tell what Fr. Bede himself thinks of the way he has been set to going, his vocation, not exactly; he will not stay for long on questions probing what it was that gave the Poor Yoricks birth—beyond the usual, God's call, vocation there within him even as a child (he freely admits this and yet will not discuss his childhood any further—will not even comment on his ties, if any, to the Ailey, Georgia, of today—Example: He only smiled enigmatically at the comments of Conroy Tucker, the gravedigger's son). But when it comes to how God reached down into Philadelphia, how it came to be that teacher-priest turned quickly into founder of an Order different from all others down the centuries, leader to a growing institute of comics and of clowns and named for no staid saint but for a playwright's fancied jester, for a skull held countless times by actors given leave in each and every age to grope their way among a kingdom filled with soul-bloat and pretenders—when it comes to that, the all-important that—he turns indefinite, grows silent, or if dressed in Yorick garb, his head nods while he smiles a little smile and sets the tiny bells to jingling softly on his tilted cap. NB: For what it is worth in the way of anything (later proof or careful detail)—on the eve of the Tour he seems no longer sad. And nothing anyone has guessed about the private him can yet be seen as right or wrong.

Darby tried to stop; the pen felt heavy in his hand, eyelids also heavy, needing sleep before the early morning came. But one more heading formed itself instead. He put it down slowly on the page:

WHAT IS IT WHY AM I HERE WHY DO I STAY?

And then he turned it around, its three parts easy enough to move–logically not demanding to be taken up and dealt with in a certain order or with fixed consideration–a personal fleshing-out, a filling-in of context that the Cardinal never had to see and read:

WHY AM I HERE?

My Job: Yes. I need my job–the money–I need the job to keep what I have in place. To keep it from going away. But–

The Cardinal: Yes. The job and the Cardinal go together–they mesh–without one, the other would not be there–not necessarily–necessarily there. The Cardinal fitted the job to me–and I owe him–owe him consideration, loyalty. And more. Like the time I went to study Fr. Craps–when the Cardinal asked me to go there, to the Charismatics. I owe him (consideration, loyalty–and more) and have tried to do whatever it was he needed to have done, whatever I could do to help. The Cardinal is a part of everything I am. Of everything I do. But–NB: Not here. The Cardinal is not here–his jurisdiction can't get through the gate. But I know that I am here because he sent me. Is he here then because of that? Because of who I am? And will there be pay phones in Pee Dee Crossing?

WHY DO I STAY?

My Job–again: I need the money. Starkly. Need it. For the house and for everything. I am here and I stay here for money. <u>That</u> much is certain. But is it all? Fear? Am I afraid <u>not</u> to be here, <u>not</u> to go where the Cardinal sends me? Money and fear. And what of curiosity?

<u>Curiosity</u>: About Fr. Bede himself. Yes. That first of all. About the when and the how exactly he was touched to do what he has done. And then the rest. The <u>what</u> it is that troubles Cardinal Spitzmulcher, that feeds his lack of trust in Fr. Bede as priest. And more: Cardinal Riga's place and the problem of Pope Hilary's purpose in accepting something most had thought would die out long before it gathered anything but disbelief and scorn. I am curious about those things, about them all. Money and fear and curiosity are equal parts of why I do not leave.

<u>WHAT IS IT—THE TRUE AND ONLY 'IT'?</u>

This is the hardest part and cuts across and touches all the rest. And it is possible that no such IT exists. That is a very real possibility—that a one and only, true and single motivation is not there at all. That nothing can be ever clear enough to stand alone.

IT-candidates grow teeming—insect-like when pushed in close and made to live all cramped together on a little space of paper:

---<u>The Little Okra</u>? <u>No</u>—but beautiful and useful like aspirin or bandaids or a taste of sugar in a cup of coffee brewed too strong. I love the Little Okra but it's not the thing itself.

---<u>The House</u>? <u>No</u>—and <u>No</u> to wife and daughter <u>No</u> to swimming pool and waterbed and big screen television sets and <u>No</u> to sauna, hot-tub, cars, and to the choice food wasted each and every day. <u>No</u>.

---<u>The Job, the Cardinal, Fear and Curiosity and the Blessed Paycheck weekly cut and signed?</u> NO.

---<u>Freedom—the chance to run away?</u> <u>No</u>. Not any more. Not for a long, long time. <u>Now</u>: Now I carry too much weight to run, a heaviness of memory turned to debt–the Cardinal everywhere but here and even here the road not fit for running and no finish-line in place, no ending point or time yet clear. No.

---<u>The Structures standing firm</u>? <u>No</u>. Not the ones of Church and State, with walls fresh-painted nearly every year, the insulation thick and wiring and especially the plumbing and most studs still strong enough through-out, the floor a trifle scuffed and chipped, a few holes here and there, a scent of mold in every room like one that comes from cleaning with detergents never strong enough, and dust upon the floors, dark grainy dust like droppings from some giant hidden thing that only feeds when change is in the air, between the time that leases end and brand-new tenants come inside to live. <u>No</u>. In-specting and repairing structures is not <u>IT</u>, not even when I write that way or let the Cardinal send me out like soap and water, hammer, nails, and good strong wood. <u>No</u>.

---<u>Purity</u>? Perhaps a yes–perhaps the IT, if IT could be a true goal, never changing and a place of rest and safety from the need to pay off debts forever. Perhaps.

Darby let the pen drop onto the page, near the bot-tom, and closed his eyes. For just a moment he could hear the laughter of the brothers, distant-seeming, shrill and with an undertone of clacking like the sound that locusts make before they leave the ground. And then the alarm clock buzzed it all away.

CHAPTER NINE

Fr. Bede drove the prop-van like it needed discipline, like it somehow had rebelled and wanted very much to leave the road and make its own way north. Darby had sat beside him dozing for the first half-hour or so, eyes refusing to stay open any longer than it took to notice Ailey passing–Court House and Lola's Café–and then a glimpse or two of the high school and Miss Hattie's satellite dish (two burly men there seemingly intent on twisting it against its will to point toward a stand of tall trees behind the house). He had sleep-walked through the Mass and breakfast and a kind of rally at the rehearsal hall, a noisy send-off of the Second Bananas that had almost brought him fully awake. Almost but not quite. Fr. Bede had spoken last, a joke before the final blessing and a short walk to the waiting vans. The Cardinal could probably not use the joke, not enough there to make a case for anything beyond perhaps treating lightly various sins and maladies that nobody seemed very much to notice any more. But Darby had made sure the tape got every word–just in case: "Ok ok–listen now–this is an old one but bears repeating. A judge was listening to the testimony of a wife seeking divorce:

'Tell me explicitly,' said the Judge to the woman, 'what fault do you find with your husband?'

And, brothers, the wife was explicit:

'He is a liar, a brute, a thief, a cheat, and a brainless fool!'

'Now, now,' said the Judge, 'I think you might have

a difficult time proving all that!'

'Prove it,' she retorted, 'why, everybody already knows it. Everybody!'

'Well—if you knew it,' the Judge demanded sarcastically, 'why did you marry him in the first place?'

'But," the wife's face got very red as she shouted out: "I didn't know all that before I married him!'

The husband interrupted angrily at this point:

'Yes, she did too,' he shouted, 'she did too!'

"Ok ok," the groans had turned to applause and then a silence, here and there broken by a cough or nervous giggle. "Ok. Let's not be like that dis-unitive couple but try to be more like the Judge. Like God. Giving us plenty of time and room to get to the truth. So, let's go and have some fun. Let's help bring healing if we can. Let's pray—In the Name of the Father and the Son and the Holy Spirit—" And every head bowed, bells jingling on their way.

"Why don't you just rest, Mr. Ross? Why fight it?" Fr. Bede's voice was soft, tentative, words seeming to jostle each other as they came out on a single breath. "It'll be a while yet. We have a long way to go." He smiled and seemed to pull the wheel away from unseen fingers, the van veering back inside the center line. "But time enough and more to get there in."

"I'm ok, Father." The Cardinal's information had been wrong. It was nearly three hundred miles to Pee Dee Crossing, and as lead van in a caravan of three, Fr. Bede's pace seemed better aimed at cruising than at making time. There was little traffic and the scenery outside had become monotonous—pine forests and ruined tobacco barns and freshly planted fields, the air coming in the windows warm, already smelling of summer. The tape-recorder was hidden under Darby's coat, beside him on the seat.

"You didn't sleep well?" In his shirtsleeves, pink cloth rolled above the wrists and red suspenders down the front snapped with outsized clips to the waistband of his lavender-colored slacks, he looked like a ventriloquist's dummy or an older child allowed to dress up one more time for trick-or-treat. It was becoming harder by the bumpy mile to see him as a Priest. And yet there was not even any hint why everything had gone so smoothly and quickly, why no one had even questioned Darby's presence on the tour. It had not been near so easy with the Jesus-Quest Charismatics.

"I didn't sleep enough, Father. Not long enough." It now seemed like seconds, the feel of the pen still in his fingers when the clock buzzed on. "I had some work to finish."

"I see." He sometimes bounced a bit on the seat as he drove, the props behind him sending out a jingle or a creak and clack in answer to the little bump and shake he made as if to help the van around a curve or through a stretch of hole-pocked pavement. They were traveling on a secondary road, a two-laned stretch of asphalt that looked like it had been laid by someone who preferred the indirect, the curve and twist and rise and dip to straight lines and the shortest way from A to B. "Your work must be demanding. Do you compose on the typewriter?"

"Pardon?"

"Or have I dated myself—it's terminals now, isn't it? Or something like that?"

"I use paper and a felt-tipped pen."

"Ah yes. A romantic. I thought so."

"What?"

"Where do you get your ideas?" He glanced over

and smiled and then bumped a bit on the seat as the van cruised into a curve. The terrain was getting progressively hillier, curves sharper and at times the sun blocked out by almost wall-like clumps of kudzu-covered trees. "Your column is required reading, you know."

"It is?"

"Oh my, yes. We read it faithfully. Our recent favorite was 'Don't Block Our View of the Shepherd.' Did you study literature at school?"

"No—journalism. I took some lit—surveys—electives. But I was a journalism major." And the Cardinal had kept him at it, finally—after New Orleans keeping him in graduate school until the master's was done and the right girl chosen for a wife. In rebellion and in near-starvation. In jail and on the street. In jobs that nearly broke his body and his soul. Ever and always the Cardinal, there and gone and come again, the now and ever shall-be, world without end. Amen.

"You write well, Mr. Ross. Not like a journalist at all. But I guess we appreciate your sense of humor best." He bounced again and flexed his fingers on the wheel. "That's not too surprising of course. Not for *us*, eh?" The van seemed to shiver, a grinding noise there briefly as it came free of the curve and started up a slight hill. "That shepherd column reminded Brother Hugo of Jonathan Swift. 'A Modest Proposal?' And your concluding survey of a modern sheepfold all cluttered up with study groups and self-help programs and shortcuts to better grazing did make us think he was right. Brother Mordecai, however, popped up with a strong argument for Sinclair Lewis. Surprisingly strong. No one had really thought about Sinclair Lewis for years until then. It quite frankly caught us all off guard. And Brother Mordecai is an eloquent speaker, you know—well you most certainly *don't* know that as yet, but you will. Yes, he very nearly carried the day until Brother Raphael pointed out the obvious—it was there all along but sometimes we dig too hard and lose the major point. Like trying to analyze a Thurber cartoon. Of course, you *can* do it—but when it's done—well, the funny part has run away to hide. What are you afraid of, Mr. Ross?" The words were spoken softly, a hint of the sadness flickering there but gone with the bounce that took the van up over the crest of the hill and helped it settle in to coast on down the other side.

"Afraid?" Darby could see the other two vans in the rear-view mirror, one and then another rolling down behind, their fronts made up to look like faces, headlight eyes wide open and a jagged grin painted on below.

"The style. We got snagged by the content. And that's common enough. The content stops most people. In that recent favorite—sheep begetting sheep begetting sheep until not one of them believes there even *is* a shepherd—or," he took a deep breath and made his voice go full and loud, announcer-rich, the line delivered like a movie title or a coming sale too good to miss, "*Tyranny of the Laity.* Yes? The content?"

"Yes. I think that's it. In general." He pushed his fingers beneath his coat and felt for the buttons of the tape recorder. "Tyranny. Yes." The Cardinal had praised the column in his Monthly Pastoral, urging its dissemination throughout the Archdiocese in a rare show of public support. Darby pressed the recorder on and watched Fr. Bede bounce the van around a slow-moving tractor pulling at a wagon full of manure. The driver of the tractor tipped his baseball cap in greeting as they passed. "The changes—a kind of tyranny has come from that." Darby couldn't tell if Fr. Bede were smiling, sunshine through the window fuzzing his features, a darkness there and moving, deeper where the face should be. But it felt as if he were smiling, bouncing and smiling and pushing them all deeper and deeper into northwest Georgia, closer by the second to a Mission Darby never even knew was there. The Cardinal had seemed surprised by his ignorance, a fragment of their last conversation forgotten until now.

The Timaquan Mission, Ross. First Jesuit success among the southern mountain tribes? You know it from elementary school. Fifth grade, I believe. The St. Pedro Lupus Journals—remember?

"I went to public school, Your Eminence."

Ah yes—I had forgotten that. Understandable. But a pity nevertheless.

And then another update on Poddy had come almost flooding out, a full account of how the Silver Beaver had received his forty-ninth distinguished alumnus award from Cardinal Hurley High.

We're all very proud of young O'Malley, Ross. Very proud indeed.

The van swerved to miss something Darby couldn't see on road ahead.

"But the style, Mr. Ross—it was the style that made us take another look. And it was good-bye Swift and Sinclair Lewis after that. Yes. And hello Mr. Fear."

"What?" There was a road-sign up ahead, nearly obscured by tall weeds but Pee Dee Crossing very much in evidence toward the top.

"Yes. The style was nervous. Like a transcribed sportscast. Have you ever read your work aloud?"

"No." The sign was gone before Darby turned to read the mileage; in the mirror, its backside looked bulged and ripped from buckshot, the tall weeds bending and then snapping up against it in the wake of the other vans.

"Well, we did. Nervous. Tense. A tension there. Now," the sun was caught behind a rising bank of clouds, Fr. Bede's face come back in focus, free from shadows, his eyes squinting at the road ahead and his fingers tightly holding to the wheel. "Now that's not a negative criticism—not at all. Tension can give punch. Like Brother Olusu's story-telling—making stage-fright funny. He can get anyone to believe he's about to die up there—and then break over into a dance and an 'Ave Maria' smooth enough to make an atheist cry. Tension can help set up a knockout punch. I've seen it done." He licked his lips and glanced at Darby. "Yes. And it's there in your work as well. But with a difference. Fear. *Real* fear. That's the difference. It comes through strong on a careful reading—a listening, really—reading it aloud. You rush your words, your thoughts—you move down the page like there was something coming after you, something," he frowned and bounced a bit on the seat, voice turning again into the deeper one, the announcer this time told to scare the children into silence, *"dark and savage, hairy and long-toothed with claws unsheathed and set to rip and tear!"* And then it was as if a laugh had clicked on the lights and turned to giggles while a kitten mewed its way up to a bowl of milk. "It's quite good—the column. It helps us get through the Bunch 'quarterlies.' You have a definite talent—a real feel for poking fun. But why are you afraid?"

"I—I'm not afraid. I write what I see." Darby swallowed and tapped at the tape recorder, fingers feeling heavy as he found the off button and hesitated. "And what I believe." Fear was safely tucked away among his papers, put already in with all the other things he sorted out and left until he had the time to think.

"And what is that?"

"The Church. I write about the Church. That's my job." He knew the Cardinal would show visible disgust at Darby on defense, at Darby sucked in somehow and made to feel like he had left his homework on the bus. He tried to get his fingers to press down on the off but-ton, but they seemed unable to move.

"About sheep and sheep and more and more sheep—and their shepherds on vacation?"

"I—yes—in that one column. Yes. That was for Voca-tion Sunday."

"And the one on 'Retail Dogma'? Last Christmas, I believe it was. Sheep again?"

"Yes."

"And 'Jung-tied Theologians'? Sheep and their teachers?"

"Yes."

"And the four-part series on nuns—my favorite title by the way—'Come Blow Your Horn' *colon*—we love titles with colons—'Come Blow Your Horn: The Bo-Peeping of the American Church.' Did you really write that title?"

"Yes." The Cardinal had almost pulled it in galley but had finally seen the point after his second reading of the text.

"We loved it. As well as the series itself. And I hope you enjoy writing your columns as much as we enjoy reading them aloud at our quarterly Bunches. But what is it you see out there, Mr. Ross? What makes you write like you do?"

"It's my job." But the words felt wrong. The job wasn't IT. Fr. Bede was laughing.

"I see. It's duty then? Your fear. It comes from that? The numbers that your column reaches—that it's somehow not enough? And your other work." He shook his head as if in pity or in understanding of a point somewhere that had not yet been made. "The other reason you are here. The reason that you came to visit us again."

"I'm—I'm not sure I know what it is you—"

"Your fear for the sheep." The voice was nearly a murmur, low and steady. "Is that it?"

"I—I'm not sure."

"That they are lost."

"I—not that—not exactly lost. I don't know."

"And leaving them alone isn't the answer?" He seemed to speak the words more to himself than to Darby, head lowered and eyebrows arched and round face pointing straight ahead. "They need the Shepherd's voice."

"Yes—I suppose that's—that's so." And the Cardinal would agree or might agree. At least his seminaries were still filling up with orthodoxy for the structures not yet marred beyond repair, to stand alternative to green-faced healers and the messengers of greed. He might just agree.

"To *hear* the Shepherd's voice. They know that voice, Mr. Ross. And they come running when they hear it." He smiled and bounced the van to a screeching halt at a railroad crossing. "And so we go." He looked both ways and bounced out over the tracks. "We go to see who's listening."

CHAPTER TEN

After settling into the Royal Wigwam Hotel (three connecting rooms and a view of twinkling lights on the higher ground outside), a Rosary and quickly-eaten meal of cheese and brownish bread, the Yoricks had gone out to work third shift in teams of three. Fr. Bede and Darby had jogged back and forth between them all evening, the Bald Mountain Ball-Bearing Company and the North Wind Novelties and Genuine Native-American Arts & Crafts each getting three shows and a sing-along. Darby had nearly fallen asleep during the final sing-along, a particularly noisy session in the expanded breakroom of the North Wind Novelties plant. Fr. Bede had sung the loudest of anyone there, standing on tiptoes at the very edge of the makeshift stage, arms flapping like some giant bird come down to rest, and voice enough to be heard back even to the place where the beaded dolls and feathered tom-toms, the plastic peace pipes, totems and the rough-cut crucifixes waited all stacked and ready to be boxed and shipped and bought and sold.

And then an encore, and another and another until the jokes and stories (little homilies embedded in each one) started up again and Darby (quarters in his pocket) forced himself outside through a warped metal door and went to find a pay phone.

It was cool in the pre-dawn darkness, the parking-lot nearly full and here and there groups of men and women stood talking and smoking, their laughter at times coming in on cue with what could be heard of the show inside. The Timaquans had loved everything the Yoricks did, Joke Break after Joke Break, at one point applause lasting several minutes and whoops so loud it took awhile for Darby's ears to settle down. The workers at North Wind Novelties had even joined in the act, occasionally on the older jokes shouting out punchlines a second before they were delivered and answering in well-timed chorus every question that a Brother asked.

"Yessir folks—it was cold!"

How cold was it?

"It was so cold we had to thaw out our words to hear what we were saying! Oh yes it was COLD!"

There seemed to be a kind of convenience store across the highway and Darby headed through the parking lot toward its tall, blinking sign, wending his way among the cars and trucks and vans, the laughter back behind him rising up and falling, rising up again and holding and then dropping into whoops and whistles and a sound like stamping feet and beating drums. There was no front gate and no traffic in either direction. The store façade looked like a fat canoe, and it seemed deserted inside. The Cardinal's quarters jingled in Darby's pocket as he jogged across the road.

"Pay phone, huh?" The man behind the counter was tall and slender, nose long and bulged across its bridge as if it had been broken more than once. His hair was black, two thick braids with silver bands around their tips that rested on the upper portion of a fringed vest. He was wearing a blue-and-white-striped shirt, long-sleeved with beaded garters just above the elbows, and leather pants belted with what looked to be snakeskin and a buckle in the shape of a spread-winged dove. His skin was dark, a reddish brown at least a half-shade deeper than the Timaquan workers at the plants. But his teeth were even whiter and bigger than Conroy Tucker's. "Yeah." He winked and showed his teeth, his face taking on the puzzled look of an old friend accidently snubbed at a high school reunion. And then he smiled and shook his head. "Yeah we gottum. White eyes want send heap big smoke signal, me betchum." The laugh was muffled, trapped behind the teeth and let out with a buzz of air. "Heap big smoke signal?"

"I—I need to make a long-distance call." The man leaned back against the wall, between two floor-to-ceiling rows of shelves with cigarette cartons packed in so tightly that it seemed a mason had fitted each one to its place and tapped the whole in plumb. "May I use your phone?" To Darby's right the cash register seemed to have been planted in a bed of candy bars and packs of gum. A yellowing bumper sticker on its front proclaimed: PRAY THE ROSARY!

"Touching base, huh? Like a good soldier?" He pushed off the wall and stepped over to the counter.

"What?" The words had sounded wrong, friendly enough but wrong in the mouth of a stranger. Darby stared hard at the man, seeking something in his face that might explain his own unease. But the face had turned neutral.

"Where you calling?"

"Florida—San Cristobel. Is the booth in here?" Darby glanced right to left. There had been no telephone sign outside and the store itself seemed almost choked by narrow aisles with mounds of everything from motor oil to giant cans of pork-and-beans stuffed onto their sagging shelves. The phones in the plants had been in use almost from the moment the Yoricks arrived and long lines had formed quickly whenever break-time came.

"Florida, huh? I thought so somehow." He nodded

his head a few times, the silver braid bands bouncing gently on his vest. "I thought you'd say that."

"What?" Again the words hit wrong, inflection, tone a shade too cordial, knowing, almost intimate from a man that Darby had never seen before.

"I lived in Florida a year once. Right after Nam. I been all over Florida. How you like th'show?"

"Pardon—I—" The face was still neutral but the eyes seemed to be enjoying Darby's confusion.

"Th'show. Over there?" He nodded toward the front door. "The Yokels?"

"Yoricks. I'm traveling—"

"I've watched them a few times on TV. Beats me what all the excitement's about. Pretty boring stuff. Pitiful." He rested his hands on the counter top, fingers slightly spread and a ring on nearly every one. "What do you think of that Father Breed?"

"Bede—he's—he's different." He wondered if the Cardinal would be asleep or there already in his office, listening to the seminary bells and waiting for what hadn't yet been said or done. Fr. Bede refused to speak directly to the subject Darby needed most to hear, most especially nothing useful there among the stories and the songs across the road. The Father-Director of the Mission School had even served as MC at both plants and four Fransciscan volunteers had helped arrange the chairs and the Altar Society of St. Pedro Lupus brought in flowers and a Holy Family banner for the stage.

"Yeah. You need anything besides a phone?"

"Pardon?" The man's eyes had begun to catch the glare from a hot sandwich sign back past the wall of cigarettes, color now changing from red to green as the letters lit up one at a time.

"Do—you—" the words came out with exaggerated

pauses in between, "–need–any-thing?" He gestured as he spoke, a brief flutter of his fingers like a movie version of a captured chief, a High Plains Lakota with not too much to say.

"No–no, I just need to make a call." Darby wondered if the phone were on the other side of the popcorn machine or perhaps wedged behind the video games that blinked and beeped a step or two away from where the rack of books and magazines began. The man was irritating.

"You sure now?" He smiled and scratched at the side of his nose. "Everything's under control?" The smile faded and he licked his lips a few times, front teeth showing briefly after each sweep of his tongue. The face seemed tensed, its neutrality poised and held in place as if against its will.

"Yes–yes, I'm sure." Darby glanced at his watch. "Is the phone in here?"

"Yeah."

"And–I *can* use it?"

"Of course. I know you need to phone home." He tried to wink, the effect slightly sinister. Darby noticed that he was wearing a crucifix, a gold one nearly lost among the fringe on his vest. "You need to phone San Cristobel."

"Yes–but–" The face was making Darby angry, unmoving, as unresponsive as a plastic mask. "The booth–where *is* the booth?"

"Ain't none."

"What?"

"There ain't no booth." And then a stronger smile came out, almost a grin in the hot-food light, the mask dissolving into creases dark and light, like the Cardinal's face had sometimes looked, just like the face he showed opponents when they stepped into some trap that he had carefully prepared. The resemblance was amazing, a long-haired, dark-skinned, irritating imitation there among the candy and the cigarettes, lips now pushing out his words in Cardinal-cadence, fast and hard like bullets nose to tail. "Never put one in. Never have had a booth. No booth." And his smile stayed out.

"Then—then how can I—"

"It's back there," he jerked a thumb over his shoulder, "in my room. You'll need a private place, I suspect." He motioned for Darby to follow him, past the hot-food and through a beaded curtain into a large book-lined room with a rock fireplace taking up nearly all of one wall. "You can pay me when you finish. I have a rate chart. Trans-Diocesan calls are a dime extra per minute. Not *my* rule." He laughed. "Southeastern Synod. Last year. Everything's going up." The phone was shaped like a frog. "You can sit here." A desk above which hung a framed diploma and various glossy prints of men in combat fatigues and one almost miniature portrait of Cardinal Spitzmulcher. The diploma said in Latin that Henry Two-Crows was a Ph.D. It was too dark to make out the inscription on the portrait.

"Then—you're not just a—"

"I'll be out front. Oh and Mr. Ross," he stepped back from the desk and unbuttoned his vest, crucifix arms pushing free of fringe and thick gold chain now visible against his shirt, "I'd make it brief. Third shift's about done. It wouldn't do to make your new friends come play hide-and-seek."

"But—" Darby hesitated, fingers poised above the desk. The frog had glowing blue eyes and its light green back was freckled black and brown. Henry Two-Crows nodded and motioned to his wristwatch. The receiver made a squeaking noise as Darby picked it up. The buttons inside looked like drops of milky water. "Why didn't you tell me?" He wondered if the Cardinal knew already of The Yoricks' plan to work the Blue Ridge sawmills for a while and then go see what was left of the textile workers, Carolina piedmont up to Richmond and beyond, a vaguer westward sweep before a spiral to the Gulf and north again back home. Henry Two-Crows waved and left the room as the frog sounded out an electronic croak with each pressed digit of the Cardinal's number.

But only the answering machine was on the other end, the secretary's voice much shriller than in person and the beep a painful squealing like a tenor chainsaw blade dropped down on steel. Darby whispered into the frog's head, the line gone dead too soon to add a message for his wife.

CHAPTER ELEVEN

Darby counted fourteen sailors in the bar–tavern Cap'n Pegleg's Grog 'n' Grub down near the Gulfstream Shipyards and the Mermaid Pleasure-Pier: fourteen sail-ors and three women with frizzed hair and wearing hal-ter-tops and hide-tight cutoffs and too much makeup on their faces–fourteen sailors, three women and several sunburnt tourists, fat and looking frightened as they sucked in oysters and sipped dark beer back toward the door–fourteen sailors, three women, the tourists and the Pope on television, waving to the crowds in Boston from a screen up high above the beer mugs on the wall– a wave and smile all bathed in flickering light, silver-streaked and caught in puffs of rolling smoke. Cap'n Peg-leg himself was tending bar. It felt good to be alone. No Cardinal. No Fr. Bede. Just Pegleg and the fourteen sail-ors and the three women and so forth. Darby had been good for ten whole years. And he was going home the day after tomorrow.

"Same again, Bub?" Cap'n Pegleg made a creaking sound as he stomped over to Darby's place at the bar, a corner, against the wall and head-level with the very bottom of a giant George Wallace poster, nose to nose (when he turned) with STAND UP FOR AMERICA, letters nearly an inch across and George's tie beginning just above the P. "'Nother one?" Pegleg pulled at the top of the carved piece of wood that together with various strips of shiny metal down the sides made up most of his right leg. The tip was polished red. Like an apple or an outsized cherry. Like a giant swizzle-stick pushed down and held inside. "Bub?"

"Yes—another." The beer was tepid. But good. Good and strong. It tasted good. The shot of Scotch he started with too raw and burning all alone. The beer helped. Pope Hilary seemed to be throwing a baseball.

"Th' guy's everywhere, y'know?" The Cap'n made his leg squeak as he filled Darby's mug, tap handle in the shape of a shell. The television screen kept streaking red and green, flashes brighter even than the beer signs or the sunshine that the padded doors let in. Pegleg filled the shot-glass nearly to its rim, just like the other times, two or maybe three, the mug set down beside it with a creak and squeal of leg. Poster-George's unsmiling eyes seemed to be watching every move Pope Hilary made. "Baseball. Jesus. What next?" Pegleg wiped at the bar with a greasy rag. "Mud wrasslin'?" The laugh came out like a gargle. Poster-George didn't seem to notice. "How you figure a guy like that?"

"I don't know."

"Yeah."

The sailors were singing and one of the women was sucking oysters with the tourists and Darby sipped his beer. The Yoricks were all fast asleep, asleep and snoring, Fr. Bede the first and loudest, back at the rooming house two blocks away, all fast asleep before the midnight show at Cam Tran Seafood USA, their last night on the tour to be a shining one out among the shrimpers, tiny yellow fishermen, smiling twitter-voiced little yellow men and women, a shining out that Darby didn't care to see and hear. He noticed Pegleg's place earlier that day as Fr. Bede had bumped them down through Pearl's Resort, past spas and condos and the Pleasure-Pier, the shipyards and the motel strip to stop at the

Queen of the South Rooms Rooms Rooms to pray awhile and eat and rest up solid for the show. Darby was tired of the road. Tired of waiting for the dark proof that had never seemed to come. Tired of being good, all sober and alert. And Pegleg didn't ask him who he was.

"My God, bub–he's gotta be in his sixties–at least sixty-five. Y'know?"

On the screen, Pope Hilary was inside a batting cage, his swing a tight one catching nearly every ball that came his way. Pegleg was excited.

"Bastard can hit, though–lookit that one! Nailed it, by God!"

But Darby didn't look, the Scotch making the beer foam and bubble and Poster-George's face now puffed and blotched as Pegleg leaned against the bar and sighed. And then he smiled and nodded almost shyly, words gone low and soft.

"Need more like *him*, y'know?"

"What?"

"Wallace. He was really somethin'–yes *sir* he was."

"Hey Pegleg!" One of the sailors, a tall skinny one with a beet-red nose was standing on a chair. "Hey!"

"Huh? Hey–get your butt down or get th'hell out!" Pegleg raised up and pointed with the frayed tip of his rag. "You hear me–*now*! Jesus."

"Well–well then change damned channels for Godssake, Peg! Change–" the sailor slowly eased himself back onto the floor, chair wobbling as he tried to sit down.

"Just settle down–boxing's 'bout to start," he glanced at his watch, "ten minutes. Need anything over there?" But the sailor didn't seem to hear. Pope Hilary was now in a motorcade, waving at the crowds again, glassed-in, a moving box that seemed to float above them with a bump and jerk like Fr. Bede was driving down below. "You watch boxing?" Pegleg's cheek was scarred, a V-shaped line nearly as long as Principal Steven's, but not as thick and not so dark and bulged.

"Yes–oh my yes–yes I do." Darby couldn't remember when or if he had ever watched a fight but it seemed to matter to Pegleg; it seemed important to his old friend Pegleg that he watch and like it and drink beer and Scotch and let the Yoricks sleep. The road had been long, too many details, all too much and proving nothing that would make the Cardinal smile and help keep Poddy well away, well well away. And the details were there forming in his mind, coming up like bubbles in his glass.

"Good one today. Middleweight championship. Marcos and Nixon."

"Yes. Yes indeed, Cap'n, yes indeed. It should be good." The details bubbled up, fat bubbles that bob awhile and then go *pop. Pop* and gone away. "They both fight dirty. It should be good." A month or more, slightly more at least, a month or more of bubbles–forming fat and rising quickly and then *pop–pop pop pop*.

"Hey not Marcos, Bub. Nixon's th'brawler. Remember? Marcos boxes. Real light-footed for a big guy." On the screen, the Pope was walking slowly among a crowd of children, Cardinal Riga's massive face there for just a second with them, pushing little bodies forward gently, gently into the Pope's outstretched arms. "Marcos'll take it back this time."

"Yes. Yes you are prolly right. Prolly right." His mouth hurt, tongue too wide to pass the teeth without a catch and scrape along the side. Pope Hilary was dancing with the children. Cardinal Riga too. "Yes. I think you are right." But the details had come out to play, bobbing now down in his glass and making little fuzzy sounds be-fore they *plumpy-popped* themselves away.

The Migrants and the Logging/Lumber/Sawmill Camps: Five in four days. Detail: Brothers Hugo and Raphael juggling to each other, juggling balls and dumb-bells and fat chunks of wood, juggling so the children squealed and old men laughed, and Fr. Bede there with the sick and dying in what someone always called in each and every place, a clinic—the sick and dying there inside and squealing like the outside children squealed (though some were children too he guessed but it was hard to tell) and Fr. Bede and jokes and blessings and letting those who could try juggling for themselves. Five in four days and then some more and details much the same in every one and all gone pop and all gone poppity-pop and pop and pop to let the next one in:

What was left of Textile and Furniture Towns With Chickens, Chickens Everywhere And All the Rest That Bubbled Up Along the Way: Fat beads on some thick necklace from the foothills to the sea.

Detail: Brother Mordecai singing, songs like birds let in to flutter for a while inside the heat and lint, the air gone thick and much too heavy for such wings but room enough and more for fear, the workers mostly young, foul-mouthed or silent, listening maybe to the tune but not the words and Joke-Breaks sometimes never heard at all. Fr. Bede weeping. And then:

Pop and *pop* and *pop* and *pop* until the details come without a setting round about them, fast and faster, bubbles in the air that float and disappear just like the pictures of the Pope now flashing one by one into the smoky room, the details *pop* and *pop* and *pop* and *pop* out in the space between Poster-George and Pegleg's moving lips. Darby smiled and nodded, Pegleg's words not loud enough to understand and Poster-George's eyes too squinty and too small to notice how the bubbles catch the light and glow.

Detail: Fr. Bede in spotlight, blue and red, the room a truckers' lounge somewhere–near Richmond or a place down further south–somewhere; his words like prayer, the jokes like some almost forgotten benediction with a laughter there that carries warmth and calm, a feeling come on Darby strong enough to almost make him sing.

And *pop*–

Detail: A carwash lunch-hour in a room that smells of soap and wax, the men there Black and Brown and White and little Yellow ones (like those he knew would live and work at Cam Tran Seafood (USA), and women too (tattooed and biceps on them like the ones the men let show), together while the Brothers dance and play guitar and lead a sing-along of old-time rock 'n' roll. And Darby sings so loud he almost loses his voice and then–

And then a *pop*–a soapy *pop*–

Detail: The Mass among the homeless, robed Franciscans there all lean and joyous and the men and women and the children for a time gone silent, Fr. Bede–the Host held high–his voice so clear it seems to let the perhaps-Purity that Darby maybe seeks–the perhaps IT peek out and show itself for just a second and then slip away to wait.

pop–pop–

Detail: The Chicken Plant–the place the chickens go to die and ride a clanging belt, their bodies ripped apart with blessings on them (Hebrew and Arabic blessings pre-recorded), repetitious, words almost a chant, an alien plainsong for the export trade. And Fr. Bede and Brother Li there out along the line, in rubber boots to keep their slacks from harm, their words still strong enough to touch a resting worker here and there and make them smile.

a *pop*—a blood-red *pop* and spray—

<u>Detail</u>: A loading dock somewhere, for furniture perhaps, hot as an oven or a woodstove freshly stoked, a sweat-soaked show with all the Brothers there, the stage a row of wooden boxes back against a peeling wall and Fr. Bede with bull-horn to his lips, pushing out a crackling stream of jokes that set the men to groaning, laughter rumbly in between, a sound that echoes off the boxes and the ceiling high above their heads. And Fr. Bede's round face caught in the harshness of the lights, an almost flash and glow that drops and deepens with the laughter's fall and rise.

A *pop*—a last *pop* up near Poster-George's nose, with bits of wet that speckled down his shirt and tie and cover his lapel pin, tiny flag moist-shimmered for a second and then clear again stiff-waving as before. It had been a long, long tour. *Pop*.

"Shrimping accident." Pegleg pushed over another mug and shot-glass, full to the very top, a thin stream of light from the slowly opening door showing up the smudges down the sides of both. "Got it caught in the prop." He tapped at the top of his leg.

"What?" The Pope was gone, replaced by sailboards and canoes and beer-drinking girls in bikinis.

"Most people think it's th'war." He shook his head. "But it ain't. Never got a scratch in Nam. Two tours. Not a scratch. Funny, ain't it?"

"I'm not sure." The door had come full open, a thick shaft of light this time that dimmed the television screen, Fr. Bede there just inside and looking for him through the noise and smoke.

CHAPTER TWELVE

The Little Okra was filled with water-hyacinths, the early morning sunshine showing clumps of them that had come together into fat islands and broad walkways bank to bank, the boat-house pylons green-booted and the ramp to Darby's office bordered in leaves and blossoms. A mile or so upriver it was clear of them, a result of the barges and steel-bladed rotors of the Apollo Bluffs Homeowner's Association's Clean River Project. And the barges were now close-by, just around the bend and the sounds of engines and the rotors, the roar and chunk-chunk-chunk made him wish that he had fought the Project while he had the chance. He liked the hyacinths and as he opened the office door felt anger at his neighbors with their speed-boats and water-skies, the condo noise now inching closer with each chunk-chunk of the barges and the blades. The office smelled of mildew and he flipped on the window air-conditioning unit and brushed the dust from his swivel chair and desk. The last of the papers and tapes were in his briefcase.

The Cardinal so far had been unimpressed, nothing on the tapes themselves or in the written fleshings-out that had made him even smile. Darby had come to hate the almost daily sessions, the early mornings and the evenings on the road, the hurried night-times with his wife and daughter, the feeling that had come to stay that everything was on the very rim of some deep pit. The Cardinal had finally told him to take the last tapes home and rest and see what might then show itself, a detail or a proof that carried with it promise or potential, something solid for the Holy Father when he came to visit. The Cardinal had paced and rubbed his hands together, shouting out the words at times, his face deep red in blotches shaped like spiders with too many legs.

"He'll be here in about three months, Ross. For an Apostolic Retreat. A first for us. One week, Ross. He'll be right here for one week. And without Riga. Just before he returns to Rome. His last stop in America, I think."

"Congratulations, Eminence."

"No no no, Ross! You've missed the point. The Bede thing, Ross. Bede. We can shut him down."

"I see."

"Yes. Yes we can do that. If, Ross—" He had glared at Darby, the look the one he usually saved for wavering seminarians. "If we have something to show him. Something real. Not conjectures. He'll brush aside rumor. You must have seen—heard something we can use. Go home—"

"Eminence?"

"Go home then and get off by yourself and think. You have more tapes—we haven't heard them all?"

"No—yes, Eminence—there's the last week—the ending of the tour. I haven't—"

"Good, Ross—excellent. You need a rest anyway. Go home and see what's there. And don't worry about *The Cross* at all. They can write and print without you, yes?" He had stopped pacing and suddenly turned to come in close and place a hand on Darby's shoulder. His eyes had looked tired, dark-circled, and his cheeks a mass of tiny veins, reds and purples mixed to make them both seem deeply bruised. "Poddy can guest your column."

"He can?" Darby had wondered if maybe Poddy were waiting in the inner office, behind the ornate doors of the Cardinal's private room, waiting and listening and planning what to say. There had been no sign of Poddy in the week since Darby's return, his office where it always was (to Darby's great relief) but somehow feeling empty and unused.

"Yes. Yes he can. And he will. You need a rest."

"But, Eminence—I've been gone six weeks as it—"

"Rest, Ross. And find something. Bring me something besides queries about statuary and the lack of liturgical irregularity. He trusts you, you say?"

"Poddy, Eminence?"

"No no no—Bede! He trusts you?"

"Yes—I think so. He seems to trust."

"Then there has to be something else—something we've overlooked. It'll be on those tapes. Somewhere. Toward the end most likely. When everyone's tired. Their defenses down. You go home."

"Yes, Eminence."

And his wife and daughter had been surprised at first and then uneasy with him there so much in daylight, the pool too noisy and the bedroom seldom better and the third day they had sent him to his boat-house office, far enough outside to keep their schedules safe. He had felt, still felt like a stranger back at the house, like somehow he had been away for years instead of weeks.

He emptied the briefcase—recorder, tapes, his journal/log and then the scraps of paper, the bits of notes and narrative, questions to himself and doodles, folded pages here and there intact on which the IT-quest came and went along the way. He would listen to the tapes, in order, the last ones day by day before he even tried to make sense of the rest. He sat down in the chair, the chunk-chunk-chunk out on the river now louder in spurts, a sputtered roar among it like the groaning of a truck set into pulling at a load too heavy and too big. But Fr. Bede's voice covered most of it, the quality shrill like it always was on tape, the place somewhere in Tennessee the journal said, a bumping cruise on mountain roads that ended at a hosiery mill. It would be a long day.

It felt like something had hit the side of the office, a slap of tin and then a thump that brought Darby up from a dream of Fr. Bede and the Little Okra, Fr. Bede out walking on the hyacinths at sundown with a sky gone almost purple, streaked with veins of red and blue above the trees, the little priest there dancing through the closing blossoms, jingling jester's cap back on his head so far it looked like it might fall. A wind had come up. Darby rubbed his eyes and listened to the tape, still running, the last one now in Georgia and the chunk-chunk-chunk was with it, closer and louder, dying down in the gusts of wind and then returning with an engine whine and knocking rumble like a thunder somewhere not quite sure which way to roll. Fr. Bede's voice sounded tired and Darby almost didn't recognize his own at all.

"—we use what we can get. We like the old jokes best—the oldest we can find."

"Does anyone write them for you?"

"The jokes? No. Not any of *us* anyway. The youngsters sometimes bring their own. But they have to be fixed—cleaned up. Toned down. Part of the discipline. What we call 'passing Moral Muster.' I generally start them out on—"

Darby fast-forwarded the tape, to get past what he remembered of a dull near-monologue on joke-books and old movies. The journal listed it as 'background/humor' but in memory the conversation had been less informational than deeply boring.

"—in Montana, I think. Seven little books in all. Privately published, I believe and—"

The tape screeched and seemed to catch on something before finally moving on. The conversation was every bit as long as he had remembered. He pressed it on again and started flipping through the papers.

"Then you use those books a lot?"

"Yes. *I* do. I like the church jokes. Religious humor. The others have their own way of going. And keep in mind in all this that it's not the material that's important anyway. It has to pass what we call Moral Muster, of course, but it's not the jokes per se that are primary. You must have concluded that by now, Mr. Ross. Must have seen it, yes? It's the going to the people. Being physically there. Where they work. Being with them there. That's the important thing."

"But those books—who wrote them?"

"Well—to be perfectly honest—there are two collections. The first one I don't think we ever used publicly. Not me anyway. And it was certainly never really offered to the brothers. That one was by a Father Ricardo Joseph—years ago—a collection of very old jokes, for the most part. Some so old they seem brittle in the telling. But put down in one place at least. Put down to rest. I think originally it was my father who gave them to me. Way back. But that other collection is the one I'm not sure about. The important one. We've used it the most, but I can't remember the author—the editor, or whatever—I just can't remember who wrote it. And that *is* strange. I've memorized many of the jokes but forgotten the jokester. That's really odd, don't you think?"

"Yes."

The tape was nearing its end, nothing there beyond

the 'yes' but repetition of surprise at not being sure about the writer's name. Darby couldn't see that it much mattered, the jokes and stories hardly worth the trouble to write down and save. But Fr. Bede had sounded worried, more so on the tape itself than what Darby could remember of that last afternoon on the road, his voice grown husky as he marveled at the strangeness of his failure, again and again returning to it until they both had finally settled into near silence, saying little then at all beyond a comment on the traffic or a word or two about the time of day. Darby rewound the tape and checked the entry in the Journal at the point the conversation had begun. He decided to put it in with the other possibles, with the four or five entries that were due to be picked up by the Cardinal's secretary later that afternoon.

It was quiet on the Little Okra, the barges waiting out the noontime heat. The flask of Scotch was nearly full, hidden under the false bottom of the briefcase. It was good to be alone in silence and the Scotch would taste good and the Cardinal might find something useful among it all. There might be what he wanted there, a weapon he could use. Or maybe something there to prove the Yoricks worthy of his trust and final support. Something. And maybe Poddy was no writer and maybe the barges wouldn't start to chunk and chunk again and maybe everything would go back to the way it once had been. Darby stacked the IT-quest papers neatly to one side of the briefcase and reached for the flask. The Scotch would taste very good indeed.

CHAPTER THIRTEEN

The telephone rang into another dream of Fr. Bede, a fuzzy setting with the tiny priest still dancing on the leaves and flowers, the Little Okra down below and chunk-chunk-chunk come now so close that Darby almost felt the spray. Fr. Bede had just called to him, to join the dance and test his weight out on the water when the phone brought back the bedroom and the semi-dark. The receiver felt cold against his cheek. The Cardinal sounded excited.

Ross? Are you awake? Is that you, Ross?

"Eminence?" Kathleen was snoring softly, her knee against the small of Darby's back as he tried to sit up.

Ross—yes. News. News!

"News, Eminence?"

Yes. And something useful. At last.

"Eminence—" Darby glanced at the dial of the clock-radio, 1:30 there in red that seemed to shimmer as he rubbed his eyes and pushed his weight against the headboard. Kathleen stopped snoring and rolled to her side, fingers reaching for his arm and holding to the rolled-back sheet instead.

The books, Ross. The books! I knew you would find something. Yes. And you did!

"Books?" 1:30 changed to 1:31, the clock-radio humming and Kathleen's snores there too, louder this time and with a whistle low and wavered mixing in. Darby had never heard this Cardinal-voice before.

The joke-books. At least the one. Not sure about the

Joseph Ricardo book–but maybe even there. Plagiarism, Ross. Bede has been plagiarizing!

"But, Eminence, I don't think he–"

Yes. I know it's not much. No. Not the big one. Not yet. But it's a beginning, Ross. Something solid. Embarrassing if nothing else. Something the Holy Father cannot simply ignore. Do you know who the author is? That second collection?

"No, Eminence. No." He closed his eyes and almost saw the face of Fr. Bede, round and worrying with his failure to remember. Kathleen stopped snoring and began to thrash about, sheet following her to the other side of the bed. She would be awake soon.

Bishop Pound. Kansas City, Ross. You've heard me mention him before. Many times. Timmy Pound! Poddy O'Malley confirmed it a few hours ago. And I've spoken to Timmy. He's–saddened, I believe he said. Saddened. Did you hear, Ross?

"Yes." Fr. Bede's face was changing itself into Poddy's, the round smoothness giving way in fits and starts to one all angular, cheekbone-sharp and beak-nosed like the Cardinal himself. "Yes, Eminence, I heard."

But he'll wait on us. He'll wait, Ross. Until there's more. I went to school with Timmy. We can count on him, Ross. He wrote the books a long time ago. Before he was a priest. But the copyright is still held by his Order. And he feels as we do–he sees the way we have to go. To meet the danger well-prepared. And Ross–you leave for Georgia the day after tomorrow.

"Eminence?" Kathleen snorted and came awake, slowly freeing herself from the sheets and propping on one elbow. As he opened his eyes, Darby could feel her curiosity, like a tingling on his skin from a cool breeze.

Yes. The news. Poddy took the call.

"Poddy?"

"What about Poddy?" Kathleen whispered. Darby held up a hand as she clicked on the light and sat up quickly, her back making the headboard shake. "Poddy?"

Yes. He was working late. On your column. Bede wants you to come with him. On a second tour, Ross. To the–let me see–yes–to the 'office workers' this time.

"A second tour? But–" He briefly imagined the scene, Poddy ever-alert, sitting no doubt at Darby's desk, the office well-lit, short-haired smiling Poddy, neat and orderly and quick, the phone picked up on the first ring, Poddy in charge of everything and thanking Fr. Bede and later thanking God or lucky stars and smiling even broader at the way things had begun to go. Darby almost groaned.

Yes–yes indeed–and he wants you to come. It's per-fect, Ross. Can you see that?

"Perfect. Yes."

"What is?" Kathleen's whisper was louder this time and Darby cupped his hand over the bottom of the re-ceiver and tried to turn sideways on the bed. "Who are you talking with?" She spoke the words aloud. "Is it His Eminence?" She bounced herself up higher in the bed and brushed at her hair.

There's more, Ross. Much more. The books are only a beginning. We'll send blank tapes and the credit cards. And a car. Tomorrow. Do you need more quarters?

"No–no, I have enough." The sack was half-full, most times no phones at all in the places where the Yoricks came to play. Or no way possible to get alone for long enough to do much good. Or something there that seemed to sap his will to *be* and *do* what he had been and done before. Always something in the way.

I'm pleased, Ross. I feel better now. I knew you hadn't slipped. Your skill at sniffing out the wrong is still intact. You still know what is wrong and what is right. You have our full support. Did you hear?

"Yes, Eminence." For just a second, he thought he heard the chunk-chunk-chunk, down on the river nearly at the boathouse/office, the clanking rumble of an engine and a touch, the barest trace of jingling bells.

No. It's like I told young O'Malley—there's nothing wrong with Ross's nose. Right? Just like before, eh? Strong and steady?

"Yes. Just like before."

But nothing was just like before, nothing, and as Kathleen's fingers touched and rubbed his shoulders he could almost feel the dream-spray out about him just beyond the bed, the feeling growing stronger with each word the Cardinal spoke that each and every 'other' time, 'just like before' atop 'just-like-before' was there within the spray in silence yet accusing nonetheless, his nose and then his column part of what had brought to light rank growth in rooms that he had gone to see, been sent to see and then to mark the hiding places and to guide in brushes, rotors, something that could scrape things clean again.

Then had he been a maker of the spray—no—helper of the brushes and the rotors? Questions now—both big and little down within and deep, churned up and bubbling clear to see. Had he run away and run away and run away and run and run and run until in weariness he went to sleep, went down to sleep a runner and woke up a nose to point the best way for the chunk-chunk-chunk to follow after, room by room and growth by growth, on point like some sad hound afraid to lose his master's favor and in debt forever for his food and bed and bitch in heat? Kathleen snuggled close and rubbed harder at his shoulders. There had been many rooms, hunts, places he had been since Jackson Square. And he had done what he was told and the structures and their rooms still stood intact but even after brush and rotor most times with the furniture all wrong inside, and sometimes with the tenants not the best ones they could be and as he closed his eyes again, the little bells began to jingle somewhere growing louder, past the spray with sounds of dancing and a laughter rising like a thunder-rumble or the moving into proper place of tables, couches, chairs and beds by some rich landlord, steadfast in his love of people and no fear whatever for the property he loaned.

Did you hear? About the support?

"Yes. Yes I heard."

Darby rubbed his nose and listened to the laughter and the bells, Poddy disappearing with the Cardinal, Kathleen fading like a negative exposed to light (the Cardinal's choice not strong enough to join the laughter and the dance), the IT-parade there briefly until one by one they tumbled down with Purity alone behind to hold its ground, but dimly like a lighthouse distant through a misting rain.

Good. Very good. I'm relieved, Ross. Are you ready to leave?

"Is it another trip, Darby?" Kathleen's voice was like their daughter's, a near-squeal there among the words just like the way it was when they had learned the house was theirs.

"I think I am."

CHAPTER FOURTEEN

Cardinal Carlton Edward Boyer, now His Holiness Pope Hilary II, was watching the sea. All afternoon, sailboards of various shapes and sizes had bobbed and spun to catch the wind, back and forth between the lighthouse and Smuggler's Point, sails nearly every color but more red ones now, the sky still deep blue, cloudless and not yet free of a sun which was just above the trees back toward the city. It was his first opportunity to be alone in nearly a month, state after state on a visit not quite half done but already troubling in its evidence of rancor and mistrust. The schedule had been set over a year ago in Rome, Pietro Riga, Cardinal Riga, studying maps and meeting delegations, writing, reading, figuring all the details of what more and more had come to seem a campaign in some distant war, a springtime and a summer to be spent in battle with an enemy of many heads and faces. The sailboards seemed to be racing now, a staggered line out to the horizon, sails full and sailors bending nearly to the water as they jumped and fell and pushed up high to crest a wave. The visit was a tiring one, the battles nearly every day enough to bring on feelings of despair.

The sky began to show the first trace of the coming dusk. Pope Hilary sighed and bowed his head to pray, the words all there and waiting but not coming when he called, a face there in their stead, a peaceful face from somewhere, Riga with it, smiling Riga like he once had always been, back when they both were boys in Illinois.

The face had come to ask a blessing. The memory was strong.

"Your Holiness remembers the new Order?"

"The Order, Pietro?"

"The Poor Yoricks, Holiness. From America?"

"Ah. Yes yes. And this is?"

"Father Bede, Holiness. Father Solomon Bede."

"Your Holiness."

"Ah yes. Dear brother—and how is America?"

But the face had not prepared him for the things he saw, was seeing yet and day by day out where he once himself had lived, had grown up among from childhood and had loved. The face had never told him of the sadness and the fear, the rude impatience and the glaring signs of slackened faith, the plenty and the greed there side by side and come so close together neither could be told apart. The face was full of hope and Pietro Riga smiled and smiled and for an instant everything had been pure again and whole.

"God's blessing, little brother. God's blessing on your work."

And that had been six months ago, a year perhaps, the time as hazy in his memory as the nearest waves and sailboards had begun to seem in the lengthening shadows of the coming dusk, the sky itself now paler than before, cloud-pocked toward the south where thunder seemed to wait. Pope Hilary sighed and bowed his head again, the words familiar and a comfort in their cadenced rise and fall, an easement through his mind sent one by one by one for others mostly, back behind him for America, back behind for every troubled place, each one seen clearly as he let the words come chanting now to meet with what he saw and heard and felt, a column

finally like a poem there for his prayer:
Angry nuns and
too few priests too few
and celibacy mixed in
as full companion in
a gone forth boil and bubble–
contra-ception contra-ception
first and mangled fetus next
and no more God–man last of all
and
Angry nuns and angry nuns and angry nuns
all in a row
all in a row–
He sighed and thought of the smiling face, the little brother close beside the almost vastness of Pietro Riga, smiling in the sunshine, pale Roman sunshine back six months ago, or perhaps a year, and one more prayer was felt:
For Solomon Bede in dark America–

CHAPTER FIFTEEN

Toad's 24 Hr. Towing Ser. had charged $85.00 to bounce and jostle the Cardinal's second car to Congo Crossing and another $25.00 to store it in the 'Sick Bay' of Toad's Deeluxe Body Shop until Toad himself could find time to see just what had made it clank and billow smoke and finally backfire to a stop out on the narrow shoulder of Highway 602 North. Toad's night-man was called 'Doobie' and seemed to see things that weren't there. He slowly counted out Darby's change near a sputtering overhead sign.

"Look out!" He ducked and whistled. "Jesus. Flamingos getting' big as ponies–that'n nearly got your head, Mister. Real close. Look out–here it comes again!" And he squatted down and covered his head with his hands. "Damn. An' they got teeth too! I don't care what you been told. Razor sharp teeth. Must be all the new-clear testin', y'know?" He slowly stood back up and brushed at the front of his overalls. "Possum're getting' bigger too. An' meaner." He flipped the last two bills at Darby and stuffed his hands in his pockets, eyes blinking and a beginning smile making his lips twitch in the corners. "You'll have to stay th'night."

"But can't you work on it now? I'll pay extra." It was a good hour or more of hard driving to Slackbridge and the Yoricks were leaving tonight. Doobie jumped back and began stamping on the greasy cement, thick boot heels slipping sideways as he pressed down and twisted with all his weight. His eyes had gone wide and unfocused.

"Jesus God–Christ–get 'em, Mister–get 'em!" He almost danced a stomping heel-and-toe, back and forth and then a sliding sideways sweep that scraped up chunks of grease and bits of what looked like wire. "Get th'queen–get her–*her*–see? There!" He jumped up and down and twisted for a second and then shuffled to a clean place closer to the office door. "Damn near got us that time–Bo-liv-an fire-ants're everwhere this summer. Everwhere." He wiped at his forehead and stepped back in front of Darby. "You'll have to stay th'night."

"But I'll pay extra if you would just–"

"Toad's in th'band. Electric bass. I can call you a cab. Hey–don't I know you?"

"No–I don't think–"

"Po' Boy Motel's just up th'road near town. It's the best. I'll get your stuff." But he ducked again instead and swung out with a closing fist. "Th'other damn flamingo–look out!" And he squatted behind Darby, holding to one of his arms and moving it like a shield from side to side. "She's a killer, Mister–watch your head!"

"But–I need to get to Slackbridge tonight." Darby freed his arm and helped Doobie catch his balance. A phone booth glowed faintly against the far wall of the garage, past the 'Sick Bay' and near a row of soft-drink machines. Doobie was smiling full this time.

"I know you. Yes, sir I do. You're *him*, ain't you?"

"*Him*?" Darby hoped the phone was working. The quarters were in his suitcase. He would call collect and pray for acceptance.

"They was wonderin' what happened–when you didn't make it for th'Battle a th'Bands. But th'girls ain't come on yet. It's on the radio. I been lissening. Th'boys all been waitin' at th'airport. Even Toad." Doobie glanced right to left and shrugged. "Getting' late. Maybe them flamingos headed north."

"Is that phone over there in order?"

"Order what?" Doobie had begun to edge closer to the office door again, still scanning the nearly black sky above the sputtering sign. "You ain't suppose to eat *here* for godssake. An' what happened to your plane anyways?"

"No–the phone–does it work?"

"Yeah." Doobie jumped sideways across a puddle of sludge and made it to the cement slab in front of the door. "But don't make too many beeps in there. An' watch th'bells too. Them flamingos like that kind a stuff."

#

A 'Fourth Banana Marvin' had taken the call, Darby trying to make sense of the words above a sudden roaring of engines outside and behind him in the Body Shop lot. Pushing a finger in one ear and pressing the greasy receiver hard against the other one, he had finally discovered that The Yoricks were gone, the tour already underway, a few Third and most of the Second Bananas and Fr. Bede all gone together on to Macon, Joke Breaks ready for the secretaries there, in real estate, five separate all-night offices and a Midnight Madness Condo City Sale-a-Rama and perhaps a little time left over for the junior college staff next day. He decided to call the Cardinal later, from some place down the road and not give Poddy any further room to gloat. Putting down the receiver, he stepped out of the booth, the engines dying down, and one voice come up from the semi-darkness out ahead.

"Mr. Morninglove–Sonny-Boy?"

Darby slowly turned to face the voice, the man,

dressed in what looked to be a gold blazer with camou-flage pants and some sort of glittering ascot pushed hard against his chin. Behind him were maybe twenty deputy sheriffs, short and tall and fat and lean and every one with polished brass buttons and campaign hats that looked freshly blocked and cleaned and Sam Browne belts whose leather glistened in the lights being held up by a camera crew, three men in red blazers and blue slacks and identically knotted string ties dangling down their ruffled shirts.

"Doobie told us about your car. I'm real sorry."

"I—can I get it fixed tonight?" The deputies were smiling, a few with tiny cameras that kept popping flashes of an almost blue light, moving now to the sides to get a better view, Darby in the center with the voice pressing in against him and the microphone held inches from his nose. Doobie was doing what looked like deep-knee bends back at the office door. The voice motioned the red blinking video camera closer in, wide dark lens nodding like a polished snout and a hesitant whir hissing up from somewhere deep within. The two other men followed and pointed their hand-held lights at Darby and the voice. Darby coughed and then swallowed a few times before speaking again. "Tonight? The car?"

"Sure thing." The voice was laughing. "Sure you can. Whatever you want. You want anything right now?"

"The car—I need—"

"'Sides that. You ate supper?"

"No—but, I can—"

"Somebody call in a burger for Mr. Morninglove." The voice raised up on tiptoe and waved toward a point behind the lights. "Hey Ransome—hey—you clostest to the cars—call in a burger," turning back to Darby, "What you want on that burger?"

"I–I don't really want–"

"All th'way, Ransome." He poked Darby in the ribs. "You can take off what you don't like–easier to take off then to put on. 'Cept for weight, of course. Fries?"

"I–"

"An' fries, Ransome–an' hell–give 'im a banana shake." He squeezed and then patted Darby's neck. "It's fresh made–sorry we ain't got no tequila shakes–like in your song? But shoot–I figure you'll need them brain cells to judge the girls. Right? Yessir."

"What?"

"Let's get the interview in th'can–everybody get quiet now!" The voice suddenly took off his blazer and ascot and dropped them carefully out of sight behind him. Underneath was a red long-john top and blue suspenders that looked painted on. He mussed up his hair and stared full into the lens just as the video camera began blinking red in several spots across its front. The lights hurt Darby's eyes.

"B.D. Laroux here for Channel Two an' a great big howdy do to all a you–my Georgia redneck friends. Tonight ol' B.D's *Country Roads* is in Congo Crossing with I guess you could say one of th'biggest country stars in th'bidness. An' that's sayin' a mouthful when you think about the great ones. But people, this ol' boy's been there with 'em all–Hank and Johnny, Ernest an' George, Willie an' Waylon, Jerry Lee an' Carl–even once or twice with th'King hisself before Hollywood stepped all over his blue suede shoes an' sent 'im on to heartbreak hotel for real. An' man an' boy he ain't never let us down. Sonny-Boy Morninglove's a country singing legend if ever there was such a thing. An' tonight? Well folks as most a you surely know by now–tonight he's here on a mission a mercy." The voice turned toward Darby and reached a hand around to press the small of his back and pull him closer to the microphone. "Now then, Sonny-Boy—do you mind me callin' you Sonny-Boy? Or would you pre-fer I call you Mister Lover?" the microphone tip bounced off Darby's chin.

"I—look—this is all a mistake—"

"An' he's modest too, folks. Just like th'magazines say. Yessir. But I'm here t'tell you first-hand that there ain't nothin' shy 'bout th'way he fights against the 'mistake' of pellagra. An' he's been battling against it near full-time th'past four years. 'Cause this ol' boy *cares*, folks. He ain't in it just for no money or awards or nothin' like that. This here is personal with Sonny-Boy Morninglove. 'Cause he knows an' I know that pellagra kills, folks, an' that's no lie, right Sonny-Boy?" the hand kept pressing into Darby's back, squeezing and then pulling at the cloth of his sport-coat. "An' this here P-2 epidemic you been readin' about an' seeing on th'news ain't just a Southern thing no more, folks. No *sir* it ain't. They got cases—real pitiful cases too—breakin' out up North an' all over th'place in California. Ever damn where. It's an American problem now. An' it kills."

"But—I'm not—"

"An' this star right here's raised millions, folks. Why that P-2-AID Concert in Houston brought in over a quarter million all by itself. An' the Three-M Research Institute over in Brunswick is mighty glad he took an interest. How long has pellagra been around anyway, Sonny-Boy?"

"Look," Darby wiggled free of the hand and tried to dodge the microphone, "I'm not—" But the voice was in a hurry.

"Right. Right. Well—that's about all th'time they'll

give us for B.D.'s Country Roads tonight, folks. But I'll be back tomorrow with some filmed highlights of the Midland Sheriffs' Miss Good-Health Competition—all proceeds to th'Three-M Institute—ever thin dime. An'—wait—we got us a few extra seconds? Ok—hey—Sheriff Bebber—Catfish you out there, son? Yeah—here he comes, folks—'Catfish' Bebber, Sheriff a Seminary County an' organizer of th'whole shootin' match—c'mon in here son an' let the folks see you."

"B.D." the man looked too big for his uniform with hair so short that the harsh lights made him seem bald. He pressed in close to Darby on the other side, a monster hand clutching at the microphone like it was a hammer handle. Darby smelled bourbon.

"Catfish—how much you raise so far—an' this here takes in 'bout five or six counties, folks."

"Twenty-five thousand, B.D. Battle a th'Bands an' the beauty contest's been sold out a week so we put th'whole thing on th'radio and'll be asking the folks t'call in their pledges long as she lasts. But we got us twenty-five in hand—countin' donations from th'merchants an' Mr. Morninglove's new record. That was real impawtant. Givin' us a dollar a sale." Up close the man's smile looked menacing, teeth protruding like they were getting ready to snap out at Darby's neck.

"Yessir, Catfish. An' I hear you got you a personal interest in all a this, ain't you?"

"Well—yeah—but it's private, y'know?"

"Right." He cupped a hand over his left ear and smiled. "Got me a second or two more, Country Boy? Talkin' to my man out in th' van, folks. Ok? Good real good." He stepped out a foot or so in front of Darby and the Sheriff. "That new record's really sellin' too—only been out a week and you hear it least three, four times

116

a day." The camera-man moved the lens closer, legs straddling a thick black cable Darby hadn't seen before. The voice was getting softer, eyes watery now and lips quivering in occasional profile. "So buy it, folks. Sonny-Boy Morninglove–Delta-Bright label–*Pellagra Took My Daddy to the Lord*. An' that's it–that's it for B.D. Laroux–stay tried an' true–ever one a you–my Georgia redneck friends." And the voice went away and the lights got dim and engines started one by one. Sheriff Bebber coughed and straightened his Sam Browne.

"Let's move it, Morninglove–show's about to start. We'll take my van an' you can eat y'damn burger on th'way. Where th'hell you been?"

CHAPTER SIXTEEN

The auditorium walls were plastered with giant Confederate battle-flags and posters of sickly-looking children, crying faces and a hint of some sort of rash-like redness on their cheeks and necks. Darby sat with the other judges, dead-center of the first row at the very end of the runway. The Channel Two crew were bunched together along the end of the stage itself, B.D. Laroux sometimes with them and sometimes not. Sheriff Bebber seemed to be some kind of general manager of the evening and had driven his van, siren wailing right into the backstage area of the medium-sized armory and personally led Darby to his seat among the judges. There had been no time to explain. The Sheriff had done all the talking:

"You just remember Miss Rebel Lanes—y'got that? Rebel Lanes if you want your cut. Go on an' eat your burger. An' lay off th'booze—we heard about Montgomery."

#

The Judge on Darby's left was a fat woman in a crinkly blue evening gown whose arms kept pressing into his shoulder, elbow digging into his ribs whenever a particularly large-breasted entry made it to the end of the runway. An Asian in a too-big tuxedo sat to his right sucking on what smelled to be lemon drops. The Asian spoke very mangled English. Miss Rebel Lanes was reading something vaguely poetic, a breathless drone of broken words occasionally emphasized by a near shout or rumbling whisper into the microphone. Some of it sounded like Robert Browning.

> *Or–or–there's–uh–Satan! One might–uh–ven-ture uh–Pledge one's soul to-to–uh him, uh yet leave such a–such a (oh what is it?)–flaw (yes!) flaw in–in the–uh–uh–uh–in the in-den-ture (whew!)–and so forth–thank ya'll–thank ya'll–*

And Sheriff Bebber had come on stage and made the applause go on longer than what at first had come out on its own. The fat judge wrote furiously in her plastic-covered CONTEST NOTES and wiped away a tear.

Darby settled deeper in his seat, trying to escape the pressure on his left arm by hugging his own CONTEST NOTES to his chest. A kind of comic had followed Miss Rebel Lanes, a tall man dressed in black and sounding like a funeral parlor director as he once again filled up time until the preliminary judging was done. He had been there in between the swimsuits and the evening gowns and had even tried to sing before the talent part began. Darby watched the band; the bass-man, Toad, was no longer there. The Comic's voice was very low. The joke was troubling. The words not clear.

> *...and so he says–'Are there any penguins hereabouts?' And the lil' Tex-Mex says, 'No, Se-ñor.' And then the guy's wife yells out from the car: 'See, dummy, I told you that was a nun you hit!'*

The fat lady was poking at Darby's arm, a long sheet of pink paper held loosely between a jeweled index finger and her outsized thumb.

"Time to mark your choices, Mister Lover." She giggled and puckered her lips into a facsimile of a kiss.

"Miss Rebel Lanes was real good, don't you think?"

"I—she seemed too—" The pink sheet felt greasy.

"Yes I know. She's my niece by marriage. Poor thing. She always does that when she's tense. But it's much better now than last year. And she looks so precious in her new evening gown, don't you think?"

"Well—yes." The Comic was trying to dance, a buck-and-wing to mostly slurred brushwork on the snare-drum. The drummer looked like a big-headed child. Darby glanced at the paper and saw that Miss Rebel Lanes was at the top of every judge's list of five. The Asian leaned in close and chuckled, a smell of lemon nearly overpowering. The audience was beginning to sound restless, and Darby noticed Sheriff Bebber glaring down at the judges from his place in the wings.

"Verra good, yes? Verry funny. Nun rooks arike pen-a-guin. Yes?" He clapped his hands and rocked back and forth a few times. "Verra funny."

"Mark your choices and pass it on. We're an hour over already." The fat lady winked and licked her lips.

"Yes." Darby tried to remember the faces of the con-testants but finally gave it up. He opened his CONTEST NOTES and then wrote down the first five names he saw: Miss Tyler Tire; Miss Friendly Auto Parts; Miss Croppy-Cromwell Community College; Miss WBIG; and the only name besides Miss Rebel Lanes that had at least a partial face to go along with what in memory had become for him a whirling mess of breasts and bulges and a dress so full of lace it seemed all troweled on instead of sewn: Miss Adams Abbatoir. The Asian almost snatched away the pink sheet to write down his own choices, pencil moving quickly in between dry chuckles and a nearly savage shaking of his head. The Comic was tapping on the microphone with his fingertips. The pink sheet was now with a sullen-looking cowgirl in red-spangled boots and a pleated evening gown.

Testing–testing–anybody there?

"Verra funny man–yes-a-sirra–boy-a howdy–I rike-a verra much."

"Well–I'm not sure that–" The Comic's words seemed more and more out of place to Darby, not appropriate to, not in sync with the event or the audience or the contestants or the judges. Darby wasn't even sure that he was hearing what the others were hearing. It was beginning to feel like somehow Father Bede had sent out one of the brothers to work the crowd for some purpose only he would know–with stolen jokes flying out with no regard for where they landed. The Comic's voice was still low but now with a bit of a whine, almost yodel-like, down in some of the words. Nothing seemed right.

...so the Mother Superior says to the Monsignor–she says: 'Did your watch stop when it dropped on the floor?' And Monsignor shoots back: "Sure. Do you think it would go through?"

"Lordy me–that Jimmy Winslow's a nut." The fat lady's arm jiggled as she laughed, thick folds of skin rippling against Darby's arm. "And him a Baptist preacher too. Lord. Think you all could use him in Nashville, Sonny-Boy?"

"Ah–good joke–watch–stop-a watch joke–ah yes! Verra good. Ho yes!" the Asian began stamping his feet and pounding the armrests of his seat as the chuckling turned to a whinny-laughter, a shrill and whistling sound that took a while to stop.

And now–c'mon back out here, Sheriff Bebber–and now the results! Girls ya'll just line up there behind us–

that's right. Good. Sheriff—it's all yours.

Thank you, Preacher Winslow. We got the judges' decision yet? He glanced down at Darby and then noticed the cowgirl waving an envelope near the runway steps. *Real fine. Let's hear it for Miss Pearlie Sue Dobbins, folks.* A green spotlight picked out the cowgirl and held her until she made it back to her seat. The applause was scattered. Turning around, Darby noticed that most of the people had left.

"Oh they'll be back, Sonny-Boy. They always come back for the questions and the crowning." The fat lady seemed to be sucking on something, her cheeks working in quick-time like a squirrel with a stubborn nut.

An' now th'five final con-testants. This here is real impawtant now, folks, so lissen up. Number One—Miss Rebel Lanes—

"That's good. Catfish'll feel better now. His baby made it."

Miss Beef-A-Rama—

"She verra big—verra big—more big than others—yes?" The Asian cupped his hands and pumped them a few times out and back on his chest. "Yes?"

Miss 491 Gospel Tabernacle—

"Now there's a surprise. She wouldn't even wear a swimsuit."

"But," the Asian leaned toward the fat lady, "she sing Gospurru-song—an' pray a ban-jo. Verra good. Nice-a teet too."

"I beg your pardon?" The fat lady tried to draw back in her seat but only her sleeve made it.

"Teet—nice-a teet." He smiled and clicked his teeth together.

Miss Adams Abbatoir—

"Best all-round figure and talent, I guess. But, Lord,

honey–look at that walk!"

An' Miss Po'Boy Motel–

"Whoa boy–she know-a Cho! An' Cho know-a her buddies! She *verra* good. Oh yes-a by God verra verra good! Mmmmmm! Cho rike-a her boy-a howdy!"

"Judges were hard to find this year, Sonny-Boy." The fat lady whispered, lips nearly touching Darby's ear. She smelled like musk.

"Yes." And the band began a tune that helped the losers find their way backstage and loud enough to reach the places where the audience had gone, to call them back inside and get them settled in their seats and mostly quiet while the Sheriff shuffled through a stack of index cards and the Comic, Preacher Winslow, slipped away to wait. And the questions went quickly, one by one, the Sheriff sliding over Po' Boy Mmmmmm and Beef-A-Rama verra big and Tabernacle nice-a-teet and stomp-walk Abbatoir, to come to rest at last and for the longest time on Rebel Lanes, blond hair in ringlets down her back and tongue so lost in starts and stops it seemed to coat its words in spray-filled clucks and trills and pip-ing squeaks:

I–I–uh–want y'know to uh–be uh–y'know a nurse–

And more:

God–umm–God uh bless–the–uh USA–

And last words came and went away the same:

Pelgra–uh–wait–pel-la-gra kills–I–uh–I hate that–I hate pelgra–hate it!

And then the Comic-Preacher showed himself as if some giant spring had jumped him out beside the Sheriff set to lead the cheers and finally motion Darby up to join him on the stage.

Let's get th'guest of honor up here, folks! Let's make

him welcome!

"That's you, honey." The fat lady pushed at Darby's neck with a hand that felt like marble. "I'll mark y'ballot– Miss Rebel Lanes ok with you?"

"I–" Two deputies and the green spotlight helped him up the runway steps and patted him toward the microphone. The finalists were huddled close together now, arms locked and weight shifting from foot to foot like schoolgirls waiting for a bathroom pass. The Sheriff stood to one side frowning at the judges. Up close, the Comic Preacher Winslow's teeth looked blue.

> *Now he ain't scheduled to do it–an' he ain't in no way ob-ligated–but let's try an' get him to sing anyways, folks. Who wants to hear Sonny-Boy sing?*

But–but I'm not– The microphone made his voice sound echoic and tinny.

The whoops and yells seemed to begin back where the deputies sat together, back in the darkness down below a flickering exit sign. The spotlight had changed to a pulsing white that took away even the runway and the row of judges just beyond. A Boy Scout handed the Comic-Preacher a slip of paper.

> *Yessir–Sonny-Boy   Morninglove–and–hey folks looky here–we just topped thirty-five thousand big ones–how about that now? Yessir– thirty-five and still climbing–so keep them pledges comin' in!* He patted Darby in closer to the microphone and whispered in his ear. "What'll it be–your latest or what? Band's all set for whatever you need." And Darby whispered back: "I–look this has gone entirely too far. I'm not Sonny-Boy–"
>
> *'You Are My Sunshine,' boys,* turning toward

the band and waving a long-fingered hand through the beam of white light. *Everbody sing it with us, folks!* He clicked off the microphone and tugged at the Sheriff's sleeve. The girls were nearly dancing now, gown hems rustling over the wooden floor and strapless tops (all but Miss Tabernacle nice-a-teet's layered neck-high) bobbing with the movement of their very-bigs. The Sheriff squeezed Darby's arm and jerked him away from the light.

"I told you lay off the booze! Didn't I?"

"But–but, I haven't–"

"Didn't I tell you that, Morninglove?" He growled out the words, a few of the girls noticing and stepping back, skirts lifted up as if to protect the fabric from a mud puddle. Darby smiled to let them know there wasn't any danger, that it was all a silly mistake. But the Sheriff growled louder. "Didn't I? Yes or no?"

"Well yes–but I haven't–" The pressure on his arm increased, a burning there now below his triceps. The people were all singing with the preacher.

"An' didn't I tell you no cut if you didn't? Right?"

"I–"

"Yes or no damn you!" He reached his other hand around Darby's back and pinched at his side.

"Yes." Darby found himself making eye-contact with Miss Beef-A-Rama verra-big, round brown eyes that seemed to understand his problem. He smiled and nod-ded, a thank-you past the Sheriff's head.

"What's so damned funny? You think this is funny, don't you?"

"No–no I don't think it's funny–it's not funny at all."

"You're drunk, Morninglove! Just like Montgomery. An' P-2-AID in Houston. Jesus! Well that's it, ol' buddy–

no cut. Nothing. An' you're leaving *now* before you even get th'chance to muck up *my* show. This ain't one bit funny, Morninglove! You hear me?"

"Yes."

"You see anything funny here?"

"No—nothing."

"You got *that* right by God. An' that's all. That's all you get. You're out! Right now!" He nodded toward the wing, toward a flat-faced deputy who seemed to be sniffing the air. "Get him out a here—get him back to Toad's—get that damned car fixed an' get him t'hell out a my county. Now!" The deputy's hands were harder than the Sheriff's. The Comic-Preacher clicked the microphone back on and raised his hands.

> *Hey folks—say good night to Sonny-Boy! He's got an emergency—personal problems to attend to. But let's tell him we still love him—what say? C'mon—put your hands together an' tell him how much you appreciate all he's done.*

And the band lurched into 'Dixie' and the whoops and yells came louder and louder and Darby let the deputy lead the way.

CHAPTER SEVENTEEN

Toad had nearly finished with the car by the time the deputy made two phone calls and took a bathroom break. Doobie was gone.

"Wiring and hoses, Mr. Morninglove. That's what it was. Most times it's something like that."

"I see."

"Yeah. One or t'other. 'Specially in these Jap cars."

The deputy had lit a cigarette and leaned against the squad car, smoking and watching Toad work. He hadn't said anything since they left the armory. Toad closed the hood and wiped his hands on a grimy cloth. His face was nearly as round as Fr. Bede's but fatter, rolls of fat in three or four chins across the top of his jumpsuit.

"Show over?"

"Pardon?"

"Th'benefit—is it over?"

"For him it is." The deputy's voice nearly made Darby jump.

"You get to sing anything, Mr. Morninglove?" Toad kept ignoring the deputy, turning his back on him as he wiped at a few spots of grease on the right front fender of the car. Darby hoped one of the credit cards would work. He was low on cash. "Sheriff sent me on back here early—to fix your car? I was in th'band."

"I—I didn't sing—you see I'm not—"

"He's got problems, Toad. Needs to get back on the road. He's one a them road men. A real travelin' man.

Y'know?"

"Problems?" Toad looked genuinely concerned.

"Yeah–that car ready or what? Catfish said to get 'im on his way." The deputy took a long drag on his cigarette, smoke curling back over both sides of his face.

"It's ready–what's the problem, Mr. Morninglove?" Toad walked slowly, one leg seeming to be shorter than the other, his movement jerky, head pitching sideways with each step. The deputy tossed his cigarette in the direction of the highway and pushed off from the squad car.

"Catfish said–"

"I heard ya Brian." Toad opened the door for Darby, standing behind it and motioning for him to get in. "An' he's doin' what you said Catfish said for him to do. You ain't drinkin' again, Mr. Morninglove?"

"Shit." The deputy made a snuffling sound with his nose as he laughed.

"Look," Darby got in the car quickly, sliding in behind the wheel and pulling the door shut almost in a single motion. Toad squatted beside the open window, head level with Darby's own. In the sputtering glare of the overhead lights, his eyes were wide, eyebrows bushy with thick white hair that seemed intent on meeting in the middle. But the eyes themselves looked kind, concerned and full of not quite pity but of something close to it, the look that Darby's father sometimes got when the Cardinal brought home the wandering son or a teacher called with news of failing grades. "I've been trying to tell everyone all evening. But no one believes me. I'm not Sonny-Boy Morninglove. I'm Darby Ross and I work–worked–I'm on assignment," the word felt good, a proper and substantial anchor, tether to the recent past, "for *Catholic Cross*–that's a kind of newspaper–I'm

a reporter, you see, and I'm trying to get to Macon before–"

"I read about the drinkin', Mr. Morninglove. But
some of th'magazines said you licked it, praise God. An'
that your wife an' sons was comin' back." He leaned in
close and sniffed. "An' I don't smell none. Nothin' fresh."
He bobbed a second or two as if catching his balance.
"It's th'pills again then, ain't it?"

"No–look–like I just said, I'm not who everyone
thinks I–" The deputy had moved to a place a few feet
behind Toad, wiping at the back of his neck with a blue
handkerchief and shaking his head slowly.

"You don't need none of that stuff–big man like you.
Folks believe in you, Mr. Morninglove–they love you.
Don't you know that?" He seemed to be speaking to a
point beyond Darby, to a place in the car beside him or
perhaps further on, outside and somewhere only he
could see. His voice was getting lower and lower and he
moved a step closer, a swarm of tiny moths fluttering
past him for a second and then as if on a gust of wind
sweeping up together to the lights. "You're important to
lots of people–people who never got th'chance you got.
The breaks. You knew Elvis, didn't you?"

"No–look I think I'd just better–"

"Yessir you did–you knew him and he knew you and
you was friends back in Mississippi a long time ago. A
long, long time ago." The words were taking on a kind of
rhythm, a blurring in their stop and start and rise and fall
like music, crooned or hummed, a solitary song. "An'
you both made it–made it out. Your music got you out.
Jesus touched you, Mr. Morninglove. Just like he done
Elvis. Just like th'king. He touched you."

"Let the man alone, Toad. Let him get on where he
needs t'be." The deputy lit another cigarette, the flash

from his lighter making his face look streaked. "Let him alone now."

"Most folks never get th'chance, Mr. Morninglove. Like me. I never got th'chance to go. Not very far anyways. Not like you an' Elvis. You don't need no booze." The song was getting louder and the deputy seemed nervous, beginning to pace now, cigarette tip glowing red, handcuffs jangling against the cartridges in his belt, and trails of smoke gone back and up behind. "An' you don't need th'pills. You need to open up an' let the Lord come in. Let Him in you like it was before. You knew Him once. You knew Him one-on-one a long, long time ago. Don't you remember how it was—how it used to be?" Toad's face was sweating, slick in places and with trickles down along his nose, the face become a round and nearly glowing thing, a dot that bobbed and dodged from side to side. "You remember how it was."

"Yes." Darby watched the face and back behind the glowing dot he heard the jangle of the handcuffs and above it the pop and sputter of the sign and almost tasted sparks, the memories sharp among the rumble of the wheels, the Giant Seahorse roller coaster that his father bought to give his son a ride and scare the tourists, high up high and swoop down quick like some crazed bird of prey and twist and shake until it seemed his skin would come apart and circus clowns and games of chance and skill and one old carrousel below the fun or nearly level with it as the jangling padded car built speed along a straightaway and rose to do it all again. "Yes. I remember." And nighttime prayers and Sunday taste of wafer, Jesus there within him, coming with him part of all the fun, to ride together for at least a day, a part of everything he did and sometimes laughing somewhere deep inside, a feeling all around him and a thought there too of freedom and that what was meant to be would come again and this time stay. A one on one one in one and up and down and side to side a power needing only to be taken whole and trusted purely like the padded bar that kept him safe and snug inside the car no matter what the rails had made it do. "Yes."

"I knew that. Yessir. No matter what them other magazines said about you—no matter what your wife an' kids said. I knew you never forgot." Toad's hands were folded on the window slot, fingers thick and caked in grease that even in the faltering light gave off a glint like polished wood.

"No." But the ride had stopped and he had run away into the dark and frightening things beyond the Seahorse lights, the Olde Tyme Arcade-by-the-Sea now mostly rust and splintered wood, his father and mother both stepped back within their fine old house among the oaks and camphors and the pines, to read and sometimes talk and pray the same as they had surely prayed back when the padded cars had held their son and all the others on a ride that always ended far too soon.

"You go on back to Jesus, Mr. Morninglove. Before it's too late. Before you lose your way like Elvis did." He reached a blackened hand inside to touch and pat at Darby's arm.

"Jesus, Toad—let th'bastid alone." The deputy dropped the cigarette and twisted it dead with the toe of his boot.

"You'll find Him, Mr. Morninglove. You'll see."

"Yes." The car started on the first try, beeping, soft and steady, a flashing tiny circle with the sound, insistent like a beacon far at sea. And it wasn't until ten miles down the road that Darby realized he hadn't paid.

CHAPTER EIGHTEEN

The Henry Wirz Rest Area had been deserted when Darby parked the car beneath the branches of a short, thick pine tree and almost immediately fell asleep. But a sound of children, squeals and shrieks had brought him back after what had seemed only minutes, back to an almost suffocating heat and brightness, sunshine everywhere and the car hood speckled with blobs of resin and his watch dial reading three o'clock. Some of the children had thought he was dead. And an ancient trucker had made sure he wasn't.

"You ok in there, Mister?"

"What? Ok—yes. Yes. Just sleeping."

"Need to be careful in this heat."

"Yes."

"It can be dangerous. An' dope fiends."

"Pardon?"

"Dopers. Lots of craziness out here."

"Yes."

"Didn't used t'be. But it is now. Dope. Used t'be folks looked out for one another."

"Yes."

"But no more though. Th'dope changed it all. Nothings's th'same no more. So y'got be careful where y'sleep. Hey—you look familiar. Don't I know you?"

"No—I don't think so."

"Well. Could be. Say—you ain't up to no funny

bidness y'self now are you?"

"No—no funny business."

But that had been yesterday, not now, back then and not at dusk and a few miles from Columbia—yesterday and hours before his escape from the Many Ha Ha Club and Wyatt Earp's 'Corral' and another night spent sleeping in his car. Darby gripped the wheel and tried to remember the directions Fourth-Banana Marvin shouted at him when the call had finally made it through. The Many Ha Ha's telephone booth was in a darkened corner in between two potted palms and near the chicken wire-protected stage. Wyatt Earp had led him there, across a kind of dance floor, at times with both hands pushing at the backs of jumping soldiers and at men in cowboy hats and women too who jerked and shuffled in among them shrieking louder than the band. Darby wished he had decided to drive on, had gone the whole way into Macon and had never stepped inside the air-conditioned cold and smoke and noise. But Wyatt had spotted him in the parking lot deciding what to do, near a blinking clown face and the ten foot rough-hewn wooden statue of a dancing brave and had clattered over from a group of drunken soldiers, his camouflage pants and khaki tee-shirt way too tight and hand grenades and bullets flashing in the bandoliers across his chest each time he turned to face the sun.

"Thought that was you over here. Come to have some fun, huh? Well let's get to it. I'm on in ten minutes."

And they had gone inside and Darby finally made it through to Marvin, listening hard to find out where The Yoricks were. The receiver had been greasy but the band had stopped and Wyatt kept his back against the door.

Columbia—they're in Columbia—left Macon hours

ago. I said–Columbia–we have a bad connection–did you get that?

"Yes–Columbia."

Columbia, South Carolina–key punchers. At ten home offices. Tomorrow. Can you hear me?

"Yes."

They plan to stay the night at Jackie Gleason House. They'll leave from there. Look for a sign at Special Exit 33. Did you get that? Special Exit 33.

#

Darby slowed down and licked his lips, mouth still dry and last night's Scotch now worked up to a place behind his eyes, the traffic heavier and added lanes and exit signs appearing nearly every mile or so. Last night was mostly a blur, hazy and shimmering like the sky above the trees or bending shoulder-grass beside the cars and trucks ahead, the soldiers and the rest a whirl of noise and glasses coming fast and full, the Scotch a burning kind that made his tongue feel raw. Exit 30 came and went almost before he saw the sign. Like the Many Ha Ha acts, one after another, Wyatt there the longest time of all, jokes that made the soldiers howl and the cowboys stomp and whoop and the women whistle and throw bottles at the wire stretched taut across the stage. But not one of them had stayed beyond the telling, Darby now unable to remember much besides a word or two or fading picture in his mind, of blood and burning bodies, 'poontang'–'slope'–'zippo' there and something like a song with buzzing sounds between the lines and everybody joining on the chorus. And then Wyatt had taken him home to his 'Macon Corral' ("What th'wife don't know won't hurt her, right?"), the sequence clear and even some of what was said, but mostly nothing left but Scotch and heat and floating faces, men and women crammed into a space too small to hold their dancing and their rage. The walls had been covered with Confederate battle flags, just like the armory, but the pictures not as sad. Darby had sat the longest time beneath a poster-sized photograph of Gabby Hayes.

"Who *is* this dude anyway?"

"An' ol' buddy–a writer–he–"

"Why ain't he dancin'?"

"He writes, bimbo–"

"Anybody ever tell you you look just like Sonny-Boy Morninglove, honey?"

"Why ain't *he* laughin'?"

"How th'hell do I know–"

And somehow he had left, had gotten through the gates of the 'Corral' and to the car and down roads that seemed to roll like waves right to a place beside a weed-choked barn, a peeling SEE ROCK CITY sign above him that the headlights caught and held until he coasted in and slumped against the wheel. A roar of jets had brought him to, the sunshine speckled on the hood this time and his watch dial reading nearly five o'clock.

#

Exits 31 and 32 were yards apart, an overpass between them and beyond a billboard filled with Jackie Gleason's face, with sunlight flashing off the silver-painted words below his giant neck, and cars all in a line and smoothly rolling up into the curve of Special Exit 33:

JACKIE GLEASON HOUSE–"Where Fat is a Four-Letter Word"

#

Darby had been shown to a small room behind the kitchen by the Director himself, still dressed in Ed Norton costume and at times even sounding like what Darby could remember of the character's voice, hands fluttering out before him in the pauses and then a rush of words each time the fingers found his vest or pushed his little hat back further on his head.

"It isn't much, Mr. Ross—but we weren't expecting the press hey? Hey?'

He had patted at Darby's arm and helped him with the large suitcase, setting it down on a single bed with the thickest frame and headboard Darby had ever seen. On the far wall a poster of a cracked and titled wooden cross stretched almost from ceiling to floor, the message at the bottom in red and its letters jammed together: WHAT IF JESUS HAD BEEN A FATSO?

Darby was tired, the Scotch-taste grown stronger in his mouth since what the Gleason people had called a Poor Soul Feast—in a room with posters on the walls of slender Gleasons and Art Carney faces, a banner too— 'How Sweet It Is'—beneath which rows of photos overlapped, 'before 'n' after' shots of 'Former Fatsos' staring at the diners who had seemed to truly like their plates of dry chicken meat and hard-boiled eggs. The Yoricks had left three hours before he made it to the swinging doors and a receptionist who had sounded and looked like Joe the Bartender and a place where everyone seemed dressed and ready for a Kramden episode so lost that even Ralph himself would wonder what to do. But the Director had been friendly and seemed truly sorry for Darby's missed connection. Darby couldn't remember his real name.

"Fr. Bede has gone to Charlotte—North Carolina hey? Bank tellers I believe he said. And they'll make camp at Belmont Abbey."

And a little flutter of the hands and jerk of the head and downward tug at the vest and a shuffle-step or two until the next words tumbled out.

"But you can stay the night, Darby-boy. You look like you could use a little rest, hey?"

#

The Director moved the suitcase to a thick wooden stand near the bathroom door and fussed with the covers on the bed and then stepped back in a slide and shake and closed his fluttering fingers on the doorknob.

"We get up every day at five in the morning. To get a jump on those fat cells hey? Hey?" And then he straightened up and let his real voice take a turn.

"But sleep as late as you need, Mr. Ross. Father Bede said you might need rest. And he was right–you seem very tired. Yes. The sleep will do you good."

"I've–I've been driving a–"

"But you're not a Fatso anyway. You look fit. In shape. You'd be an Early Norton here. An inspiration and a goal–if you'd care to stay awhile."

"No–I'm–I'm on assignment." Darby tried to remember when it was that he had last called the Cardinal. There had been a phone at Wyatt Earp's corral, back in a kind of narrow hallway in the semi-dark, but a long-haired cowgirl had kept giggling in his ear. He hoped the big bottle of Scotch was still in the suitcase, resting beneath the socks and handkerchiefs, the supply bottle for the briefcase flask. He had left the briefcase in the trunk of the car along with the tape recorder and the packet of unused tapes and all his paper and his pens and how he wanted the Director to just go away and give him time to stop the shaking in his stomach and the throb and fuzzing in his head. The bed felt marble-hard as he sat down and stared at the poster with the cracked and tilted cross. The Director was laughing.

"A present from a Kramden Graduate–an Early

Norton now. An advertising executive from Boston. Effective. We have one in every flat."

"I see."

"Sleep good then, Darby-boy." He tugged again at his vest, both hands then fluttering out to the side and brushing the door into a glide toward shut.

"Yes." The Cardinal had hung up on him back at the corral, the cowgirl giggling something to him, her lips close to Darby's own as he fought to keep the receiver free. She had told the Cardinal that Sonny-Boy was being good.

"And come back soon and stay longer." The Director's real voice flickered in and out of the Norton-sound. "We love your column here. We really do." The door closed with a click.

"Thank you." He turned away from the door and listened for the jingle deep within a chunk-chunk-chunk that somehow had come up behind his eyes, a clank and spraying rhythm like a feel of wheels on bumpy track or heartbeats, thumping muffled in the quiet of the room. Sonny-Boy was thirsty and alone.

CHAPTER NINETEEN

Fr. Bede had left him, had been told to go, angry words in Jackson Square that frightened several tourists and made others stop and stare; but he had finally gone away into the late afternoon heat and his little cap had jingled out behind him for a while until the big bells clanged and seemed to make the people and the pigeons there grow louder than before. The jingling had not lasted long at all, not near so long or loud as what had been a part of everything that Darby did and everywhere he went, the weeks he followed after what his ears kept telling him was just one town or state ahead, the sound sometimes grown weak but still the jingling like a fog-choked buoy where it was hard to see, out waiting for him with a power in it that had promised him a padded car to ride and final resolution of the way his life had gone. But close at hand the jingling brought no light or comfort and then anger came into the place where cars and resolution should have been.

They had walked and talked for hours, days now since Darby had caught up with the jingles in some office complex back toward Mississippi, back toward somewhere, back toward the East—the 'when' no clearer than the 'where'—so many times and places since the Gleason-people fed him grapefruit and a piece of unbuttered toast and sent him on his way, so many many times and places and then Bede alone, in Jackson Square again—New Orleans—and walking round and round the General on his horse, the boat horns on the river coming in and a sound of guitars and singing and a poet nearby shouting out his work and artists good and bad and everywhere a smell of coffee and fat tourists all around, red-faced, yellow too with tiny cameras, whir and click, the black men laughing at it all, the easy mixture and the clumsy dance. At first they had talked quietly enough. The question:

"Are you planning to go home, Mr. Ross?"

The answer—words about the same as all the other times but three full Scotches now to help them waddle on their way and make room for the disappointment, anger in it building slow and strong:

"Uh no—no—no—no I think I will stay here. I have time to stay. The tour is over. I can just stay here now. For a few days. Or more. To think. My room is paid—paid-up for a week—I think a week. And I need to stay here until then. To get my money's worth. I have a credit card, you know. Several cards. And I have a good place to eat. And I need to stay."

And then more talk, more and more, the little priest in costume walking through the camera whirs and clicks, full on him as the tourists turned to stare, some smiling as they notice what they must have seen on television, Joke Break Time or on the news, The Yoricks highly visible in each and every place that Darby followed after on his long long chase to catch them standing still.

"Hey Yorick—how small *was* your home town?"

"Ok ok—my home town was so small the fire department consisted of three squirt guns and a seltzer bottle."

More and more talk and walking round and round the stiff-tailed horse with (call 'it' what IT surely had become, had perhaps always been since padded cars had left their rails): PURITY gone flickering like a candle flame or moth wings up against a window screen, around the words the little priest let free and in among the memories Darby kept, a flicker and a peeping strongest deep within the many, many times he heard the laughter they had made. But IT would not come out to stay and nothing called his name. And anger gained a little more in strength.

"You need to go home, Mr. Ross. To your family."

"No! No. Well–well yes I know that–I certainly know that. That I know. And–and I will. I *will* go. But my room you see is paid-up. And I've found a good place to eat. And I'm on assignment you see."

But soon the tourists had come even closer in, each step at times a bumping near inspection of their backs and fronts, their sweaty flowered shirts and hands that seemed to drop like giant spiders, heavy and thick, pressing in but less and less on Fr. Bede and more on Darby then–the many sudden fans of Sonny-Boy come out as well–like in the other places he had been–to show surprise that he was still alive.

"It's for my sister, Mr. Morninglove. Esther. She's in a home now. We're from Texas. Can you sign it–love?"

"Sure thing–For Esther–"

"Can you give my boy here some ad-vice, Mr. Morninglove? He's a singer like you. Plays guitar too. Just like you."

"Never give up your dream, son. An' practice."

"Did that TV preacher ever get your wife an' kids t'come back home, Sonny-Boy?"

"Not yet, Sister. Not yet. But be in prayer, y'hear?"

"Hey Sonny-Boy–you playin' here anyplace?"

"Naw–I'm just restin' up. My room's all paid an' I got me a good place t'eat and set. I'm just here restin'."

"Let 'im alone now–can't you see he's busy? He's

talkin' with that lil' hippie–let 'em both alone now."

But by then the talking had begun to sharpen, Fr. Bede turned earnest, his face a contrast to the outrage of his clothing as he gently guided Darby to a nearly private place beside a tree. The jingling bells had fast become an irritation, mocking what there was to see and feel of PURITY, IT now playing hide-and-seek among the words that came out clear and hard. A cluster of tourists stood nearby and watched, a whir and click and murmur with them like the popping trill of locust wings back hidden in a piney wood.

"This is sad, Mr. Ross. All those people. It's dangerous for you to stay here. You need to go home. Today."

"No! No dammit no! I've got to have IT first–I've got to–I *need* IT!"

"What, Mr. Ross? What do you think you need?"

The face was rounder than it ever seemed before, and blander too, a neutral smoothness tilted cap-line down to where the neck and chin got blurred, the eyes wide-staring, barely blinking, color less distinct but mostly green-flecked pale and nose and lips like putty waiting for a sculptor's change of mind.

"What *you* have–I want *IT*."

"And what do you think I have?"

"You know dammit! You know what I need!"

"I think you need a rest, Mr. Ross. You need to go home to your family and rest."

"No! No no no! You sound like–like *him*–like all the others–no!"

"Him?"

A few of the tourists had squatted down to let the ones behind them see, to give them room to fill their lenses–and children now in greater number than before and babies in their funny-looking buggies, dogs and one thick-chested black man with a parrot on his arm, three old-time nuns in black-and-white despite the sunlight and the heat, a sidewalk preacher with an outsized Bible flapping slowly in one hand, a Cajun fiddler thrumming out a tune, a legless veteran riding on a cart, and faces everywhere that seemed to hope someone would take the time to tell them what the show was all about.

"You know him—dammit Bede—*Him*! Cadinal Spitzmulcher—him!"

"A servant of God."

"Pardon me? Servant? *Him* a *servant*? My God—he's after you! He's after *you* Bede! He's—"

"I know that."

"And—and I'm a spy, Bede—I'm the Cardinal's—"

"I know that as well."

"—a stinking spy—you—dammit! You know? You *know*? Did you say you know?"

"That you were sent by Cardinal Spitzmulcher? Yes."

"I see—oh yes by God I see now—now I see!"

"And what do you see, Mr. Ross?"

The face had showed him nothing, nothing there beyond the smoothness of its skin, untouched by even locust click and whir and voices sometimes rising up out past the tree shade where the tourists stood and watched or squatted down to let their neighbors see or shooed away the dogs and propped their babies up to catch a breath of air. But the jingle had come and gone and come again, faint but there a jingle-jangle with each movement of the head, mocking now a distance turned too great to reach across and touch the other side.

"That's why you won't help me—that's why. You

know?"

"Yes."

"All along–you knew?"

"Yes."

"Then–then–you're a fool!"

"Oh yes."

And he shook the bells with his long fingers and let the smooth face break apart, a smile so strong it made the wrinkles crash into each other, bunching up and twisting like the current of a swollen creek. The tourists had gone silent.

"Dammit–dammit Bede!"

Darby had reached down and taken hold of the green blazer, fingers spread across its front, yanking the face up closer to his own almost as if it were a doll, a torso filled with straw. But the face had never even hinted at surprise, the smile grown wider and the eyes alive, a deep blue now without a trace of fear. Darby let the blazer go and stepped back to the tree.

"There's nothing here for you, Mr. Ross."

"But–he'll–he'll ruin you–he'll do it Bede. Like the others."

"No."

"Yes Bede yes! Yes yes yes!"

"You go home, Mr. Ross. And I think it best you do so on your own. Begin there."

"Begin? For Godssake what begin?"

"Your listening."

Yellow tourists had come in along the edges of the crowd, an ordered group with thick green tags upon their blouses and their shirts, all shuffling in a perfect line and stopping just as Fr. Bede began to dance, a back-and-forth step through the tangled grass with mocking bells to keep the beat.

"Listening? Bede dammit–let me help you, Bede. I'll help you and then you can give me what I need–Ok? I can save you. I know him well. I can save you and then you can help *me*. I know you can–you know the way–IT's with you Bede!"

"Go home–go home and listen. You can't hear if you don't listen–"

"Bede–"

But the dance had nearly taken him away, a slide and step-step toward the sidewalk and the street. He stopped beyond the circle of tree shade and adjusted his cap. Darby licked his lips and tasted scotch. The voice came loud enough for everyone to hear.

"There's nothing here for you but noise. And error."

"No! I need to stay–or–or can I go with *you*? Can I stay with *you*?"

"Go home, Mr. Ross–and listen. On your own. Go home. You'll be a better writer if you do. And a better man perhaps. And your wife and daughter need you there."

"You go to Hell, Bede! I don't need a damn one of you! Go on then–you hear me? There's nothing to go home to–*nothing* Bede–do you hear me?"

But the man had danced away, a tinny jingle quickly lost among the sudden clang of church bells and the lo-cust buzz and Darby had sat down to feel the sun and think ahead to supper at the good place he had found. The tree's rough wood had fitted snugly up against his back.

"Don't go near him, Sissy. Can't you see he's drunk?"

CHAPTER TWENTY

It felt late when Darby jerked awake, head banging once or twice on the rough wood of the tree until he got himself faced forward. The Square wasn't as crowded now. Dinner time but he wasn't hungry. The flask had somehow gotten twisted in his pocket, cap pressing sharply into his thigh as he pulled it free and tried to gauge the level of the scotch. Bushes blocked his view of the Cathedral. And Fr. Bede was gone.

"You Ok, Mr. Morninglove?"

The voice was a young one, a skinny teenager of un-certain gender who seemed to work at the good place to eat, at PAPA LINDA'S BAR & GRILLE: 'Where Gay Meets Straight and the Food is Great!' Darby didn't know his/her name.

"Uh yeah—yes sir-ee. Fine. What time is it?"

His watch had been gone since Baton Rouge, since a night too vague to stay in place, a missed connection with The Yoricks and then hours in and out of smoky bars and little shops and crowds of men and women who had taught him dance steps and a better way to eat boiled shrimp. The teenager came closer. She/He seemed to be wearing lipstick.

"Nearly eight. You sick again?"

"No. No. Just resting for a while."

"You don't look too good."

"No—no really. I'm fine. Just tired."

He/She sometimes seemed to be a waiter/waitress or a busboy/girl at Papa Linda's, sometimes even there in the mornings sweeping the sidewalk and taking out the trash, sometimes alone and sometimes with others looking just alike, sometimes a girl and sometimes a boy and sometimes too far in between to tell. But they all loved Sonny-Boy at Papa's. Darby took a long pull on the flask and snapped it shut. It just fit in his back pocket.

"You can't sleep here, Mr. Morninglove. Po-lice'll get you."

"Oh—hey look I'm not sleeping *here*. No—oh no. I'm just resting. I have a room y'know. All paid-up too."

"Where is you stayin' at anyways?"

" I'm —I'm over at 'The OK Corral'—no my God no—uh—uh—the—uh 'Honeymoon Hotel'? No no that's a cartoon—you ever see that one? Old cartoon. Lil'guy sings—they all—all sing—they're bugs, see? It's a singing cartoon—everybody sings—the bugs—this one bug—the one I remember goes: *I'm the guy who carries in th'luggage—I work at the Honeymoon Hotel—I see all the kissage and the huggage—and many other things as well—*No? Don't remember it? It's an old cartoon—an old old one. No? Well I have a very nice room—I just can't remember where it is right now. But—but—look I'd know it if I saw it—it's—it's near the river. Y'know. It's a big place too. With all this fancy grillwork on it—balconies—"

"Most every place got 'em some of that down here in the Quarter, Mr. Morninglove."

"Oh yeah look I know that too—yes—but this place is different—it's got a different name too—nothin' French neither—oh damn what is it?"

He/She squatted down and seemed to be studying Darby, eyes moving up and down and back and forth as if all part of some private linear estimate, inches to feet, 1234567 and on and on, or maybe it was weight, Darby feeling heavier now than he had ever felt before, his stomach empty and growling but head and shoulders, arms and legs gone throbbing like they all were pushing outward, growing bigger and bigger and almost at a point too hard to lift or move. He wanted to leave the Square but didn't trust his legs. She/He was smiling. It was getting dark under the trees.

"Papa say to come find you. And I did it."

"Yes you did—oh yes. What's good at Papa's to-night?"

"Crawfish gumbo goin' pretty fast. But Papa say—Papa say—"

"What did Papa say?"

He/She was frowning, little face all wrinkled up like a crying infant, new-born and deeply red and puckered everywhere at once. The crawfish gumbo would taste good, and Papa's drinks were always strong and tall and Sonny-Boy could eat and drink and set awhile and think.

"Papa say you come on back quick an' see you a su-prise. Papa got you a su-prise."

"That Papa." Darby made his legs work just enough to start the rest of him moving, back scraping along the tree trunk and hands now pushing off the ground. He felt better standing up. She/He tried it too. Quickly. "That Papa is something. A surprise, you say? For me?"

"Yes sir. Papa say to come and find you."

"Yes. And you did. You found me."

And the other voice was strange but almost familiar.

"And so did I—finally! My *God*, Mr Ross—where have you been?"

#

Later, hours or perhaps a day or two beyond when everything was said and done at Papa's and the hotel name remembered ('The Malibu Porpoise'), Darby still could feel the icy spray that seemed to chunk-chunk-

chunk out from the semi-darkness with the other voice, Poddy O'Malley (the Silver Beaver) there beside the him/her, Poddy with his clothes just-so and hair styled short and neat and as he came in closer smelling clean and with a hint of fresh-cut flowers there or some exotic fruit each time he moved his arms. The Him/Her giggled and began to pat at His/Her own hair and full-front shirt and stepped aside just enough to make young Poddy brush against an outthrust hip.

Later, hours or perhaps a day or two beyond when Darby woke up in his hotel bed with Silver Beaver Poddy pacing near the television screen, he did remember thinking Poddy's eyes looked strange back on the Square and that he seemed to tremble when the Him/Her giggled and began to tug at both their arms. But that was hours or days beyond with Papa's coming first, the Her/Him like a guide-dog made to double-lead the master and a friend, down into noise and heat and light, clean through a theme-park Sodom with young Poddy never looking up but holding on to Darby's arm, his fingers painful on the skin, an angel surely come to save the Cardinal's long investment and to drive home squarely one last time the fact of no escape but one—a jurisdiction coming down as quick and surely as the night sky up above the smoky lights on Bourbon Street.

But later Darby learned the truth. Past Papa Linda's su-prise and with just a trace of jingle-jangle come back in to mix with Poddy's chunk-chunk pacing, back and forth before the Pope's face on the screen.

CHAPTER TWENTY ONE

Papa Linda had given the Him/Her a crisp five-dollar bill and then had winked at Poddy. Darby noticed right away that the Bar & Grille was louder and more crowded than usual, even the 'Hard-Hat Hideaway' over by the jukebox filled to overflowing with what looked like oil-rig workers free on a one-day shore leave. But everybody had gotten mostly quiet when Papa raised a jeweled hand and motioned toward the bar. The Her/Him brushed past Poddy in a half-jog toward the kitchen as a cowboy slipped slowly off a padded stool and started walking slowly across the floor between the tables and the booths. He seemed somehow familiar.

"Papa promise you the su-prise—and here she is!"

The cowboy put on a large black Stetson and came to a stop a few feet away. His voice was soft and slow.

"This here th'wrangler you was tellin' me about?"

"*Mais oui*—yes. This is that exact same man."

"What?" The room had gotten even quieter, Darby not able to hear even so much as a clanging of pots back in the kitchen. And then a few of the hardhats had begun to move toward the front, other people coming with them as they passed, tables and booths emptying like a fire alarm had sounded and the front door was the only way to safety. The cowboy had stepped closer, into a circle of light from an overhead fixture, his polished boots glinting, silver band across the toes and flaring eagle wings along the sides. He had been dressed in spangled, black, skin-tight, leather pants and a shiny shirt with rhinestones where the buttons should have been.

"Well well well—"

"Oh—this is too precious—*two* Sonny-Boys! Together at last!" Papa had almost skipped in place, hands clicking together and short yellow hair bouncing and Poddy had backed away almost to the door. Darby had smiled and held out his hand. The cowboy's words had come out this time with a hissing sound around them.

"So this here's th'bastid, huh? I thank ya—uh—ma'am. Y'see he's been settin' fires ever damned where. Who th'hell *are* you, pod'ner?" He had scowled and hooked his thumbs in his outsized belt and watched Darby's hand die away. Papa had begun to pant and wheeze.

"See? Come and look everybody—like I have promised—*oui*? Two Sonny-Boys! But," the skipping stopped and Papa had nearly slid to a spot between the two, off to the side where a cluster of bald-headed black men leaned against each other and showed their teeth, "but—*maintenant*—who—who is the real one. *Réel. Oui*? The Judging then—that's Papa's way—we will have The Judging and find out. *Oui*?"

The crowd had shouted out *oui* but Poddy had come back in close and whispered fast for Darby to just tell them he wasn't who they seemed to think he was, to tell them he was Darby Ross instead and not some cowboy who (yes—on the surface and amazingly) *did* look a lot like Darby but there was no point at all in staying with these people any longer just because of *that*. Right? He had even pulled at Darby's shoulder, trying hard to get him turned to go outside, words coming hot and fast and louder than before.

"For Godssake, Mr. Ross—let's go! Now! Just tell them who you really are—please! I need to talk—I've got to talk with you! *Now!*"

But scotch and (he would later tell himself) the disappointment over being left behind by Fr. Bede, the priest's refusal to accept one Yorick more and let him ride and stay the distance this time all the way to PURITY, to IT at last and on forever, to IT made permanent and not just promised in a jingling out ahead or moments when a dream came in to trick him with a feel of freedom gone too soon—all that and (this he knew without a linger of a doubt) much more had made him pull away from Poddy's hands (damp fingers cool and feeling slick) and give himself up meekly to the voices of his peers.

"Let the people decide! Let the people speak!"

And the voices had come in around him then, deep and shrill and rasping out their pleasure, croaking out their need in chorus with a clang and jangle, scrape and thud of tables being moved and chairs pushed back to let a kind of platform rise up in the middle of the room. The cowboy had seemed angry, slapping at the people as they helped him take his place, to Darby's right and just above where Papa Linda jumped and giggled, shrieking for the people to get quiet so The Judging could begin. And then a spotlight had clicked on, lesser lights dimming everywhere at once, and the voices coming slowly down to murmur-level and below. Poddy had slipped away back into the sudden darkness near the door.

"Oh my—they both look good yes? So so good. But this one—" Papa had reached up to rub a hand slowly down the cowboy's leg, making him jump and shuffle sideways. "Oh yes—*trés bon—oui?*"

The crowd had roared out '*Oui*' and clanged and stomped and whistled, the black men shouting *tout ce qu'il y a de mieux* and going on and on till Papa leaned in close to squeeze at Darby's ankles, fingers pressing hard a few times then relaxed into a rubbing motion mostly with the thumb.

"Ah me ah me—but this one too. *Aussi*? Ah me—*trés magnifique*—yes? *Oui*?"

The '*ouis*' had sounded less distinct, covered quickly by the '*nons*' and several shrieks of 'That ain't Mister Lover' and a chant of 'Fake Fake Fake' beginning like a grunt and growl from deep within the crowd. The cowboy had finally turned his face toward Darby and touched two fingers to the brim of his Stetson.

"They know the real thing when they see it, Son. Ever damned time they do. Who th'hell are *you* anyway?"

But Papa had not given room to answer, all the voices roaring in at once (the Him/Her and the just-alikes, the hard-hats and the wayward fans of Sonny-Boy), come in together with their hands and arms and shoulders in a bumpy wave-like crash that swept away the platform, feet there too as Darby rode up on the crest, their sound like chunk-chunk-chunk way down below and coming closer in his rise and fall and bump-bump through the open door to fly for just a little while until the street and Poddy (drenched by spray with chunk-chunk echoes of his own) both finally there to help him get away.

#

The desk clerk at The Malibu Porpoise had not looked up from his magazine as he handed Darby the key. A silent television screen flickered shadows out across the mailboxes just beyond its metal perch. The Pope's plane had landed in New Orleans.

CHAPTER TWENTY TWO

Darby woke up slowly, one eye at a time, his head a mass of tiny points of pain that seemed to pulse and sting out in a grid-work side to side and up and down and make his face flash hot and cold and skin and hair feel brittle to the touch. Poddy was pacing in front of the television screen across the room and near the only window, talking in a voice that seemed to fight against the volume he had set, now loud now soft now harsh now soothing as announcer followed announcer, news-analyst to reporter-Priest to many voices all at once, shouting in collective outrage over some vague wrong that Rome had not put right. Darby raised up on the bed and eased his head against the wall. The Pope's face now filled the screen, riding once again above the noises down below, a jingle-jingle with him there in spite of Darby's efforts not to hear. But Poddy's words came out in chunk-chunk loudness and a spray that made his head look clouded over, window light behind him bright and painful and a darkness going with him bouncing with each step he took. The Cardinal's odor seemed to be everywhere.

"Look—he's going in the Cathedral—and—and I was supposed to be there—with the delegation. Look—see? There's Monsignor Gramland. And—oh my God—and Monsignor Austene! I was supposed to be there with them both. And—and later at the special session. I was supposed to send you home and catch up with the delegation—oh my God—"

The Pope had stopped to wave, just past his car and in the shadow of St. Louis's steeples, smiling, waving, and a word or two—*jingle—jingle*:

> *America is a vast country, my brothers and sisters—We have come home to visit but more importantly, to listen—*

But *chunk-chunk-chunk* took clean away the other thing the Pope had come back home to do:

"I'm frightened, Mr. Ross—that—that boy was diseased—my God—he told me—he—"

Jingle and *chunk* stopped fast as if someone had paused a tape to fix a sandwich or go see about the kids.

"Boy?"

Darby tried to move his head up higher on the wall, but his shoulders were too heavy, and his neck felt vise-gripped, and his hands refused to carry things alone.

"What boy?"

Poddy stopped pacing and turned toward the bed, his face completely blotted out by sunshine and his voice not *chunking* quite so steady as before.

"The—the black boy—the one I told you about last night—the boy, Mr. Ross—*the* boy." He seemed to fall backwards into the light. Darby guessed he was leaning against the radiator. "What should I do now—I—I can't get tested back home—someone will find out! They always find out—always." The words were nearly a moan.

"Yes—" Darby fought to remember last night, closing his eyes and trying to bring up something solid there beyond or even out around The Judging and his sudden loss of Sonny-Boy. But nothing came except a picture of a woman, framed by tiny print all glossy on the page the clerk had left, huge breasts and something like a teddy bear between her legs, and on her head a graduation mortar board with tassel twisting down into her golden hair. He opened his eyes and tried to lick his lips. The words hurt as he forced them out. "A *boy*, you say?"

"I–I did it again, Mr. Ross. I couldn't seem to stop it–and–that's what's tearing me up! I thought I was through with all that–a long time ago–and my wife has been so under–oh my God my wife!"

"Where?" Darby's head banged twice against the wall as he tried to turn his body toward the door. Poddy's *chunking* had grown softer, more a clicking hum and not half so full of spray. The Cardinal smell was going too, and good Pope Hilary had turned into a rerun of THE WILD WILD WEST.

"She'll have to be told, Mr. Ross–I know that–that's only fair–but–my God–I'll lose her if I do! I can't expect her to forgive me again–not after all my promises–that–that's why I tried to do away with myself last night–that–that boy was definitely diseased–"

"A *boy*?"

"It's happened before–carelessness–only once–years ago–not long after the wedding–before anybody knew about the extra danger–before all that came along–but nothing happened–nothing came of it–and–and I told her and she forgave me–and God forgave me, Mr. Ross. But–but this time I know it's different–I saw it! He was diseased–clearly diseased–and he laughed–afterwards–he–he told me–showed me–and he laughed."

"He laughed at you? This was the boy, right? The boy laughed at you?" Darby's head was starting to feel better. This present Poddy looked and sounded nothing like the Poddy back at *Catholic Cross*.

"Why did you stop me, Mr. Ross? Why didn't you just let me end it–like I tried to do–why did you stop me?" The voice was tinny-sounding now, far off at times and hard to hear.

"Wait a minute wait a minute—wait—are you saying that—that *you* tried to kill yourself last night?" The *clicking-hum* was coming closer, the New-Poddy making the bed bounce as he sat down and moved his face free of the window light. His skin was flushed and twitching, nothing like the Cardinal's Silver Beaver and Scoutmaster of the Year. "*Here*? You tried to do it *here*? In my paid-up room?"

"Yes—but—but I would've gone to Hell—that's where they send the suicides—to Hell—and maybe she'll forgive me, Mr. Ross. I can find a way to get a test made—somehow—a secret test—right? And maybe I'll be Ok—maybe I won't have to worry her at all." The Old Poddy was flickering back to life. "So—so I'm glad you stopped me, Mr. Ross—I'm glad I didn't go to Hell."

"So am I." Darby needed a drink, something, his head still clearing but his memory not joining in, his hands and legs gone cold, a shaking come back in his stomach too, a feeling there like fingers squeezing hard and quick. "What happened?"

"I think it's this place, Mr. Ross—it—I've never been here before."

"Where are we?"

"New Orleans—it's—it's evil, Mr.Ross."

"We're still in New Orleans?"

"I drank too much, Mr. Ross. On an empty stomach—right after I got here. His Eminence thought you'd be here—in the French Quarter—near the Cathedral—somewhere. And he was right. Finally. I went to Mass in the cathedral—and found you afterwards—on the street. He wants you back—he said to get you home—he's had reports all along but—"

"Reports?"

"—he said to find you no matter how long it took. And he wants you back home reports or no reports. He said that. Almost those exact words. But it took too long, Mr. Ross. For me—it took too long. And now that everything has—"

"Reports?"

"—changed—The Yoricks—"

"Yes—they've gone—Father Bede—"

"—their success—and everything—he didn't want a scandal—not now—he wants you safe at home—to take care of you—he thinks you're sick and—"

"The Yoricks—success? Did you say—success?" He could almost hear the last *jingle-jangle*, the last one when the little priest had gone away, the dance and bells and then a too-short rest against the tree. His back was sore as he shifted his weight on the bed. "Success?"

"—and I guess you are sick—I can see that now—you *are* really sick—and—and I'm—I'm—oh my God, Mr. Ross! Will you forgive me?"

"What?"

"For my joy at your trouble. Before I saw you were sick." Poddy had begun to wring his hands, the New-Poddy re-forming, fingers twisting palm to palm in his lap, his skin still flushed and twitching and with deeper swirls of red beneath the eyes. "I felt—I felt joy—His Eminence called me 'Son' and told me all about The Yoricks—and your assignment—the trouble you were in—he trusted me, Mr. Ross. Me. He hinted at a better job. But—but now? My God! I—forgive me—forgive me my joy." He whispered the words, a rasping rush of sound that seemed to leave in stages, jerking like his chest was being squeezed by giant hands. The New-Poddy had returned in force. "Will you forgive me?"

"Yes—I think so—sure." The first segment of WILD WILD WEST was finished, a panel there for just a second like the face of Artemis Gordon. And then a kind of Joke-Break seemed to flicker on, a close-up of a younger Yorick dancing on a box marked PRIDE, letters bold and black and other boxes side to side and out before, like stair-steps or like broken columns, POVERTY and DEATH there on their fronts, and also LONELINESS and WAR and GREED, PESTILENCE and GLUTTONY and SLOTH, and LUST along the very edge and then a sweep back left to right to take in ANGER and a few he couldn't see, the Yorick dancing in a ballroom glide and dip like Fred Astaire. Darby couldn't hear the words. "Yes—of course I forgive you." The New-Poddy seemed very grateful.

"Oh thank you—thank—"

"The Yoricks—what did you say about The Yoricks?" The dancer was gone, Artemis Gordon there instead inside some dungeon with his arms chained to the wall.

"Yes—their success—the performance for His Holiness in Baton Rouge—"

"Father Bede and the Pope?" Darby's head was fuzzing again, just a little bit, a feeling in behind his eyes like what had been there on the Square, with rough wood up against his back and clanging bells to block out all the rest. "He never told me about—"

"And the donation of the casino and—"

"Casino? Did you say, casino?"

"Yes—His Eminence calls it that—since it's in Las Vegas. But—it's not a real casino—it's mostly a big building— it was given to Father Bede during his tour—there's a kind of theatre there—a stage. It was even in the secular press. Every day for a week." He took a deep breath and let it out slowly. "The press calls it 'Solomon's Temple'—

I think that's right—everything has moved so fast—I think that's what they call it. No one knows just who it came from or—"

"Las Vegas?"

"Yes—a big building—a warehouse maybe—but new and in a good location. His Eminence was very upset—he said to find you and tell you everything has changed—to come home immediately. He's very angry, Mr. Ross—and tired—very tired. He's tried so hard and nothing seems to work. Even Bishop Pound has pulled out—the Joke Books? The Plagiarism? Father Bede apologized to him and gives him credit now for the jokes. So that's all over. And nothing else has surfaced—nothing but rumors—nothing we can use. But His Holiness is coming to San Cristobel—did you know that?"

"Yes."

"So there's still hope—isn't there still hope?" His hands had relaxed, fingers clasped and resting in his lap. "His Eminence can still stop it, don't you think? All he has to do is—is convince Pope Hilary of the danger—right? They're friends—old friends—and His Holiness will listen and stop the disrespect—the mockery—" He seemed to be near tears, the words the Cardinal's own but the voice not anything as strong as that, jerking again and pausing and his head now bowed and shaking in a rolling motion side to side. "He—he said to find you, Mr. Ross. And I did—at least I did that much—even though flying makes me sick—I did it—I came here and I found you—but—but too late—for me too late—it's all over for me—lost and gone—his trust—when he finds out—all gone—the better job—I—shouldn't have gotten drunk—but the place looked clean and everybody was friendly—and I was lonely—the black boy was my waiter–"

"Black boy?"

"My waiter–the black boy–the one who's diseased? He–he said his name was Sammy."

"Sammy?" Darby rubbed a hand over his face and finally got his head up high enough to ease the pressure on his neck. The room was getting darker, sunlight going and James West gliding down a slender wire above a courtyard full of sleeping soldiers. "This can't be real." He needed a drink.

"But it *is*–it's–"

"No! Not now. It's not real–and you're not really here at all. No." But the New-Poddy looked so sad, so frightened and alone, a parody of what had come to life at *Catholic Cross*, a something there that begged for close attention and a careful dance between its idled blades. THE WILD WILD WEST was over now and bells were ringing somewhere in the dimming light. A drink might help his legs to move.

"What–what can I do, Mr. Ross? What can–"

"Stop–stop. Get me that suitcase over there. The big one. See it? Get me that suitcase–bring it over here," he patted at the covers down below his aching head, "and then we'll see."

CHAPTER TWENTY THREE

The visit was nearly done. Pope Hilary sat up above the other Bishops, his chair a gilded one with armrests in the shape of lions' heads and legs like deer and a cushion in its seat that puffed out dust each time he moved. The meeting with the Southern Bishops had been a long and tiring one, the issues and the anger much the same as what had greeted him in all the other places he had been. He shifted in the chair, dust curling downward when he stopped, motes dancing in a shaft of light that came in through the ornate window back behind and up above him, up above the altar and a crucifix that when he first had seen it earlier that day had made him wonder what the artist had intended to portray. From a distance, the Jesus there looked like an exclamation point, the torso long and thin and feet encased in what up close had seemed to be some kind of amber ball, the dotted hands on arms too slight to matter and the wounds in feet and side a color nearly the same as orange juice.

The place was filled with light, with windows everywhere and massive fixtures in the ceiling holding light-bulbs enough he guessed to make the night as bright as day. But the sessions he had sat through had brought in a darkness from the outside much too deep it seemed for windows or for light-bulbs to turn away. The present speaker, Bishop Andreas Krull of Bayou Grand, was in his second hour and showed little sign of flagging, voice as booming now as when he started and his gestures growing ever more pronounced the longer he endured. The issue here was to be the ordination–of women mostly and of married men and women both. But yesterday the flow of words had shifted, changing slightly with each speaker, one and then another turning to the very source, the Godhead and His Nature, His Human Nature, rising up in robes and miters in a challenge to a Father, Son, and Holy Ghost that sought a kind of savage levelling, androphagous in its method and androgyny its final end. Bishop Krull was close to jumping now beside the lectern, robes flapping and zuchetta slipping and his bald head glistening in the light, arms and hands in constant motion, slapping at the air and falling briefly down to rise again and punch this time with fists that seemed to move like pistons in amongst an almost crash of shouts and deep applause.

And God is Mother to us, Our Mother in the Timeless, in the co-eternal and co-equal union with the Father-Self, a Both-And there that makes us what we are, that creates us male and female in that selfsame Image, both together with the Spirit open freely as a channel holding Love!

And the applause intensified the jumps and more words come and more dust puffs out into the thick and mote-filled shafts of light.

Pope Hilary gripped the lions' heads and finally found where Pietro Riga sat, two empty spaces on either side, the chair too small to hold his bulk. He seemed in pain, his hands pushed deep within his robes as if to hold his chest in place. The trip has lasted far too long, Pope Hilary thought, too many voices and too little time between them, too much the clash of weapons and too little time to pray. And Pietro had received the sharpest blows, had stood and taken to himself the sharpened points that seemed to fall like thickened rain out on a land unlike the one they both had left so many years ago. Pietro smiled and nodded, hands come free of his robes and tensed upon the silver cross that Pope Hilary had given him, its outsized chain wrapped like a tattered glove about his fingers.

Bishop Krull was jumping harder now, a heavy sound of slippered feet that blended with the clank of metal from his own long chain and cross, a slap and clang out in a shaft of dirty light, a memory there as sudden as the cheering and applause, the little priest, Pietro's Bede and Brothers with him dancing in a joy as pure as what had once been there in moments when the call of God first came. The little Priest had danced and sang, the jokes he told the same ones left behind in Illinois, in rectories and banquet halls and in the homes of sheep now surely dead. Pietro had relaxed, his fingers smoothing down the chain and pressing at the cross. The little Priest had jingled as he danced, his cap in jingling rhythm like a belt of sleighbells bouncing on a running horse. There was one last place to go, a careful progress through the bursting parishes of Florida, and then a rest with Cardinal Spitzmulcher, old friend and at the other pole from Krull, far distant from that thudding clank, the sound he made a chopping one, yet pushing like the other ever inward to the places where Pietro's little Priest would dance.

CHAPTER TWENTY FOUR

The Journal-Log had gotten very fat. The Father-Doctor had been very pleased with all the paper. Very pleased indeed. He had even smiled and shut his note-pad without writing down a single word. Just yesterday. In the air-conditioned private office.

"Your progress has been remarkable, Mr. Ross. Excellent reports from everyone."

"Thank you, Doctor."

"No harmful side-effects from the medication. No sleep disorder. Appetite good. Coherence and motor skills returning nicely. Everything in order."

"Thank you, Father."

"Just call me, Chuck."

"Yes—of course—Chuck."

"And your journal-therapy?"

"I keep it with me, Chuck. Just in case."

"Just in case?"

"I need it. If I need to write. In case I get another idea. You know. Something that needs to be written down."

"I see. Well it certainly *looks* healthy."

"Pardon me, Chuck?"

"The journal—it looks full."

"Oh yes. Yes. I try to feed it every day."

"Ah—a joke. Was that a joke?"

"When can I leave here, Chuck?"

"In time, Mr. Ross. Very soon I'd say—judging by all these glowing reports. And my own observation. Very soon."

"I need to go home, Chuck. My family–"

"Yes. Yes I appreciate that."

"And my job–"

"No need to worry there. Your medical leave is good for another six months. Or even more. His Eminence has been most generous. Most generous indeed."

But Chuck had not read the fat journal, not a single word in all the weeks of talking. He had only watched it grow and touched it with his fingertips and smiled. He had not read anything beyond perhaps the title–MY JOURNAL–or the credits–BY DARBY ROSS, Senior Editor, CATHOLIC CROSS–so all the poems were virgins still and every stolen thought and borrowed phrase and fear were safe and snug inside the plastic cover and the pages crisp and sturdy when he turned them one by one. Chuck had shaken his hand and led him outside to the long long hallway and the helping hands of Mario D'Angelis, his own and personal steward, guard and gossip.

"Mario will see you back to your room, Mr. Ross."

"Yes. Thank you, Chuck. Thank you, Mario."

"We'll talk again on Friday."

"Yes. That's the day after tomorrow isn't it, Chuck?"

"It is indeed. That's very good, Mr. Ross."

"Thank you, Chuck."

And Mario had left him (with an hour yet to go) to wash his hands and get to supper at the Special Cases Table near the statue of Our Lady of the Cookstoves, five tall chairs and plates, fat cups and silverware that bent like rubber if you pressed too hard, and Darby's place between the Purple Pig's own Principal Thaddeus Stevens and a former monk who thought that he could fly. But the food was better than the jailers in Jacksonville had served to all his cursing, sweaty new-found friends at Table 16-A. And the Cardinal never came there.

But all that was yesterday, today all done and gone now for at least an hour, nighttime everywhere but where the light made one large circle on his bed, supper over and the prayers, the movie done and Doris Day still chaste in body and in dialogue, the Journal in his lap and plans to get away to Vegas crisp and sturdy in his mind just like the pages that he touched and read and tore in pieces small enough to stuff down in the hole, the narrow slit above the mattress handles near his thigh. Mario's had been the last voice he had heard, but past the daily summaries (of weather, food and dinner-talk), and past the poetry (some his, some half-remembered bits of textbook pieces—*The World was all before them, where to choose/ this place of rest, and Providence their guide/they hand and hand with wandering steps and slow,/Through Eden took their solitary way*), past questions (fewer than the entries he had written with The Yoricks in their Laughing Place) and past the lists of drinks that he would like to try, and many many other things that he had written in a fruitless hoping for a healing good enough to move the fingers that would sign him past the gate and back among the others of his kind—past all of that the Journal's heart at last lay open to the light, the fat all trimmed away and mixed in with the mattress stuffing (white and yellow clumps of rubber-puff)—the heart come folding out, a hidden packet (newly written) thick and plump and Mario the first thing there, the gossip like the veins, an unclogged channel filled with blood enough and air to keep the rest alive.

Darby smiled. He would keep the packet with him when he ran away. He would keep it with him in his shorts. Somewhere. Until he found a better hiding place.

Las Vegas maybe or the desert out around. He would keep it with him safe and snug until the echoes of the jingling stopped, until he heard himself the rustling sound of Shepherd's robes and thumping of his staff.

He read:

My Own Good Gossip's Good Good Facts To Know:

(1). I arrived here in early August–the date most probably the sixth (a Saturday–Mario is guessing about this of course because he was off-duty that particular weekend–which means the actual arrival might have oc- curred on the seventh or after five o'clock on the after- noon/evening of the fifth).

(2). I was mostly unconscious when I arrived and was admitted to the clinic by the Cardinal's secretary. (I obviously have no memory of any of this beyond a vague image of an angel with a sword–the statue is presently near the nurses' station–and a few pieces of discon- nected dialogue: *stench–needs a thorough washing–Boston 6/Atlanta 3*).

(3). <u>Poddy O'Malley</u>: More later, less now. But–here is one pretty big less-now fact: He apparently drove me from New Orleans to San Cristobel and then arranged for my transportation here to St. Gadarene's (ca. 50 miles or so). Although Mario overheard this much while polishing doorknobs in the administration building on the Monday morning following my admission, he under- standably is lacking in further information. More later.

(4). <u>The Poor Yoricks</u>: And it is here that Mario has been the most help–the television and newspapers, magazines and radio in the staff cottages are uncen- sored and Mario is off-duty every other weekend–all of which gives him ample opportunity to 'hear things' and 'see things' which the patients are kept from hearing or seeing for their own good. He has confirmed that: (a).

Most of the Georgia Yoricks are on a national tour. (b). Fr. Bede himself has been featured on the following television shows: TODAY, TONIGHT, 60 MINUTES, B.D. LAROUX'S NEW-COUNTRY PROFILES, the OLD-TIME CATHOLIC HOUR, and something called CIRCUS ROMANA on PBS. (c). The national tour will end at the 'Temple' in Las Vegas on Labor Day (my goal) with a Benefit for Hospice Workers. (d). The jokes are getting older and worse–<u>Sample</u>: "One night a circus clown was searching for his rubber nose in the cook tent. 'Are you sure you lost it in here?' one of the cooks asked. 'No,' he replied, 'I think I lost it back in the last town, but now I'm hungry."

(5). Sonny-Boy Morninglove is dead. Mario brought the news and stayed awhile to talk–"the Meester a-Love he is a gone–you twin a brother die lasta night. Man-o-man you look just th'same like heem. Just-a the same. But a course you ain't a-dead like heem. What *is* this pelly-gra thing, Meester Rossi?" he asked fussing with the bed cover and smoothing down the pillow. "That's a-what the story say–pelly-gra. Pelly-gra, pelly-gra–to me it sound-a like a bird." He frowned and seemed about to cry. "He gone a-now to be weeth the keeng–up a there," he pointed toward the ceiling, "up-a-stairs, y'know?" And he put a brown brown hand on my shoulder. "You think a bird done it? Whew boy-a-howdy— whoa buddies—some new t'ing alla time, y'know? Like a keeler flamingos an' all a them bees from South A-merica. Yes? What a-you t'ink them pelly-gras look like, Meester Rossi?"

(6). Pope Hilary is in Florida, down South and moving slower than expected town to town.

(7). The Little Okra River is free of hyacinths. Mario never misses a t'ing: "I t'ink a-you come from there, yes? I'member some-a-t'ing 'bout that place," he said right after lunch one day the second week—"I hear the doc-tore say it—Leetle a Okera—Meester a Rossi live a-there he say. Yes?" And I said "Yes" and he said "On a th'news a-show—the Leetle a Okera she's all clean." And then he said: "She dirty back a-before?" And I said, "No."

Darby carefully placed the Mario page face down-ward on the bed and patted at its crease. The rest would follow soon—visitors and one co-patient (Thad Stevens with his cheek scar and his story and his black black skin)—the other names gone funny sounding as he whis-pered each one quickly, over and over again—Poddy Kathleen (Cindy too) the Cardinal's secretary and Brother Mordecai the last—Poddy–Kathleen/Cindy–the Cardinal's secretary (Eugene is his name)—and Brother Mordecai—like destinations called out in a terminal—like all the towns and cities he had traveled through in nearly never finding Fr. Bede—from Charlotte on to Winston-Salem on to Asheville, Knoxville (Oak Ridge by the way) and Nashville, Memphis, Little Rock—then El Dorado, Shreveport, Baton Rouge, a jump back east to catch the jingling and to hold it long enough to turn and re-turn to the Square again and lose it all there one more time, the jingling only echoes really after that, brief sounds that sometimes now seem much too far away to hear. But each place with an image of its own, a flash of scenery or perhaps a face, each one a kind of moving Prelude to the People-Notes and then tomorrow to the jagged hole that he would widen and slip through, among the bushes and the trees a portion of the western wall whose stones had cracked and fallen, a door not locked at night and only maybe twenty yards back from the road. He had hoarded the money his wife had brought. Crisp new bills all safe inside an old tobacco tin someone had dropped along the jogging trail. Father-Doctor-

Chuck had given back his clothes. Money and clothes. There was more than enough of both. And he would leave before breakfast, when Mario let him out for Mass. He smiled and shut his eyes and let the Prelude skip and jump along–himself–whoever that might finally be–down in it strong.

In Charlotte: Not quite in Charlotte–south–near darkness and the startling lights of PTL–a Pentecostal Avignon against the sun-streaked sky–the moths grown thick upon the windshield–soft wings flattening there until they pass like rolling balls of dust into the nighttime further on–

Winston-Salem: An old man on the shoulder of the road, a burlap bag beside him in the grass bulged full of cans, his hand reached out to find one more, near crushed but glinting in the sunlight down below a Baptist billboard, open Bible, dove and Jesus-face and toll-free number for a prayer–

And Asheville just at dawn: A misting rain to soak the trees and slick the buckshot-pitted signs that point the way to some long-ended tent revival and an all-night Gospel Sing–

A blur of mountains, Knoxville and then Oak Ridge gone and nothing else no matter what he tried, shimmered roads and traffic, Sonny-Boy there more and more in people's eyes, in faces full of awe or pity, hands of every color reaching out to touch him and to take away whatever thing they could, the Yorick-jingling always just ahead but never close enough to hold, and bright lights finally and more scotch than he could ever hope to drink:

Nashville: Just one place among the many, one sad bar where no one seemed to notice who was there, the jingling strongest in among the stories of defeat and songs that had a touch of rawness in the way the fiddle squealed and skirled, and voices too as rough as what the faces of the men let show, failed crops and hard times on the factory line, but delicate defiance all the same, defiance there a rare fine thing and savored, brittle like the fragments of a dream pushed out to catch reflected light–

<u>And Memphis</u>: A pilgrim-face, a child, eyes wide and staring at a Cadillac that Elvis owned. And one motel.

And on and on–to Little Rock (the steps of Central High) and El Dorado (two straw-hatted black boys and a dog), to Shreveport (nothing but a blinking cross and well-lit fishbait sign), to Baton Rouge and Huey's tomb at sunrise and a jingling sound come in so strong it led him almost blind to Fr. Bede. Darby opened his eyes, the Prelude gone and People now there one by one down on the crisp and sturdy page–first-person also there to move it all along:

<u>PODDY O'MALLEY</u>: Although he visits me in dreams and often in brief memory-flashes, the man himself has only come three times in flesh-and-blood–the first time after I had realized just where I was (St. Gadarene's Retreat Center, Inc. Welaka, Florida 32601); the second (brief and pain-filled) just before I found the jogging trail and stone-wall opening to the road; the third time is more recent, in the morning, while I was admiring the stubbornness of an ant struggling with a candy wrapper (half a wrapper actually)–bits of melted chocolate on it, once a ZERO bar I think–one ant, one half a candy wrapper, in the taller grass beside the only park bench near the sink-hole pond. The visits have helped enlighten several stretches that before were blank or like a kind of murky stew, with bits and pieces, chunks and slices, scenes and sequences that wouldn't fit together in the

bowl. I wrote them down in my Journal—strong sentences and carefully constructed paragraphs—abundant detail and transitions running smoothly, like a story slowly building to the only ending it could find. I'll make a list to see how much I still remember. Then bring in Poddy proper for the rest.

<u>Papa Linda's/The Judging</u> (Sonny-Boy much older than I thought he'd be)

<u>The Mermaid Tavern</u> (I remember where my room is by the time I drank my second scotch)

<u>The Malibu Porpoise</u> (My room is on the second floor):

--scotch

--Poddy's secret

--Poddy and the razor blade

--scotch

--much sleep

--Poddy's pacing

--the Pope on television and THE WILD WILD WEST as well

--Poddy-talk

--much scotch

<u>And then</u>—and then the bits and pieces rise up like the things I saw out on the road at night—

<u>A passenger in the Cardinal's second-best car</u> (at dusk, at dawn, in full sunlight)

--through Mississippi

--through Alabama

--In Florida forever all the way to Big Red's private home—

Bits and pieces, little things like strange bugs on the wing that flap and curve into the headlights: A Pizza Den and Parlor Pizza Kitchen Pizza-Pizza Pizza-Italiano Inn Best Pizza #2 Fast Eddie's Pizza Pizza Paradiso JEB Stuart

Pizza and the Tico Taco Chili Pot the Taco Tavern and one lonely EATS and Food-A-Rama and more pizza and Burger Barns and golden arches by the dozens burgers crowned and lassoed some with smiling faces hot dogs too and somewhere east of Pensacola my most favorite thing of all: LO'S CHITTLINS all alone and slowly blinking at the rising sun.

Bits and pieces after that more fuzzed than brightly lit with strong arms lifting and the others come to wrap me up and drive and drive to here, to Father-Doctor-Chuck and Mario and jogging trail and broken wall and pizza in the dining hall the first night I could get there on my own. And Poddy come to see me right away. That much and things that happen after that are clear. He came wearing slacks and flowered shirt (his one day off a week), not chunking much at all, not looking like himself but still he came and walked a little way inside the Grotto of Perpetual Hope, beside me sometimes or in front, his face like what had been there back when Sonny-Boy was still alive. I've drawn the setting full of detail in my Journal. My version of the words fits better here:

"He's—he's very upset, Mr. Ross."

"Call me Darby—has anyone found my wallet?"

"He said to see if you needed anything—I—I haven't told him about—about you-know."

"You-know?"

"My—my mistake—you-know."

"The Sammy-sin?"

"My God, Mr. Ross—don't talk so loud—he—he just thinks I'm tired. After the trip—the long time finding you.

And the drive home. He doesn't know."

"But you said he laughed."

"Laughed?"

"Yes—he—I think you said—he showed you some-thing—that part still won't come clear—he showed you something and he laughed."

"No—my God keep your voice down—no—not His Eminence! That was the *boy* who laughed."

"Sammy is in San Cristobel then? Still laughing?"

"No my God no, Mr. Ross—he's—"

"Darby—just call me Darby. Or Meester Rossi. Mario calls me that. Have you met Mario?"

"Please don't shout—I—I can't tell him—not yet. Can you understand?"

"Not telling?"

"Yes."

"Of course I understand. I understand perfectly. I don't tell everything I know either. Nobody does. It would be terrible if everyone told *every*thing they know. That would be terrible. And noisy. Don't do that *here*. You're not planning to do that *here* are you?"

"No—for Godssake Mr. Ross you're shouting again—please—"

"Don't ever do that, Mr. O'Malley—you'll never get ahead doing that kind of thing. You'll never make a rise. You'll never prosper. And you'll frighten people."

"I'm replacing you at *Catholic Cross*."

"What? What did you say?"

"I'm Senior Editor now. Two days ago. His Emi-nence—"

"*You*? *You* are Senior Editor?"

"Please, Mr. Ross—don't shout—those people over there can hear us—they—"

"Where? *Those* people? *Those* people think they're

the Marx Brothers and that fat one—the one dressed up like Harpo—doubles as a horse when they need one. What do you mean *you're* Senior Editor?"

"Please, Mr. Ross—I'm sure it's only temporary—until you're well again—His Eminence said you'd understand. He said exactly that—'Ross will understand.' It's temporary I'm sure. Just until you come back. You're on a leave of absence. Full pay. Benefits. He—His Eminence said to tell you that your wife would visit soon. And your daughter—you can see why I couldn't tell him—this is my chance, Mr. Ross—he gave me his blessing and—"

"Full pay, you say?"

"Yes—yes and benefits. I'll be filling in most likely just until you return. Everybody thinks so. Temporary. Until His Eminence feels you're strong enough to—"

"That's good about the full pay. And the benefits. That's good."

"So you can see why I couldn't tell him—not now—but I'm watching it closely, Mr. Ross. For signs. And—and I *will* tell him. Later. When we publish a few more issues—we've already increased circulation—I'll tell him—I will."

"It's in your bloodstream then? Circulatory? Whatever *it* is—it's gotten worse? The Sammy-sin?"

"No—*Catholic Cross*, Mr. Ross—circulation is up."

"And Sammy? What about Sammy?"

"Sammy?"

"Yes. What will become of him?"

"I don't know, Mr. Ross."

"Poor Sammy—he was a waiter. Right? You said he was a waiter."

"Yes. A waiter."

"Poor Sammy. Alone in New Orleans. Waiting there.

Was he fat?"

"Fat?"

"Yes. You said he laughed. You said that, didn't you?"

"Yes–he–he laughed. Look, Mr. Ross, I–"

"Darby. I'm Darby. Fat people are jolly–he must be fat."

"No–no he was slender–very slender, Mr. Ross."

"Like Harpo over there–he laughs. He's fat and he laughs. You can't hear it of course but he laughs. When he's a horse you can hear it. Sometimes it wakes me up. The laughing."

"I need to go, Mr. Ross. I only wanted to see if you needed anything. And to tell you His Eminence cares about you. He really does. He cares about us all. Like a family."

"Yes."

"And–and to make sure you haven't told anyone about–about you-know–"

"The Sammy-sin?"

"Yes. You haven't–haven't told–"

"No. No I won't tell."

"Good–very good–thank you, Mr. Ross–it'll be our secret."

"And Sammy's."

"Yes–well–yes but he's not here. And doesn't know my name–and–and your job is safe–there'll be a job for you when you return, Mr. Ross. Everybody knows that. But–but this is my chance–I just know it is–and–I–"

"Yes yes I understand. Yes. But of course you'll need to see a doctor. That's obvious enough, isn't it? And a Priest. You'll need to tell a Priest. Perhaps you can find a Doctor-Priest. Like Chuck. Have you met Chuck? He's both in one. A doctor. A Priest. But if you have to choose–go find a Priest. You need to do that. For the good of your immortal soul. You know the reasons. To be absolved. Made pure again. Yes. Some things you need to tell. Go find a Priest."

I'm not sure where he went but when he came the second time, his legs were bowed and body slightly angled to one side and he had nearly waddled out to find me at the Chapel of the Pines. I was sitting in the grass. His face was twitching and his eyes seemed glazed.

"My God, Mr. Ross–there's–there's a rash!"

"A rash, you say?"

"Yes. A bad one. Just like–like the one that you-know–that–"

"Sammy?"

"Yes–and it's–it's getting worse–and I'm in pain, Mr. Ross. All the time. And my wife–"

"She has a rash too? Your wife?"

"No! Oh my God no–no, she dosen't know anything about it. I haven't told her–"

"About Sammy?"

"Yes–no no I haven't told her! My God–how can I tell her about something like *that*?"

"Yes. Yes I certainly see your problem. Yes. I certainly do. It's like Sammy's, you say? The rash?"

"The same–like–the same thing he showed me–"

"When he laughed?"

"Yes–my God, Mr. Ross–I've got to do something–but–but what can I do?"

I'm not sure what it was he did, but he was gone for what seemed like years until a morning just a little while ago–a week or so ago. The ant had made it nearly to a patch of dirt beyond the tallest grass, a brown-stained ZERO clearly visible, a jagged cape that bounced and floated out behind. The face this time, Poddy's face, was calm, an older version of the one that I first saw long months ago when it was newly hired, but this time with a touch of coldness in the eyes and teeth much larger-seeming than before. And chunk-and-spray there too, the Cardinal close at hand behind the words.

"Mr. Ross–they said I might find you down here. It's lovely. A lovely view."

"They?"

"It's a lovely place. And you look *much* improved."

"Who exactly told you I was 'down here'?"

"His Eminence sends his best. And his special hope that your recovery is total. And permanent. He also sends his congratulations on your new position."

"What?"

I remember now most clearly how the eyes had seemed, young Poddy's eyes all bright and deep deep blue but with the coldness in them growing deeper also with each word he spoke.

"The at-large slot. Senior Editor."

"Senior Editor-at-large?"

"Yes. And I want you to know I pushed hard to get you that particular slot. Your old salary plus ten-percent. A bonus. Light duties. Or no duties at all. A fabulous place to be. And you've earned it, Darby. Every last bit of it."

"And you?"

"Oh now–no need to dwell on *that*. This view is stunning. I like it very much."

"Well I don't. I don't like the view at all. In fact–this place stinks, O'Malley. And what about you? *Your* job?"

"Oh–Senior Editor. Your old stand. Basically that."

"I see."

"Yes. His Eminence and I thought that would be best for everyone. Did you know His Holiness is in south

Florida?"

"My job. You took *my* job?"

"And he'll be in San Cristobel in a few weeks. The Retreat is all prepared. It's best this way. His Eminence thinks the chances for further upset will be lessened by this arrangement. I'll serve as Diocesan Press Liaison. For the duration of the visit."

"And what about *me*?"

"Beg pardon?"

"*Me* O'Malley–*me*! What am *I* supposed to do?"

"Recover. Get well. You'll still have your column. We can't feature it as often as we have, of course. The *Cross* is changing. You'll find things much changed in fact. When you get well. I need to go. I envy you this view. Do you come here often?"

"What about Sammy, O'Malley? Remember Sammy? What about the rash and–"

"Oh. Yes. But I thought I told you. No? It's gone."

"Gone? What do you mean it's–"

"I went to a doctor. Finally. Took your advice. The rash was a severe case of *tinea cruris*. Can you beat that? Jock-itch. Yes. Really. Jock itch! It's gone now. All gone."

"Gone?"

"Yes. Just look at that sparkle on the water out there. Are those ducks I see?"

"Sammy had jock-itch?"

"Yes. And he knew it all along, I suspect. A joke. It was all a joke. Nasty and mean. But it's over now. Over and done. Would you like me to walk you back to the Center?"

"No. I'll sit here awhile."

"Of course. I don't blame you. This looks like a good

place to sit and think."

"Yes."

"You get well, Darby. We all miss you back at the *Cross*."

"Yes."

I remember him turning to walk away, his last words staying with me as he faced the grassy hill and path that curled in through the pine trees toward the office and the gate.

"His Eminence will find a way to stop The Yoricks. He said to tell you that. Nothing has been in vain. And you have his full support in getting well. His full support."

And then he left, long strides and swinging arms, up and up the grassy hill until the pines and shadows were the only things I saw. But the ant was still there, wrapper bumping on the dirt and friends come out to help.

The other People now were free to come, their names in bold print and the rest a sometimes hurried script that looked too small to be his own. KATHLEEN/CINDY there together on the page—the date now unremembered but indoors this time, with chairs and tables in the room, in Father-Doctor Chuck's own study with a ticking clock against the wall and shelves of books and dirty windowpanes that let in very little light. The words were bold and black down on the page:

KATHLEEN/CINDY: I talked with Kathleen and Cindy for exactly twenty minutes early this afternoon. Kathleen kissed me on the cheek and Cindy touched my hand. We talked about how clean the Little Okra River had become and Cindy's parties by the pool and how much better off we seemed to be and all the help His Eminence had given. I'm getting very good at remembering dialogue:

"We'd have come sooner but he thought it best to

wait. He's called nearly every other day, Darby. With reports on your progress and news and–"

"Reports?"

"–offers of help. Sometimes it's just his secretary
doing the actual talking–but it's at His Eminence's request. And–oh yes, they deliver your check to the house.
Special–"

"Did you say, reports?"

"–delivery. The raise and bonus came at a good
time. Everything is in order at home. We're free of debt.
Have they given you the money I sent?"

"Yes."

"It's all so wonderful, Darby. Everything is in good
shape. Waiting for you. And everyone has been so nice.
Even Poddy O'Malley has called to–"

"Poddy? He called *you*?"

"Yes. With an offer of help. I didn't accept of course.
It wouldn't have looked right to accept Poddy's help."

"No–that's so. No."

"He sent me a bicycle, Daddy."

"Who? Poddy?"

"No no, Darby. His Eminence. Special delivery with a
big red bow on the handlebars."

"How old does he think I am anyway, Daddy?"

"I don't know."

"*Nobody* rides bicycles, Daddy. *Nobody*."

"I see."

"He meant well, dear. Didn't he, Darby? Isn't that
so?"

"Yes. I'm sure he–"

"But Daddy–what do I *do* with it? It's ugly!"

"No it's not, dear. Tell her it isn't ugly, Darby."

"But it may *be* ugly–I haven't seen–"

"And anyway it's the thought that counts–isn't that

so, Darby?"

"What?"

"The thought."

"Thought?"

"I know–you can give it to a poor child at Christmas. That's just the thing to do."

"But I don't *know* any poor children, Mommy! All my friends live in Apollo Bluffs. Why don't *we* live in Apollo Bluffs, Daddy?"

"Apollo Bluffs?"

"Oh–that reminds me. We *did* receive an invitation to join the country club, Darby. It came yesterday. We'd be the second Catholic family. We have until Thanksgiving to decide."

"Can we, Daddy? Oh can we can we? All my best friends–"

"Don't bother your father with all that now, Cindy. He looks tired. You look tired, Darby. Aren't you resting well?"

There was more (and what I *have* might not be certain but it seems so in my mind–it seems so now)–but listening did not help me hear whatever Fr. Bede had wanted me to hear. They (Kathleen and Cindy) might have come to see me many times but what I have put down can give back what it all was like. Chunk-chunk.

He paused to rest his eyes and listen to what sounded like a howl, a long and undulating wail come in all muffled through the air-conditioner hum and thick locked door and windows double-paned and made of something near impossible to scratch. The howl was like a dog's but somehow different too, a wobbling of the note too shallow toward the end and swooping down to rise again with sounds like cries of 'help' and 'no no no' there as it came to a momentary pause. Someone had woke up too soon. Darby opened his eyes and read. The words put down two days ago:

<u>SECRETARY EUGENE—FAITHFUL EU-GENE WITH THE PAPERS IN HIS HAND</u>: I signed each page that Big Eugene—broad-shouldered, trim-waisted, white-toothed, smiling Eugene put down on the table near my resting hands, my fingers spread until they took the pen and signed each page beside the bold black X that someone had made sure I'd see with very little effort. No matter what they were. No matter just so long as they were signed in Eu-gene's presence (Notary Public Eugene with an official Seal snug down in its little bag)—and once I did it I would have a friend no matter what no matter what else happened and no matter what I failed to do no matter what had happened up to now, the signing of my name, the Cardinal wanted only that and never mind the rest. And chunk-and-spray had come along in force, much louder and much wetter than what Poddy had brought in.

"I'm sorry there are so many of them, Mr. Ross."

"That's quite all right, Eugene. I don't mind. Why is this one purple?"

"Diocesan Requisition. It's new. Something to do with office supplies, I think."

"And this Kelly green one here?"

"The new insurance forms. So your total coverage will continue."

"I see. And the white ones?'

"Ah yes—Liability Wavers A, B, and C. For the damage done to diocesan property and so forth."

"The car?"

"Yes. And the credit cards. The quarters. As I understand it, they'll deduct a straight ten-percent from your new salary which is—"

"The pink one?"

"Yes—you'll notice that you've received another ten-percent raise to cover the waivers. Now then—oh yes—here—the red one."

"The Cardinal's own?"

"Yes. The General Form. No title yet but welcome, Mr. Ross."

"Welcome?"

"To the diocesan staff. His Eminence said to tell you that. Welcome."

"But—but what about the *Cross*? My column. O'Malley said I'd—"

"All in good time, Mr. Ross. As I understand it, you'll be on loan there now and then. But His Eminence said not to dwell on the details. He'll fill you in at the proper time. When you're well again. Sign here. At the X."

And I signed. Without reading what my job would be. Without a whimper or a bang but with a scratching, creaking sound instead, a sound of heavy pen on rich thick paper and a pat pat pat of Eugene's hand upon my shoulder and his voice turned soothing and come down so low the chunk-chunk-chunk had almost carried it away.

The howling was gone, no noises now but Darby's breathing, in and out and with a little wheeze and whistle as he smoothed the next page into place—Thad Stevens and then Brother Mordecai, a Yorick-incognito come to see them both, just yesterday, the writing here the newest part of all. He read:

I never saw a purple pig–
I never hope to see one–
But sure as bald men need a wig,
I'd rather see than be one.

And that was the verse Thad Stevens said had finally set him free. Although we have talked quite a few times since my arrival here (*he* was already in place by a good three weeks or more) and have eaten nearly every meal together, this verse keeps coming back and coming back until it seems in memory all there was to each and every time we met. Yesterday was no exception. And is a typical meeting because of that. And since it also is the last one we will have, I put it here as sum of all the rest. Even the fact that Brother Mordecai appears toward the end (disguised as a pharmaceutical salesman) does nothing to detract from its typicality. For me, however–for me personally, his arrival means much more. I know that this is also true for Thaddeus. But the point here is that it (the sudden appearance) does not really add or take away a single thing from what had gone before. And I come in to help, to prod and question, like the other times a voice to play against and use, an auditor to note the facts and point to new things struggling into view.

I never saw a purple pig–
I never hope to see one–
But sure as bald men need a wig,
I'd rather see than be one.

He, Thaddeus, usually says the verse twice, recites it with clenched teeth and with a force near anger, almost biting off each word and bending forward to rest his head in his hands at the very end. Then he slowly straightens up, smiles, and begins to talk pleasantly enough but with an undertone of anger there that never seems quite gone away and done.

"And I heard it every day for two months, Mr. Ross. Every day."

"The poem?"

"Every day. Even on weekends. Radio. Television. Shopping. Once I even heard it at Mass—afterwards. In the parking lot. A quartet was singing it. Four old men in striped shirts and straw hats."

"Straw hats, you say?"

"It was everywhere I went. Summer school was a nightmare. Sixty-five students. Our worst. And they all sang it differently. Each one managed to make it sound different. And then I found myself singing it."

"*You*?"

"Yes. In my car. I was getting ready to park it in my reserved space. It was a Friday. I remember distinctly. A hot Friday. No clouds. Muggy and hot. I suddenly heard singing. And it was me."

"What did you do?"

"I left. The last thing I saw was dancing. On the sidewalk. In the grass. At *my* school. Dancing."

"Dancing?"

"Yes. Students. Around the pig."

"Around the statue? You mean around the statue, don't you?"

"Yes. And I never went back."

"But how did you get here? Why *here*?"

"I told you I was Catholic?"

"Yes."

"I subscribe to *Vocation Digest*."

"And you read about *this* place *there*?"

"Yes. Last year."

"So you left your home and came here? You checked

yourself in?"

"No. Not right away. Not the first thing."

"Yes?"

"I drove around. First I drove. For hours. With the windows open and the radio on. I drove for hours. Mostly around the new lake. Lake Scattergood. And then I stopped. And you know where I was?"

"No."

"A cemetery. A big, modern cemetery."

"Modern?"

"No gravestones. No crypts. Only fields of bronze pots with plastic flowers in them. And I walked. I–I got out of my car and walked. For hours. Mount Gerezim. That was the name of the place. Mount Gerezim. I walked for hours in Mount Gerezim. And I heard it even there."

"The song–the poem?"

"Yes. Gravediggers. Singing it and laughing. Near a statue of praying hands. Giant praying hands."

"The purple pig."

"Yes. Singing it even there. And I prayed."

"In the cemetery?"

"Yes. And I left."

"In your car?"

"Yes. And you know who was on the radio?"

"The Purple Pig?"

"No. Bede. The Yorick. The cult leader himself."

"He was singing then?"

"No. He told a joke. An old, tired joke. He didn't sing."

"Do you remember the joke?"

"Yes. Yes I do. And that's the funny part."

"The joke?"

"No–that I remember it. Until then–until that

minute really, I had never been able to remember jokes. Or stories. But that's no longer true."

"You can remember them now?"

"Yes. That particular joke was brief—a short joke--A teacher asked the class: 'In which of his battles was King Gustavus Adolphus slain?' And a student on the front row answered: 'I'm pretty sure it was the last one.'"

"That's it?"

"Yes. Old and tired, I'm sure."

"So you came here?"

"Yes. I'm not married, you know. No family really. And I felt something—"

"At the cemetery?"

"Yes. Bede's father is there. And his mother. At Mt. Gerezim. I saw the graves."

"I knew that. No really. I saw the other place. When they were moving the graves. Conroy Tucker was in charge. I remember that—"

"It was peaceful there. And I very much wanted peace. For a long time now. Ever since Times Square."

"Times Square?"

"Kennedy. The assassination. Remember? I was eating a hotdog. At Nathan's. It had mustard on it. And pickle-relish. And then I became a Catholic. And Vatican II came. And the South caught fire. And the job at the Purple Pig came. And I came to hate it."

"The job you mean?"

"The pig. I hated the pig. And everyone in Caladega County. In Ailey. And in Slackbridge. Bede the most. I hated him the most of all."

"But why? How could you *hate* him? Father Bede? I mean—I know how he is—how he can be—he's angered *me,* but *hate* is so–"

"No. His father."

"His father? Marcus? You hated Marcus. But he died a long time ago."

"And his mother. I hated her too."

"Marcus's wife? But why?"

"I know things now, Mr. Ross. I finally listened. To the stories. I researched records. The ones that were left. But I mostly listened. Stories. Long or short. And everybody back there has one. Believe me. Everybody. I listened to them all. And I discovered things."

"Things?"

"I've suffered, Mr. Ross. For a long, long time. You must have noticed that much. When we first met."

"Yes. I think so. But you said, 'things'–what things?"

"Facts. The truth. From the stories and the records. I researched it all. The Purple Pig was her idea."

"That song? The poem?"

"No–the song and the poem were originally about a cow, I think. A purple cow. Way back in the Nineteenth Century. Way back. No. I'm talking about *the* Purple Pig. The statue. She gave the land."

"For the high school?"

"Yes. And that was when it started. It began there. They couldn't keep it to themselves after that. That pig changed Ailey. I know it. And so do they. Everybody knows it. They lost the county seat. The dam project money. The new lake. The new highway. They lost it all. And got back jokes. The Purple Pigs. That's what they're called. The people. Purple Pigs. I heard about them in Atlanta. But I thought I was different. I thought I could beat it. I thought I could win. For years I thought that. But it was probably already too late. And then Bede came back home."

"Father Bede?"

"Yes. But not to Ailey. Even him. He went to Slack-bridge. That land and house and all? She gave him that."

"His mother? Father Bede's mother? But she's dead too."

"Before that. It's in the county records. You have to dig to find it. But it's there. And now he's taking it to the world."

"It?"

"She knew he would. Hattie Peese thinks she was a witch. Hattie has many stories. More than anybody else. She claims Bede's father walks the land. She says she even talked to him once."

"She did? To Marcus Bede—the ghost of Marcus Bede?'

"Yes. Years ago. In the wintertime. When Solomon Bede was gone. He asked her how to get to Philadel-phia."

"He did?"

"Yes. Hattie knows the Bedes. She knew about the land. And the Purple Pig."

"The statue?"

"Yes. And how the mother knew her boy would come back home. And take it to the world. She knew he would. Like all the Bedes. She knew he'd take up what his daddy left undone. And now the Bedes are every-where."

"You mentioned 'it.' What 'it' is that?"

"And that song and the cemetery. I stayed there praying for a long, long time. And then I was singing it myself. Again. That song. I was laughing too and it felt different then. I was laughing and I felt different. Like—oh I don't know—like I was free. So I came here. That song helped me see my need. Helped me to *see*. And I'll probably join them now."

"The Yoricks. *You*?"

"Yes. There's nothing else left. Nothing else seems worth doing. Nothing in the world. It all seems to be ending in comedy anyway. And they can use me. I'm a good administrator. They can use me now. In the meantime. In Georgia. Or Las Vegas. I've written them. And mailed the letter myself. The last town trip. Last week. I'll join them if they'll have me."

"But you mentioned 'it'." What 'it'?"

"It?"

"You said they've taken 'it' to the world. Which 'it' is that?"

But Brother Mordecai had come, in well-coordinated coat and slacks and shirt and tie, a tiny businessman with sample cases and knowing wink, and Thad had smiled and told a joke or two and tried to get his feet to move in something like a dance. And I had followed after them, the little Brother and his black black friend, with sounds of singing drifting back, my own feet clumsy in the taller grass, not keeping up until the two men stopped and waited, singing then together up ahead, the words and tune an undertow that seemed to pull my memories free, one last one there a skull and bones I never saw, old Marcus Bede upon the water barrel come down hard to clatter for a while and make the people laugh.

#

A bell began to toll, muffled in the distance like the howls had been, single notes with pauses in between, a creak of doors there with it up and down the hall and Mario and western wall come closer with each clank and rattle of the keys.

192

CHAPTER TWENTY-FIVE

Darby had missed the Labor Day Benefit by nearly a week, the lights of Vegas just now up ahead, an impossible brightness past the darkened landscape, desert sameness zipping by for hours before he fell asleep (in sunlight then and Jeeter Baldtrip singing with the radio). It had taken a long time to get here. And Jeeter wasn't singing anymore.

"How's about that up ahead there, Buddy-Boy?"

"It's bright."

"'You sure got that much right about it. Yes *sir*."

Jeeter was a clean-lined man, fifty-four with sunburnt skin and squinting eyes and a voice that rasped and almost seemed to grumble over being used at all. He had given Darby his fourth ride since wiggling through the western wall. At a truck stop in north Louisiana. Jeeter was hauling bulls, two dark and heavily sedated chunks of glistened hide and rolling eyes that took up most of what there was of air-conditioned trailer back behind the sleeper of his nearly paid-for Peterbilt. Jeeter had found Darby near the magazine rack.

"Don't waste your time, son. Ain't nothin' fittin' to read in all a that. Nothin' but trash–bare skin an' hatred, filth an' dirty words. You wasn't fixin' 'buy none, was you?"

"No–no I'm just–"

"Good for you, son. Good for you." And he had walked a few times around Darby, squinting eyes mostly fixed on the face, staring finally for what seemed like hours before he spoke again. "You look like Sonny-Boy Morning–"

"I know–I've been told that I–"

"All but the eyes. An' the mouth. Close but wrong. I'm Jeeter Baldtrip."

"Pleased to meet you–I'm–I'm Darby Ross and I've been trying to get to Las Vegas but–"

"Vegas, huh? Well I'm going through there. Yes sir. Man but you do look like Sonny-Boy though. Like he used to look. You're a Christin ain't you son?"

"I–yes–I think I am."

"Knew it. Eyes an' mouth. I can tell. Sonny-Boy started out a Christin too. But somethin' happened 'long the way. I'm hauling bulls to th'coast. Matched pair."

"Bulls?"

"Pell an' Agra. Sonny-Boy's favorite two. I'm his foreman. Lovestar Ranch. The Florida ranch. The working one. Not that Hollywood mess his wife lives on."

"You work–worked for–"

"Yeah. Thirty years. You don't drink, do you? Whiskey?"

"No–well–I did–I used to but not anymore."

"Praise God for that. Pills? Dope?"

"Pardon?"

"You use any dope?"

"No."

"Praise Jesus. That stuff killed Sonny-Boy, y'know? I tried to stop it. Oh I know I know–papers, television, everbody tried t'make out like pellagra done it. But I know better. He had that stuff under control. Veggie an' fruit diet. Special treatments once a year at that clinic in Brunswick. Nosir. He had ol' pellagra whipped. It was booze an' pills. An' that so-called wife of his. An' them two nasty kids. Bled him nearly dry. Got near 'bout everthing. 'Cept them two bulls an' me. It's all in th'will. Th'bulls is mine ok. He give 'em to me. I got me a ranch of my own, y'see. California. I'll call *you* Buddy-Boy. You want a ride?"

"I—yes—I'd appreciate—"

And Jeeter had stuffed Darby's rolled-up blanket in the sleeper (extra shirts inside and the Journal's Heart and some underwear and one fresh pair of socks) and got him buckled safely in beside him in the softness of a leather swivel chair. And Darby slept and woke up to a sound of Gospel music, slept and ate and listened, talked and watched the rig while Jeeter slept, the road pushed out now like a river in his memory, blacktop mostly state to state like something rushing westward on its own, the people met along the way expectant, waiting as it came to seem, alert and tensed like ancient children straining to be first to hear the long blasts of a showboat's horn. And Jeeter had preached to them and sang songs Darby had not heard before and laughed full into choking fits each time a Yorick Joke-Break crackled through the speakers in his cab.

"They're Christins too, y'know? Even if they's Cath'lics. Even if they are. Christins all the same. An' don't you let nobody tell you different, Buddy-Boy. You hear me?"

"Yes."

And on and on the river went, straight toward the sun, the land beside it gone at last to sand and rock and whiteness like a skull, with jingling and a clatter overhead and sometimes coming in so strong that Darby half expected Marcus Bede to drop down from the sky out on the cab's long nose and ask if anyone had seen his son. And Darby slept, one last time just at sunset with a bumping sound there mixed with all the rest, a muffled tap and beating like a staff on rocky ground.

"Nearly takes away y'breath, don't it?" Jeeter was laughing. "All them lights."

"Where are we?"

"Sodom and Gomorrah, Buddy-Boy. You sure this is where you want to be?"

"Yes—I need to visit someone."

"Well it's your life, son. You look more'n old enough to vote." He cleared his throat and shook his head, face green-streaked and soft-lined in the dashboard glow and semi-dark. "Where 'bout in all a that mess you goin' to? You never have said."

"I'm—I'm not sure."

"Not sure? You come all this way an' you ain't sure where to stop? Man oh man but you're even *sounding* like Sonny-Boy now."

"Solomon's Temple."

"Do what?"

"I need to go to Solomon's Temple."

"Well we all do, Buddy-Boy. An' some day we'll all *see* it too. Praise God an' we'll all walk abound in it an' make a joyous noise unto the Lord. But not in Vegas." And the laugh choked off the rest of the words, the cab slowing down as his body shook and his head bobbed up and down and his fingers flexed and unflexed on the wheel. The lights were getting closer and brighter by the second. Darby wondered if old Marcus Bede had already made it there, had slipped away from Mt. Gerezim when Conroy Tucker and his boys were eating or asleep, to float (ghosts would surely float or glide not walk or run) straight back to Hattie Peese to get the mileage and the best route west to find his son. "You got kinfolks in Vegas, Buddy-Boy?"

"No. Not kinfolk. I need to see somebody there

about something."

"Must be real important."

"What?"

"I said it must be real important—to come all this way."

"Yes—yes it is. Important."

The lights looked cold, still and cold and waiting like the people on the riverbank with jingling and the tapping of a staff now louder than before and in the place of showboat horn, no clatter really there at all and Darby guessed that Marcus Bede was safely locked away behind the Gates of Gerezim. But Fr. Bede was free and somewhere deep within the lights, at work and doing what his father had begun, perhaps the very 'What' that Marcus told him he must do, in Philadelphia, steel-plate sparkling in the moonlight as he floated in (an Elder-Hamlet-Yorick all-in-one) to carry with him some high message straight from God, not tainted in the least by Denmark's sin himself but sent against the seemers all the same, against the greed and soul-bloat and permitted one and only one more visit (skull and bones on water barrel notwithstanding) and his words a jolt that set his son to dancing in a jingling laughter that had risen up at once and never stopped. A grinning skull at first within a hood, white bones within a heavy cloak that slowly take on flesh and give a message clear and to the point: *Bring laughter to the workers of the world!* And then perhaps a bit of conversation, father-son across the

years and past the fastness of the grave:
Mark me.
"I will–I do."
I am thy father's spirit.
"Yes."
Dost thou believe?
"Yea. Yes. I dost."
Good. Ok Ok–knock-knock–
"Knock-knock?"
Yea verily–knock-knock!
"Oh. Oh yes. Forgive me. Who's there?"
Punch.
"Punch who?"
Gesundheit!

The laughter shrill, a piping squeak like a tiny bird had risen up in protest, on the wing and fleeing in a sudden flurry, feathers left behind to whirl and spin across the cold dark pavement stones. And Conroy Tucker maybe there, come all alone from Georgia in the night, to find and take back home the one who got away:

"Don't you give me no more trouble now. Just say good-bye and get on back in your box."

Fare thee well at once. The glowworm shows the matin to be near and gins to pale his uneffectual fire.

"Y'know, that's good–that's really good. I like th'sound a that. But you can't stay out here no more."

"Father–"

Adieu, adieu, adieu!

"He can't stay out here like this, Sol! And don't *you* give me no trouble neither."

Remember me!

"We all do, Mr. Bede. But there'll be big trouble if you don't start stayin' where you belong. C'mon now–and don't you worry none. Your boy there'll turn out real good. Not good as you was a course, but still good. Real good. Let's us go on back home now."

And mist and cold perhaps come thicker and with just a touch of whistling wind thrown in, his visitors gone the little priest is filled with awe and gratitude, down on his knees he goes and thinks as he kneels how best to make it last.

"It's like dreams, Buddy-Boy." Jeeter coughed and slowed to miss an armadillo. "Evertime I see it. Hear it. It just ain't real."

"Dreams?"

"Vegas. You sure you want me to let you out *here*?"

"Yes."

"Well you watch y'self close, Buddy-Boy. I spent time here once. And this ain't no Christin' place."

"Thank you for–"

"Don't mention it. Just be careful. Hear?"

"Yes."

"An' you ever get to California look me up. Me an' Pell an' Agra. We'll be there. Lake Morden. Down south. You're always welcome. No need to warn us. Ok?"

"Yes. Down south."

"Ok. Here we go, Buddy-Boy. Heading out of town– finally. I'll let you out up here. Looks ok. Better than back yonder in all that mess of lights. Yeah–right up here. Over by them bushes there." And he smiled a quick smile and shook his head. "I hope you find what you're lookin' for."

"Yes." And maybe then the little priest had slept, alone and dreaming of the road ahead, the vision and the time to come, with Caladega County as his starting place and hallways through the structures room to room all out from there and waiting for a jingle and the tap-tap-tap that Darby wanted most to hear. Jeeter helped him with his blanket and then climbed back in the cab. It was noisy and cold outside, the rumble of the truck lost almost at once as Jeeter eased back into traffic, the trailer lights bright and dim by turns and heading west. Nearby but hidden by a stunted stand of barrel cactus, a neon Elvis danced atop a thick and blinking cross, his legs flared wide and then come back together arms and guitar slapping in an ebb and flow of blue and red and green.

CHAPTER TWENTY-SIX

The main room of the 'Temple' sloped downward to the stage. It was 'Homeless Week' and every seat was taken, a smell and noise there rising up from two thousand laid-off oil-field workers, hoboes and liberated mental patients, burned-out families and migrant farmhands stranded by a dying bus or truck, run-aways and the veterans of three wars who mostly wandered in the aisles or hunkered down to talk or think out loud back in the lobby. Fr. Bede had taken Darby to a room behind the stage, a green-walled place of props and trunks and costumes and a smell of mothballs heavy in the air. He had left him there to rest until they had a chance to talk. The last show was about to start.

"I need to see to the lighting and introduce the first few acts. Why don't you find the couch and take a nap?"

The couch had been hidden behind a bamboo screen and its top was stacked with pillows of various sizes, a few drooping down almost to the tattered cushions. The screen had a seascape on it, shrimp-boats and a harbor neat and filled with water the color of dark wine. Darby had sat down at the end nearest the door, a pillow behind his head with a clown's face on its cover. It was warm in the room and he kept dozing off, the Elvis Chapel there each time he did, the inside nearly screaming out in clashing color and in sparkled flash and glow. The receptionist had been fat, an Elvis-copy bulging out the glittered cloth of his white jumpsuit in a dozen places as he stepped up behind the desk and settled onto a padded stool. 'Love Me Tender' crackled through guitar-shaped speakers up above the crowded doors across the deep blue carpet of the room, from mini-chapels, four of them and Elvis-Pastors at the ready with a song or two and special blessings for the young folks starting out. The receptionist's voice had been nearly a whisper.

"Yuh f'get somethin'?"

"Pardon?"

"Ah said—did yuh f'get somethin'? Somethin' real im-portant?"

"No. I just need directions to—"

"Oh. Ah get it. Well don't yuh worry none—she'll be 'long directly ah'm sure. Yuh got a res'vation?"

"No—I'm not here to—"

"Sorry but ah cain't take no walk-ins tonight, Bub. Nosir."

"But I don't need a—look—I need directions to—Solomon's—"

"No-sir. Not tonight. We cain't handle none tonight. Maybe next Tuesday. Yeah," he flipped at a pink-covered ledger, "next Tuesday'd be cool. Got a open block at two in the afternoon. Two full hours open. Chapel '57. Duboise Raven. He's 'bout the best we got too. Knows *all* th'early stuff. Yuh want me put yuh in there for that two o'clock?"

"No—can I use your telephone?"

"You bookin' a chapel or aintcha?"

"I don't need a chapel!"

"Whoa now—lookit ah know how it is—yuh look like a first-time t'me—an' y'chick late too—ah sure know how *that* goes. Nerves all 'tore up. But yuh gotta stay cool, Bub. Ah run a quiet place here. No trouble." He had tapped his fingers on the pink ledger cover and frowned,

202

a stray lock of his shiny black hair tumbling down toward the bridge of his nose. "Cain't never use no trouble. Ya'll jus' settle down now an' let me he'p yuh de-cide on a time. Ok? Will you jus' let me he'p yuh? Thas what ah'm here for. Yuh ok now?"

"Yes."

"Cool. Thas cool. Now—two-thirty's just as good. Shoot fire maybe even better. Give ol' Duboise a chance t'warm up on th' two o'clock. Yeah. Yuh look like a two-thirty anyways. Cool. Now what would yuh like him t'sing? Y'chick got a fav'rite? Maybe ya'll got a 'Our Song'? Or jus' th'Sun Years Special? It's all th'same to Duboise. An' everthing's figured into th'one low price. Now then—what was the'name again? Hey—where yuh goin'?"

The cold air had felt good outside and Darby finally found a cab and let the mostly silent driver take him to the 'Temple.'

The couch had become sticky to the touch and Darby pushed himself up and began pacing in front of the screen, back and forth across the harbor and the shrimp-boats and the wine-dark sea, back and forth and then a jingling in the hall and the door swung open, old round-face there and all in place and smiling and a jester's cap pushed forward on a shaking head. The noise outside was brief, the door a thick one padded in red circles that thumped loudly as it closed, the laugh-ter, shrieks and thousand jingling bells cut off or lowered to a clanking hum as Darby tried to give a smile back to the one that bounced now up above the shuffling feet of Fr. Bede.

"And what did you hear, Mr. Ross?" He stopped the dance and came in close, to lick his lips and smile some more at Darby, face and hands no longer pink but sunburnt red, the wrinkles there but fainter than before and something-else there too upon the skin and in the way he moved his eyes that seemed all wrong. "We heard you finally made it home."

"Father Bede—I—I'm sorry for the things I said to—"

"Yes yes I know all that. That's not important now." The something-else had color in it, color the first thing noticed really, a faint but nearly rigid gray. But the rest was mostly like before, reddish now, much redder than it had been on the Square but still a moving thing that never seemed to rest. "That's not important at all."

"But—what can I—"

"There's little time, Mr. Ross. Very little time. Don't waste what you've been given. What did you hear?" The voice was different too, not like the private one that calmed and soothed but now clipped and hard and with a touch of rasp and wheeze that made it sound much older than it was.

"Hear?"

"Yes. Back home. Right back where you started from. Home sweet home. Where the heart is. The place you'll be for Christmas (if only in your dreams)." He shuffled his feet in a weak parody of a buck-and-wing, arms flapping only once and fingers turned to fists and coming back to hide within the outsized pockets of his best green coat. "Home. Where your music's playing. Home. Where the old folks are. Home. There's no place like it. Home?" The laugh was nearly a cackle.

"There wasn't much to hear." The face seemed streaked with gray, rigid bands which laced the red like skinny ribbons on a birthday box, the skin now pulsing, red on gray in battle back and forth. "There was talk. Everybody talked. They put me in a —"

"We know. I know. They even wired us to expect you

here."

"They did?" The face was smiling, up from the bat-tlefield like a sudden burst of peace. But the gray was gaining ground.

"Yes. His Eminence personally. They sent your wal-let. And money. They want you back."

"At the hospital?"

"In the diocese. They also telephoned. Twice. His Eminence has a very kind voice. A warm voice. Full of hurt. And disappointment. Fear. But love the most of all. I don't think he wanted to call me. I *know* he didn't. But he did it anyway." The skin was almost solid gray across the forehead and around the eyes. But the smile kept flickering down below, cheeks flushing red in patches and pushed hard into the gray. "They want you to come home."

"But—but there's nothing there for me!"

"Then you heard nothing?" The face was nearly gray from hairline down to chin, a rigid mask that stared up with a smile turned frozen and with eyes deep moving inside circles smooth and dark. The bells were silent as his fingers, gray like all the rest, slipped off the cap and brought to view a scalp with something like caked dust between the traces of a hair once brown or red or golden yellow, but only dusty now and blended with the color of the mask. "Nothing at all?"

"They cleaned the Little Okra. And Sonny-Boy is dead."

"Did you pray?"

"Yes. I think so. Yes I prayed. Of course I prayed. I must have prayed. But I never heard a thing except—

except—"

"Except what? What did you hear?"

"Your bells. I heard your bells and—"

"And?"

"The blades. The ones—I heard the rotor blades—the barges—"

"The river. On the river?"

"Yes. And other places. But I never heard anything else. Just talk. And sometimes screams—howls—howling down the hall or in another cottage. Somewhere. And laughter. And thumping. And shouts for help. In the night. At night. Nearly every night."

"And that's all?" The mask seemed larger now, expanding like a tire pumped up too full of air, with flecks of gray spun off in places where the pressure pushed the most. "That's all you heard?"

"No." The mask was cracking, tiny fissures glowing red along the cheeks and out across the chin, the gray not holding anywhere intact but falling in upon itself, to disappear in spots and patches like an ointment rubbed into the skin. "No—I heard—no I wanted to hear—more. Something more. To stop—"

"The other sounds?"

"Yes."

"And so you're here?" The mask had almost gone away, the contour of the face, the moving skin and wrinkles and the smile the most of all returning little bit by little bit, the voice again the soothing one and calm and tap of wooden staff there in the words.

"Yes."

"Can you throw a pie, Mr. Ross?"

"What?"

"A pie. Can you throw one?"

"I–yes–"

"Good. Let's find a pie to throw before you leave."

And the skin was free of gray, the mask all gone away and in its place a face just like a child's, a smooth and rosy-cheeked and trust-filled face that caught reflections in its eyes of Darby and a Kathleen and a Cindy, laughing, young and close together down beside a Little Okra flowered over bank to bank, green and rippling and with strength enough to bear their weight.

CHAPTER TWENTY-SEVEN

He had dropped the Journal's heart (torn from top to bottom and again from side to side) into a large garbage can shaped like Woodsy Owl, the open beak not touching any of the pages and a voice come back when everything hit bottom–saying (with a crackle and a beeping hum): *Thank you Thank you Thank you–Hoot!* The bus depot had been crowded and noisy and too cold as Darby bought his ticket with the help of Fr. Bede and picked a place to sit as close as he could get to Platform A. The priest had been out of costume, dressed in a flamingo-pink silk shirt and pants that bagged in the knees and covered his green suede shoes altogether. But the face was nearer the right color (less red than slightly pink) and the voice almost the same one that he used in Georgia and the seats were decent and in order as they sat and talked.

"This is for the best, Mr. Ross."

"Yes."

"But are you sure you want to travel on–"

"The bus?"

"Yes."

"I like the bus. The time. I'll have more time to think."

"And pray?"

"Yes. Of course. That too. Yes. I like the bus. And thank you, Father Bede."

"For what? I'm afraid I've been able to do very little

for you. No need to thank me for that."

"Last night–I–"

"Yes?"

"I loved it. I was afraid at first. For a little while. But it went away. And I loved it. The lights. The people. Their laughter and applause."

"And the pies?"

"Yes. The pies most of all. Especially the pies."

Fr. Bede had smiled and rubbed his eyes. The 'something-else' was gone but he had seemed tired all the time. No. Tired wasn't right but Darby couldn't find another word to do the job. To cover what he saw beside him in the depot waiting on the call to board. They had talked and talked and people came and went and the noise had grown stronger with every passing minute. Last night he had seemed younger than the children that he brought on stage to help him with the show. And Darby had stood beside him, stacks of pies there on a kind of cart, standing all together in the brightest lights that he had ever seen, Brother Mordecai behind him (back from Georgia just a day ago) and the others, Second Bananas and the younger Yoricks in a row, the pies soon passed from hand to hand and to the children last of all, and then a horn began to bleat like some crazed ram was there and free to chase whatever it could find and pies went flying through the brightness, multi-colored froth gone spinning everywhere at once, and more and more until the cart was empty and a new one took its place. And the laughter was as loud as thunder-rumble on the sea.

"The children love that part. Even the saddest ones."

Darby had been hit many times, dodging and afraid at first until two chocolate creams had found him down beside the cart and landed almost joined together on his head. There seemed to be no let-up after that, pie after pie on face and chest and back and one tall thick one sticking for a second to his upraised forearm, a soggy buckler that had knocked away two cherry tarts and one lost blob of blue before it slid off out of sight. And it was then he let himself be pulled inside to fight, with chocolate mostly but a few times using anything that could be scraped up from the floor, a mix of colors that he sailed toward anyone that moved. It lasted for a long time, music building and the shouts and laughter holding at an almost painful pitch, The Yoricks and the children and then others in their seats, the first four rows or more a blur of color, pies and splatter, globs and gooey chunks and Darby feeling, hearing and then nearly touching, in the noise a jingling louder than the Yorick bells, a bump and knock and tap-tap-tapping close within it, soft then rising like a padded car about to fall, pushed free of every other sound, footstep-cadenced as he licked his lips and wiped his face and saw for just a second, eye-blink flash and gone, a shepherd's crook pass slowly in the air above it all.

"It makes the children laugh. And when *they* laugh— the older people laugh. The children help them laugh."

And when it ended, Fr. Bede and Darby talked, showered and clean, for hours in the quiet of a tiny chapel down a jagged hall and past the green-walled room, on pews that sparkled red and green and gold and blue and multi-colored shafts of light upon the walls behind the crucifix, the crown of thorns deep red and wounds like polished rubies mounted deeply in the side and hands and feet. They had talked. About many different things. And finally about going home.

"Start again, Mr. Ross. At home. Start there. With

what you have. Can you do that now?"

"Yes—I think so—yes."

"Good. That's very good. You're needed there the most of all. And listen. This time listen. It's really very simple. Like throwing pies."

"Yes."

But when the bus had come and Fr. Bede had walked away into the crowd, when Darby gave the Journal's heart to Woodsy Owl and settled down into a window seat and scrunched against the inside wall to let a fat man in an orange jumpsuit push beside him thigh to thigh, the simple thing seemed far away and gone. The window glass was greasy and the fat man smelled of onions and the desert landscape passed like some far country in a dream. Hours now had also passed and more, a feeling growing in him mile by mile that he had gone too fast alone, that home and Big Red's 'just-like-before' might still be there for him, intact and as a comfort and a hedge against the road. And somewhere in New Mexico he found he wanted very much to go back home and stay. And he cried into the pillow he had rented, his head turned toward the window so the jumpsuit couldn't see.

CHAPTER TWENTY EIGHT

Pietro Cardinal Riga had not wanted to leave, his bulk seeming even to rebel against the pacing steps his feet had taken back and forth before the rectory door, hips and stomach pushing out his robes a beat or two behind each time he turned to go the other way. Pope Hilary had remained seated on the padded bench near a brightly painted statue of Our Lady of Mt. Carmel, in place exactly as Cardinal Spitzmulcher had left him, hands folded on his lap and smiling with a visible effort. Pietro was coming very close to anger.

"You have to know why he wants you here alone."

"But I'm not alone, Pietro. I'm never alone."

"Don't make light of this, Sparrow. It's dangerous to do that."

"Ah."

The nickname had sounded strange back at the rectory, in the latticed sunlight waiting for the return of their host, Pietro almost never using it except when he was angry. Little Eddie Boyer, 'The Sparrow,' most of those who used the name now dead or memory-damaged, Little Eddie 'Sparrow' Boyer the smallest of the boys, the weakest but the one who never cried. Pietro had been 'The Ox' and sometimes had to carry Little Eddie on his back.

"He'll push hard for what he wants."

"But this is to be a retreat, Pietro. A rest. Renewal. In devotion to the Blessed Mother."

"You'll get no rest in *this* place, Sparrow. No rest at

all. He'll fight you—smiling, yes and praying, yes—but fight you all the same. At every turn, he'll fight."

"To change my mind?"

"Yes. And more than that."

"Ah. You make him sound—evil, Pietro. You make him sound like an enemy."

"Not evil, Holiness. Not evil."

"An enemy then?"

"Yes, Holiness. One of many. Almost openly now. An enemy."

"Of what? We've both known Heinrich a long time. He's never disobeyed."

"But this time everything has changed. You've seen America. For yourself."

"Yes." The months had stretched behind like lakes of mud, shallow bogs with trails marked plain for all to see, but trails that led to nowhere, trails that deepened as they lengthened in the mud. And he had come to think that the Church Herself (here most of all) seemed hesitating, like the runners of a race set in their starting blocks and waiting for the gun to sound. But he had found the runners barely civil, each one facing toward a different goal, the common track ignored or kept as bare convenience marking where they all began, a sentimental contrast to the better place each one was sure that they would reach. And few there were still centered on the track itself, still there and running to the scattered cheers of those who shared their hope.

"He'll go after Father Bede the hardest. You know that." Pietro had stopped pacing and turned toward The Sparrow, the sunlight caught behind his massive back like wings, golden and glowing out around his shoulders, feathery shafts and moving as he breathed.

"Yes. Your little priest upsets him greatly, Pietro."

"And not just him, Holiness."

"Yes yes. He upsets others as well. I know. Bishop Krull is thumping at the other end. Spitzmulcher and Krull agree on something. Just think of it. Almost a miracle in itself. Your little priest has stirred much dust, Pietro. He's made the Bishops' world untidy."

"Don't give him up, Sparrow. Don't sacrifice–"

"Enough Pietro! I know his worth. We need to pray now. You and I. For the Blessed Virgin's intercession. For peace. That the runners find the track again."

"Runners, Holiness? Track? I–"

"Can your little priest help lead them, Pietro? That's the question now."

"Holiness–you talk in riddles. You must be tired. You always talk this way when you are tired. Even as a boy you–"

"But can he help, Pietro? Your little priest? Can he be belled and still be–"

"Belled? Like a cat? Father *Bede*! Him–*belled*, Holiness? What are you–"

"–made to lead from deep inside the troubled flock?"

"Runners–track–bells–flock–your metaphors, Holiness, are–are mangled! We need to leave here. We've stayed too long. We need to go home."

"You saw him in a dream, Pietro?"

"Holiness–what–"

"Your Father Bede. You saw him in a dream, you

said?"

"Yes, Holiness. In a dream."

"And he danced for you there. And you felt joy?"

"Yes—I've told you about all—"

"I know. And he brings joy. Yes?"

"Yes."

"And stirs up dust? Untidiness for the Bishops. And makes the other runners nervous. Yes?"

"He's like a child, Holiness. A wise child."

"But touched by God, Pietro?"

"Oh yes, Holiness. And he leads others. Already. He leads them to God. Even now."

"And when he's gone? What of the leading then?"

"I'm not sure I—"

"When Father Bede is dead. What then?"

"There are others, Holiness. The Order has grown and—"

"But are there others like *him*?"

"I—I don't know."

"No dreams to help you this time, good Pietro?"

"No."

A knocking at the door had come and made Pietro's shoulders jump. Pope Hilary had told those on the other side to wait—'a few minutes more—we'll call you when we're done'—and stood up slowly, Pietro's hand there at the last to give him balance. The Ox's eyes were wide and puzzled-looking, wrinkles on the forehead deep and cheeks and jaw gone tense and twitching from the effort that it took to keep them still. The Pope knew that Pietro had waited. In place out on their portion of the track and looking backward. The runners had not yet been given any signal loud and clear enough to spring them on their way.

"The gun will not sound from here, Pietro. Not from

San Cristobel. Not now."

"Holiness."

"But Father Bede must be belled. At least the bell must be in place. And good strong leather for a collar."

"For a compromise, Holiness?"

"For what comes after Father Bede, Pietro."

And they had knelt and prayed, the Virgin's eyes in shadows as the golden light was lost among the clouds outside, broad thick ones growing darker by the time the limousine had left the city far behind, a silent Heinrich there beside a Sparrow deep in thought and dreaming every now and then of migratory flocks together on the wing.

CHAPTER TWENTY-NINE

It had been a good year. Darby slipped the wolf-man head down over the top of a dock pylon and adjusted his furry shoulders and arms. It was getting dark out on the Little Okra, sunlight nearly gone and the dark water barely streaked with gold toward the far bank. He was dressed for the Monster Ball and Crawly Creep-Show Masquerade, his second one and first as a junior director of the Apollo Bluffs Country Club, and he had come to the boathouse for a drink. Kathleen and Cindy, Joan of Arc and Vampire Princess, were not yet ready, Kathleen polishing the visor of her helmet as he tucked the wolf-man head under his arm and started for the river. Her voice had sounded muffled back behind him in the semi-darkness of the house.

"Don't forget we leave in an hour, Darby. Don't forget. Did you hear me?"

He had heard but didn't answer, nearly through the front door when she spoke, the wolf-man costume she had helped him choose making heavy squish and plop-plop sounds on the giant paving stones of the veranda. But the costume itself was remarkably lightweight, not hot or itchy at all as he squished and plop-plopped to the boathouse, down the graveled path among the pines and scrub oak, golden light all patterned in a lat-tice-work spread out above him, swaying there like spi-der webs connected side to side.

The boathouse door had been locked, keys left on the nightstand, so he had squeezed around the side to make it to the dock. The river was clear, a speedboat churning up the water down toward the bend where the barges used to anchor, not one hyacinth there, not one thing bobbing in a rippled sway and dip in the stiff breeze from the distant sea. The speedboat had disappeared by the time he put the head down on the pylon, fangs clacking together and the fur gone flat between the ears and the eye-holes dark and nearly turned to slits. Kathleen had found the costume, almost hidden beneath a row of dangling tights and tutus in the farthest corner of the Sumptuary Shoppe's main room. They had spent the day together, yesterday, no a week ago yesterday, four days after his return from Big Red's annual Retreat and gentle Eugene's watchful care. It had felt good to hear her laugh, a furry arm and claw-tipped glove pulled free of tights and crinoline, slashing at the air and resting on his back to scratch and tap and tangle in his shirt. They had laughed a lot that day. And it had been a good, good, year.

The coming night seemed filled with voices, the good, good year in jumbled echoes on the water, breeze cool against his face (the only exposed portion of his body), voices rising up and gone out where the light was dying, bobbing markers of the long, long way back home. He patted at the wolf-man head, slit eyes lost each time a furry glove touched down, listening now, closely, the voices there and quickly gone like jumping fish or sandflies in the wind:

Poddy there and gone–gone far away–to Rome as Big Red's special present to the papal press–young Poddy gotten older now and leaving Darby with *The Cross* again and mostly free. But Poddy with the other voices in and out, a new-old sound that made the past seem far away.

"It's my big chance, Mr. Ross. Everybody says I'd be a fool

not to go—

not to go—"

And Big Red himself, the Cardinal's voice bass-sounding through the rest, just like it did when Darby's bus had rolled in finally from the desert, Jurisdiction waiting in its biggest car and smiling Eugene down on Platform B to guide him back within its tender chunking care at last:

"My son, my son. Come—sit with me. Here. Sit here. We'll ride and talk.

Just like we used to do. We'll ride and talk and take you home."

The other voices mixed, wavered in a rise and fall above the deepest water he could see, out where the barges cut and dredged the longest time of all, his own voice with them bobbing on the crest of months which gave him back his column and a soundproof place to pass his days and Kathleen's soft warmth to push away the darkness of the night. The good, good year was ending in a rush of voices floating like a Marcus Bede between the condo clutter on the riverbanks, bounced back and forth between the insulated comfort of the visible and known:

"You will take *The Cross* as part of your duties."

"Yes, Eminence. Thank you."

"But keep yourself free for other work. More important work. Here in the Diocese for now. Close to home."

"Of course, Eminence."

And more:

"Oh Darby—it's—it's like we were still newlyweds—it

feels like it used to feel."

"But we never had enough to eat. Back then. We lived on garbage. Don't you remember?"

"You were happy then, Darby. All the time. Happy. You even sang for me. What was that song you used to sing?"

"I stayed drunk–every day, night. I worked as a janitor. And you worked in the Burger Barn. Third shift. You brought home stale bread. And our apartment–the bathroom floor sagged and the rats and–"

"And you wrote poetry, Darby. Long poems. And we went to Mass every day."

"*You* went to Mass every day."

"And you sang me songs and played guitar and we laughed."

"I sold the guitar for a fifth of gin–at Christmas–and punched our landlord in the nose and he threw us out."

"And you made love to me, Darby. Like you do now. Just like you do now. You were so gentle and sweet."

"The police came–to our new apartment–I hadn't punched the landlord yet. It was Easter. We fought. You and I. For days. You told me you were pregnant and we fought. I broke a window and the police came."

"We were so young, Darby. Like now. We did it on our own. No help from my parents. Or yours. We worked hard."

"And we nearly starved. For years. We lived on garbage. And the Church had gone away. They took the Church away. Don't you remember? Nothing held together. And you were pregnant."

"His Eminence loves you, Darby. Like a son. He told me he does. And he sounds like he used to sound. When he came to help us."

"I was in jail again. I punched a cop that time. Don't

know why. Cindy was a baby. I worked in a car wash. He drove in one day. The Cardinal. I washed and waxed his car and we talked and he left. I thought the Church was with him. That he had somehow saved Her soul. I got drunk. To celebrate. And I punched a cop."

"He loves you, Darby. Just like when he came to help. When he baptized Cindy and gave you a job."

"I've tried to remember why. I remember his face. The cop's face. And his name—R. Sanchez, Jr—but I don't know why I hit him. That was the last time in jail. R. Sanchez, Jr. He had blond hair and blue eyes. They said I broke his nose."

"I love you, Darby. And we're together now. He told me how he loves you. Like a son. Like the son he'll never have."

"But his Church was silent. Something even there had gone away for good. I don't know what. It looks the same. Mostly just the same. He saved that much.'

"And Cindy is so happy now. She really is. Her daddy's home for good."

"It could be how it sounds that's different. Not the words. Not the obvious. Not that at all. Something else. I knew about the English. The Mass in English. So it couldn't have been that. Something else. A certain sound. There was something I couldn't hear there any more. In his Church. In San Cristobel."

"All her friends' parents are members. And now us too. It's quite an honor. Apollo Bluffs is very selective. His Eminence was very pleased."

"And other places. IT just wasn't there anymore. Not often anyway. Not all the time like what used to be. Like what probably still is there with The Yoricks. But Father Bede won't let me stay with them. Or help me find IT. And make IT last. He told me to go home. And I did. And

IT's not important any more."

"We're happy now, Darby. All of us. I've prayed for this. Our happiness. I've prayed for so long. And now it's here."

And more and more and dismally on and on:

"Yes–what? What did you say?"

"Who is it, Darby? Is it His Eminence?"

"Dead–both–did you say both of them? Dead?"

"Oh my God! Who? Darby!"

"My parents–what? What did you say? A wreck–yesterday–my parents are dead–are dead–are dead–are–

And moving right along, and moving clear and strong–on back to Poddy once again:

"It's my big chance, Mr. Ross. A chance of a life-time."

"Yes."

"He wants you here. You're his man. I've always known. Nobody can replace Darby Ross."

"No."

"And something's coming. Here. I know it is. He's different now. Since the visit with His Holiness. Something's different. Can you feel it?"

"I think so. Yes."

"He never mentions The Yoricks anymore. Have you noticed?"

"Yes."

"He's waiting for a victory. He expects one. It must be that. And he wants you here. Can I help you before I go? Is there anything I can do?"

"No."

Final voices now—moving swiftly in the dark and sad:

"Mr. Ross?"

"Yes? Eugene—how are you?"

"Mr. Ross—His Eminence thought you'd like to know—he just found out himself—"

"Yes?"

"Father Bede—"

"Father Bede?"

"—is in the hospital. In Las Vegas. His heart."

"Father Bede?"

"His Eminence thought you'd like to know. Before reading about it in the press. Or seeing it on the television. He thought you'd like to know."

"Yes—yes. Thank him for me. His heart?"

"Yes. It happened this morning. One of our Nevada people telephoned the news. They're moving Father Bede to Georgia as soon as possible. That's all we know for sure."

"Thank you, Eugene."

And back and finally back upon the dock again:

The sunlight was just a flickering glow on the docks up river, the boathouse lights now sputtering on and the new electric torches snaking through the pines beside the pathway to the house, showing the way back, to Joan of Arc and Vampire Princess and the time for one more drink before the Creepshow at the Club. He tugged the wolf-man head free of the pylon and smoothed down the fur above its eyes. The house was visible through the trees, rising up on the bluff like a multi-layered cake, light-streaked and clean-lined and beautiful. They had eaten prime-rib that afternoon. With tiny potatoes and a spinach salad filled with fresh mushrooms.

And a wine the Cardinal gave them on their anniversary. And they had sneaked away from Cindy and her friends and made love on the new waterbed while the speedboats chased each other up and down the Little Okra and the sky began to slip toward night. His parents had left him their one-story house and several acres, some books and savings and a near-dead car, their will a short one with a codicil providing for the shipping (straight to Darby) of a life-sized mermaid statue, sole survivor of the Old-Tyme Arcade-By-The-Sea. The box was stored inside the boathouse office, unopened, blending with the dust and resting up against a bookcase near his desk.

He turned his furry back on the river, water lost to sight beyond the circle of the boathouse lights, the voices lost to other sounds, to fireworks rumbling at the public landing and a sputter and a whine of smaller boats down where the river widened and the Interstate cut through. He licked his lips, almost tasting Kathleen's acrid perfume and he smiled remembering how her breasts had felt, his tongue licking taut the nipples as she pressed him to her, his cheek against her like a baby and her long long fingers smoothing down his hair. He squeezed around the boathouse and caught hold of the rope bannister on the other side. The plank bridge to the graveled pathway was well-lit, thick slats of light across the places even underneath, dark clumps like grass down in the mud and nestling there against the bank, swaying in the water's whirl and flow. He had sent a card to Fr. Bede, had told him that he hoped he'd soon be well and signed his name and mailed it after work, a month or more ago. The news since then had been spotty but he did remember that the priest was back in Georgia, home and resting at The Laughing Place.

But all that seemed so long ago and done, The

Yoricks less and less a part of what he did, a year stretched out behind to buffer any nearer sound but Kathleen's breathing as she slept and Cindy's squeals and music by the pool. He felt good. Safe. His stomach full of beef and scent of Kathleen's perfume now to mix in with her taste, her breasts and down below all moist and springy to the touch. He stooped and watched the water bubble by beneath his feet, the grass-like clumps turned thicker now, stretched out to either side like ocean swimmers bobbing on a swell, familiar as he knelt to see them better, the hyacinths and somewhere near at hand a bird cry like the laughter of a child.

CHAPTER THIRTY

The Wolfman had eaten six finger sandwiches (green-flecked cream cheese with a dominant flavor of dill), several rolled slabs of medium-rare roast beef, a mound of boiled shrimp that a liveried waiter was returning to the kitchen, three somethings in the shape of chicken wings that tasted like steamed clams, and after his fourth scotch-and-water began singing Buddy Holly songs with Friar Tuck. The friar's belly bobbed beneath a thick rope cinch each time he reached for a high note and his face glistened like a roasting turkey freshly basted and waiting to slide back into the oven. The Wolfman liked him immensely. They sang well together, arm-in-arm before an ornate fireplace in a busy corner of the ballroom.

Something resembling Joan of Arc had tried to stop them, several seconds into "Not Fade Away" but a group of hunchbacks had shouted her down and clapped for more and pushed an Elvis in to beat out rhythm on an un-tuned guitar. The Wolfman was having fun with his friends.

Friar Tuck began to laugh, belly bobbing and the rope cinch bumping with it and his brown robe rising up calf-high on his thick and hairy legs. The Elvis kept on beating at the strings of his guitar.

"Whoa—man—wait—wait till—I—catch my—breath—man!"

The Wolfman waited, feeling love for the fat friar and the Elvis, for the hunchbacked men and women, for the vampires and the scarred and bleeding faces in the crowd, the dancers and the eaters and the drinkers one and all. He hugged the friar and flopped a paw down on the very top of his tonsured head. Their audience was leaving.

"Whew—man—I love them old songs!"

The Elvis had found a shrouded skeleton to play with, dirty long hair down its front, bulged like a woman where the golden ringlets stopped, the face a skull and fingers pasty white. He left his guitar leaning against the fireplace. The band was coming back on stage across the room. The friar wiggled free and fussed his robe and tonsure back in place. The Wolfman was thirsty.

"Who *are* you anyway—under that furry thing?" The friar looked tired, fat face beaded with sweat but a good face all the same, concerned and feeling, full of pity surely for the ugliness he saw. Joan of Arc was nowhere to be seen. And there were many Vampire Princesses, many of them, here and by the pool. The friar adjusted his tonsure and smiled. It was a good smile. Lips made for easy absolution, for penance quick and short. "You're th'only one here. Where'd you get that thing?"

"Do you need a more private place, Father?" The Wolfman brushed at the friar's shoulders and patted him gently on his sturdy back. "Or should I kneel here?" It felt late and the band was playing again, recorded music changed for live, the dancers never noticing, going on just like before, a bump and jump and shake and glide, hunch and fang and bloody faces, skulls and bones and rotting clothes, bump-jump swish and crinkle, moans and groans and laughter like a wounded cat, a hundred wounded cats dropped down together in a pit. "Or sit? I see chairs over there. I'm not opposed to face-to-face." The Wolfman reached for his fifth big scotch, the glass just where he left it on the mantle, up above a spangled blue guitar. All Saints was coming in and All Souls close behind. It was best to use the love he felt and seek God's pardon here.

"You say somethin' ol' pal–ol' fuzzy pal–ol' fuzzy-wuzzy pal?" The friar had a glass of his own, deep brown, dark and deep, a long glass full of deep-dark sloshing as he tried to hug a furry arm. "Who th'hell *are* you any-way? Hey–why'nt ya take off th'mask huh? How ya drink through that thing ol' wuzzy-fuzzy–ol' pal fuzzy huh?"

"Bless me, Father, for I–" The music was getting louder, dancers almost blended to the Wolfman's eyes, the holes wide slits that jiggled as he turned his head to see. "For I–I–" He fought to hold his love, the dancers every one, the ugly and the lame, to hold it long enough to say the proper words. "I have–I have sinned."

"Yes *sir*–I sure enough done me some a *that*. Done a whole lot of that. You–you *do* know me, don't ya ol' fuzzy-pal–you know me!" The Friar sloshed his deep-brown down his robe to splash about his sandaled feet. The face looked different, red-tinged all about the fore-head and the ears. The smile was jagged. "Josh With'spoon? With'spoon? Real 'state? West Wind Devel'ment? Ev'body knows *me*. Huh? Are ya a member here ol'fuzzy? Ol' buddy-sinner-fuzzy?"

"I–" The face in the flashing light was nothing like a priest's, the eyes all wrong for reconciliation, darting back and forth across the room, feral in the shift from light to dark, the lips thick curled and leering at the dance. "Yes–yes I am." The Wolfman felt foolish and drank his scotch and let the love go burning down his throat, down quickly and then hot inside, a solid lump that seemed to send out waves of flame.

"I knew it! Yes *sir*–that voice–ol' fuzzy–ol' pal." He

hugged the Wolfman, splashing deep-dark all around, the tonsure twisting as he moved and Joan of Arc some-how popped up behind his head. "Whoozis? Who we got us here ol'fuzzy?" He lurched and pulled her closer in. "Hey–it's–it's a fee-male in there–lookit–see?" He tried to push the visor further up but St. Joan got away and clattered to the Wolfman's side. "What y'got under them lil' iron pants, darling'? Huh?"

"Darby!" St. Joan was hiding now, behind the Wolf-man, holding on to his fur while the friar drained his glass and put it wobbling on a passing tray.

"Wha'd she say ol' fuzzy?" The band had left again, a tape come on that crackled shrill and popped awhile before the beat pushed clear with moans and screams around it and a sound like plainsong rising just above. "She your woman or somethin'? Huh? Lil' iron-pants? Let's get us a can opener, what say ol' sinner-fuzzy? Huh? Whew-boy–lookit them go!" The dancers were jumping, in pairs and groups of four or five, bandages unravelling, bloody rags and shrouds and bindings flar-ing thick and fast, the light now multi-colored, dimming and then flashing like explosions big and small. The friar seemed unable to move.

"Darby!" St. Joan hissed almost louder than the dance. "I've had enough. We saw you–heard you–I sent Cindy to the powder-room–someone tore her dress, Darby! I–I fixed what I could–she felt sick again–I told her to come here when she's done–she threw up twice the other time–right after they tore her dress–she'll come here when she's done. Take us home–*now*!"

"What–what did you say?" The Wolfman noticed that the friar was swaying, just a little bit, his belly flop-ping side-to-side and moving ever closer to the beat.

"That's not funny–not one bit funny, Darby!" St.

Joan let go of the Wolfman's back and stepped to one side.

"What? I only said–"

"Don't–don't do that! That growling frightens me–I don't like it here–"

"We'll go home then. We'll leave. I've eaten. Have you eaten anything? The shrimp was very good. And the sandwiches. Did you try the clam wings? And Cindy. Where did you put Cindy?" The love was all gone, no more burning where it hit, but coldness now, a stabbing pain like fingers left too long in snow and held and rubbed above a fire. The Wolfman felt alone. "I've had enough to eat. And drink. But I don't like the music. I'll mention that I don't like it at the next Director's meeting."

"Stop it! Stop that growling right now!" St. Joan's visor seemed stuck, halfway up and obscuring her eyes–nose and lips there in the light and cheeks mascara-stained and wet. "Don't do that–don't." The friar was dancing, pulled into the outer frenzy by a mummy and a bouncing lizard with a bra around its neck.

"But I'm not–" The Wolfman shouted to be heard, at St. Joan and a crying Vampire Princess, both so tiny-looking and alone, their voices lost down in the shattered plainsong and the shrieks, their fingers clutching, holding to his sides, beneath his furry arms and well behind his slashing claws, the dancers parting one by one to let them pass.

CHAPTER THIRTY-ONE

The Wolfman costume hung on a peg on the bedroom closet door. Darby had put it there while Joan of Arc went clattering off to see the Vampire Princess safely into bed. The zipper had stuck a few times and the head-mask had pinched his ears and the skin of his arms looked crisscrossed in red, fabric marks and matted hair from shoulders down to wrists. The shower had felt good, steam and soap, the water hot and washing everything away, bits of fur and lint and sticky places on his neck, hair foamed clean again and squeaking to the touch. He had stood a long, long time and let the water take away all trace of what he'd been. Joan of Arc was stacking her armor in a box when he came back in the room. He pulled his bathrobe close about his waist and sat down on the padded platform of the bed. St. Joan was down to undertunic, tuille and cuisse. The helmet rested on her vanity, visor up and insides dark. It was cluttered in the room, the bed unmade, warm and close and scented with the perfume Kathleen always used.

"It was horrible, Darby. Horrible. Poor Cindy. Did you see her dress?"

"Yes." He could still taste the last scotch, acrid on his lips and tongue and mixed with shrimp and dill. A wind had come up outside from the river, the big oak at the balcony creaking, stray branches clattering and scratching against the side of the house in an almost rhythmic play of hard and soft and pauses in between.

"It's ruined—and we lose the deposit." She

unfastened the tuille and cuisse and tugged the tunic over her head, breasts rising with the movement of her arms, pale blue bra and panties down below, hips still firm-looking and pushed out just enough, her legs long and pale white contrast to the shadows out around. Darby watched her bend to press the final pieces of her costume down into the box. "I'll find a bag for the helmet. I can't make it fit. Not tonight."

"Is Cindy sleeping?" She had cried most of the way home, softly, little sobs and gasps like she was out of breath. A gang of satyrs had danced with her and torn her dress.

"I don't know. She's tucked in. I hope she sleeps." Dropping the bra and panties on the box, she sat down on the wing-backed chair near her side of the bed, bare skin almost mixing with the colors there, her ankles crossed and Wolfman torso and the mask behind and up above, its eye-slits covered up with fur and snout and teeth pushed out and pointed slightly toward her head. Her red robe lay in a lump on the carpet near her feet and she snagged it with her toes. "It's gotten colder. I'm glad the bed is heated. Did you check the thermostat?" The robe went on with just a flash of breast, white against the red as she leaned forward to smooth the cloth behind her and then settle back slowly in the chair.

"Yes. I turned it up a little. Furnace'll click on in a minute."

"It was frightening, Darby." She crossed her legs and wiped a hand slowly across her face. The robe was open slightly in the front, her knee and thigh a crooked V of white that moved with her foot, tapping at the air toward the bed, big toe pushed down and coming near the floor. "I–I–got there just in time."

"Who were they?"

"No one knows–a security guard tried to find them. Afterwards."

"Which guard?"

"The–the big one. I don't know his name."

"Robin?"

"I don't know."

"Must have been Robin."

"He tried. But they had disappeared by then. They did the same thing to two other girls. It was so–so ugly."

"The satyrs?"

"Yes. And everything. It was nothing like last year's. And why did you drink so–"

"I only drank enough. Just enough. I didn't get drunk. I'm not drunk now."

"But–that horrid little man–"

"Friar Tuck?"

"And the singing–you frightened me."

"Like the satyrs?"

"No–of course not! Not like them at all. But–but you–"

"The old days then?"

"What?"

"Like the old days. Like they really were. Just-like-before? Is that how I seemed?"

"Not–no, not like that. Nothing like that."

"Nothing?"

"Well–maybe just a little." She laughed, legs un-crossing and the robe now open further, knees and thighs come out and darkness pushed up higher in a V. "Just a little bit. The growling. Yes. Especially that." On its peg, the Wolfman seemed asleep, head drooping, snout and teeth slipped deep into the fur awhile to rest.

Darby crossed the room quickly, kneeling in between her feet, his hands come gently down upon her thighs. "Darby—it was horrible." She pulled the robe together.

"Yes." He kissed her knees and slid in closer, the big oak's clatter-scratch behind him, its beat and wait and beat again, like drums or booted dancers on a hollow stage; he listened and he closed his eyes, his lips now moving upward in the mostly dark, a gentle pressing toward her face, full down upon her lips a moist and settled fullness there.

CHAPTER THIRTY TWO

Fr. Bede was perched on the armor box like a tiny statue balanced on a column much too small. In the dream. He was there in the dream for sure, and Darby always would believe, for seconds or for minutes after it had gone away. They had all been dancing, again, out on the Little Okra and everyone was there—the Cardinal and good Eugene, New/Old Poddy and Thad Stevens stepping high, Kathleen and Cindy and himself, all dancing with the jingling Yoricks and the Pope, with Conroy Tucker and his singing boys and Hattie Peese and Wyatt Earp, the Bideawhile's fine Host and Henry Two-Crows all alone, with Darby's parents toward the last and Sonny-Boy and Jeeter on their bulls, and Fr. Bede a skipping fiddler testing out the strength of hyacinth leaves and blossoms all grown back and thicker than before. The dance had lasted for a long, long time and then the others started leaving one by one, a wind come up from where the water moved to take them on a bumpy ride away. But Fr. Bede was left behind, alone out on the rippling green, and on the armor box when Darby left the rising wind and jerked himself awake.

"Mr. Ross."

"Wha'—where?"

Kathleen was snoring softly, snug beside him in the bed, the taste and feel of her still there between them, resting warm and filled with sleep. The Crucifix above the bed sent shadows of itself out almost to the walls on either side. The dream had seemed so real.

"I only have a few minutes–no, don't bother to get up. It's gotten colder now. Don't leave your bed. It's taken long enough to get you there, Lord knows."

"I–I'm dreaming. I'm still dreaming. Right? This is a part of my dream. The last part. Right?"

"We have only a few minutes. Just this once. A few minutes to talk. It's almost dawn."

"But–you–you're so small–how can you sit on the box like that? Was it the heart attack that made you small?"

"Would you rather I stood? I can stand if you'd prefer. I'll stand."

"How are you here? Why have you–"

"Your wife is very beautiful."

"*That's* why you're here? To tell me *that*?"

"And your daughter–she has a sweetness–a gentleness clean and simple. Underneath. Still growing but there. She's very beautiful. Like your wife. Do you know that?"

"I–yes–yes I know that–I've heard that before."

The Little Fr. Bede went silent, like a string-pulled version of a talking doll, its sounds jerked slower and with nothing more to say. But then the program changed, the string yanked hard to set it off again.

"And your home is beautiful. This room in particular. A comfortable room. A good place to begin."

"Why are you here, Father Bede? If you *are* here. And what about your heart? I heard about it. Awake. You can't be here. Are you dead? You must be dead."

But the doll jumped down and skipped across the floor, a mouse-like burst of speed that seemed to blend in with the shafts of moonlight just then reaching for the bed. The room was full of movement, dappled forms and near-mist everywhere, silver-gray and rolling gently like a peaceful sea. The doll stood taller on the footboard, dressed in Yorick bells and with a fiddle in one hand, the other with the bow pressed down just like a cane to tap the covers and to test the ground. To balance for a while until the moonlight took it in. And then the bow whipped up to meet the strings, to rest there while the doll began to smile and nod its head.

Kathleen giggled in her sleep and rolled toward Darby on the bed, the blankets and the quilt pushed up against him and a hand there too, her fingers taking hold, long fingers holding to his waist. His eyes were itching, the warmth beside him and behind a tugging thing like river water forced to whirl and eddy out around a tree stump or a log, the fiddle playing now, the bow pushed back and forth and sometimes tapping on the strings, a jingling in among the other sounds, of tiny bells and laughter and a clicking of strong wheels on new-made track. And sleep there too, and dreamless rest until the dawn, and Kathleen's wondrous body rising with him, rising in a tune so pure the grave itself would hear, and maybe breakfast then high up above the greening river, fresh eggs and sausage, coffee, toast and oranges, autumnal light upon their table, Cindy sleepy-eyed and hungry and the three of them and more sat down to eat.

EPILOGUE

Heinreich Cardinal Spitzmulcher was smiling. He had even hugged Darby, twice, in the long corridor from the cathedral to his private office, the deacons and gentle Eugene scurrying behind like puppies just let loose to play. The Christmas Mass was ended, bells ringing in the coolish air outside, a breeze there too that smelled of frying fish and seaweed, wet and salt-tinged from the darkness toward the bay. The office was well-lit, a glowing log in the ornate fireplace and His Eminence had made the others wait outside.

"Your wife and daughter will join us in a few minutes, Darby. I've sent Eugene to see to their needs. A joyous, joyous day—good from apparent evil. Always good from apparent evil, yes?"

"Christmas is always a special—"

"And yet it's almost more than anyone thought possible. Much more. As you know, His Holiness called earlier this evening. We spoke at length this time and—"

"His Holiness telephoned?"

"Yes, yes—I thought you knew."

"No, Eminence—we were almost late for Midnight Mass." From preparations for the party later, with Cindy's friends and parents of the friends, old carols and a special punch, co-workers at *The Cross* and twinkling lights and peace enough to carry everything along right through the rising of the sun.

"Ah—I thought Eugene had told you. But no matter—*I'll* tell you. Yes. It's better that I tell you." He motioned

Darby to one of the chairs nearest the glowing log, taking the other himself, red cassock rustling as he sat down quickly. His face looked fuller than before, more flesh in cheeks and chin, zucchetto on his head almost too small and slipping just a little bit each time he moved. It was very warm in the room. "Yes. We are moving northward–the Archdiocese. And to the west. Consolidation. Charleston and Atlanta. New Orleans also. From the Carolinas to Texas. A new and much larger Archdiocese. He'll announce it at Epiphany. I had hopes, of course. That much you know. Since the Papal Retreat, I never gave up hope. And we have been in monthly communication with the Holy See. Our people there have kept us up-to-date. But I never expected such a thing as *this*. Never. You look surprised yourself."

"Yes, Eminence–Atlanta too?" The log hummed in the fireplace, a mumbled sound that seemed to throb, soft to loud with tongues of blue curled up and dropping back, the log itself unchanging in the patterned flames. It seemed a muffled chant, an echo of the Mass come over somehow with the volume much too low to catch and hold its words. "You did say–Atlanta?"

"What? Yes, yes. And there will be other changes as well. In the country as a whole. To bring the picture into better focus. But for us–north and west. And yes–Georgia. All of Georgia now."

"All?" Darby's house was decorated, every room with green and red, pine and holly and tiny lights along the pathway to the water's edge, right down to where the remnant of the river-green lay growing stronger underneath the bridge. And the house when they left it smelled of pine and ham and something deeper, like a sound might smell, like tap and jingle, staff and bells might scent the air, the past there too to hold the rest in place. "Then—then that means that—"

"Yes yes—the obvious of course. Our original request. Slackbridge and The Yoricks. Under my general jurisdiction now." He smiled and stretched his slippered feet toward the dancing tongues of blue. "Under my pastoral care. But," he crossed his ankles and patted at his knees, huge ring slipped sideways and nearly lost in crinkling red, "compromise was necessary. I know, I know—I have had much to say on *that* subject, eh? But we've lost nothing by agreement. And much has been gained."

"Compromise?" And he had transplanted the river-green, hyacinths, a few at a time, along the bank in sheltered places nearly to the bend, their leaves now thick and reaching for the light.

"The Yoricks. They still answer only to Rome. Riga—Cardinal Riga is still their protector. But," he straightened up and slapped his hands down on his thighs. "We will have a Visitator. Yes. A *lay* Visitator. A watchman. A man to guard against excess. Our own observer there from time to time. At our pleasure. His Holiness has seen the need. Since Father Bede's untimely death. He saw the need himself." He stood up, slowly, robes rustling and then mixed in with the strengthening plainsong of the log, the tongues now licking higher, red tips up above the blue and steady in a nearly even line of splintered flame. "You, Darby. You will be our man."

"Me?" Fr. Bede had died in Slackbridge, All Saints Eve or on the day itself, the timing never clear, so many pictures moving with the news—of requiem and Yoricks by the hundreds, full network coverage of the jingling dance to Gerezim. And *The Cross* had gone there too, a new reporter sent out on his first assignment, a young,

young man that Darby found and hired himself. "Me."

"Yes. We will install you formally. On Epiphany, I think. Yes. To coincide with His Holiness's own announcement. You will be in place that way—for the canonical election of Father Bede's successor. To see that all is well-ordered. Tidy. Yes. Epiphany will be perfect." He held out his hands to the singing flames, to the red-tipped tongues of blue that seemed to tap and clack together back and forth, a different sound down in their deepest part like laughter barely heard but surely there beyond an unfamiliar door.

Other books by James Louis Fortuna Jr.

Available now from Lightnin' Bug Publishing:

Story Collections:
A Rock in a Broken Land: Scenes from the Progressive Apocalypse
The Gator and the Holy Ghost and Other Stories of a Slightly Reconstructed South
A Burning of Ducks and Other Stories

Novels:
A Rumor of Appomattox: Confessions of a Georgia Klansman
Hell Broke Loose in Georgia

Forthcoming:
One Welcome Child: A Love Story
From Sea to Shining Sea and Other Stories

About the Author

Specific, factual biographical information about the author can be found attached to the six other works already published. Pertinent insight into the man, into James L. Fortuna Jr. himself, proves more difficult. Suffice it to say that he taught various courses (English, philosophy, ethics, The Holocaust) for many years. He has retired. He lives in North Carolina. He remains happily married to a woman much better than he deserves. He continues to be a struggling Christian pilgrim—better on some days, worse on others—hoping all along the way for permission to keep on writing until he no longer can.